AND THE ANGELS SING

a novel

Fr. Brawn Sullivan

I

By the same author

SEVEN SUMMERS FROM THE SHORE

THE ROSARY AND THE GOSPELS
(with Sara Sullivan)

THE SEASON OF GRIEF

Front cover photo: Erick Villa

Back cover photo: William Rolf

Cover design: Erick Villa

Book design: Miguel Vargas

Published by Catholic California Press/Sullivan Media Group,

Los Angeles, CA.

Sullivan Media Website: www.greenearthprintanddesign.com

Catholic California Press: www.catholiccaliforniapress.com

To Ruthanne,

for reasons which only she would understand

AUTHOR'S NOTE

AND THE ANGELS SING is my first novel in twelve years. It is also the only novel I have written as a priest. This latter fact in particular suggests the wisdom of a foreword to the book: novels do not need forewords, but maybe a priest who writes them does. I wrote six novels over twenty-three years before giving the effort up under what I perceived to be Divine guidance in the spring of 2002. I've written about this elsewhere (SEVEN SUMMERS FROM THE SHORE) and the only comment I am going to make on any of it here is that the Lord made clear to me, in April, 2002, that He intended one day to resurrect me as a writer. I scoffed at the thought and applied myself to completing my preparation for priesthood.

Three years after I was ordained I began to publish non-fiction and I took this to be the fulfillment of the Lord's promise: I was no longer a novelist but I was very much once again a writer. This past winter, three mornings after my birthday, the climax of a novel presented itself to me. It happened on a vacation day while I was still in bed. The climax was powerful; it drew me in and held my attention. In the climax I caught many glimpses of the novel's earlier scenes, of the plot leading to the climax, and I sensed the presence of a character, the character whose story this was. The character was Kendra Collins. I had known Kendra (in that way that an author may know a character even if as yet there is no story) since 1980. I knew Kendra so well that all I had to do was follow her: the story unfolded almost effortlessly in whatever stolen midnights and early mornings I could find for it this extremely heavy Lenten and Easter season just past. When I was with the novel, it was like being on vacation. I was astonished to find that I had another novel in me, but as I say, its writing was a smooth and graceful joy. I do not know if other novels will follow, or whether through Catholic California Press I will bring some of the earlier ones into print. For now, it is more than enough for me that AND THE ANGELS SING exists.

Novels speak for themselves. They need no introduction. But as I take my role as a public person for the Church seriously and want no misunderstandings, I think it a good idea to make the following points, not so much about AND THE ANGELS SING, but about novels, novelists and the art of fiction in general.

The first point really should be obvious, but I do not want to take anything for granted. This is a novel. It is a work of fiction. I am not in it. None of the characters are "me." There are, of course, writers out there, claiming to be novelists, who place themselves at the center of their books, "creating" (poor use of that term) a central character that is really only a stand-in for the writer. I do not write fiction that way. It violates the whole concept of fiction, in my view. If I wanted to write autobiographically, I would not write a novel. I would write autobiography. And of course, I have done just that. A reader looking for me in one of my books need look no further than SEVEN SUMMERS FROM THE SHORE.

As surely as none of the characters are me, nor do any of them "speak" for me. My characters speak for themselves. Their views, opinions and convictions are theirs, not mine. My job as a novelist is to present those views, opinions and convictions as honestly, as transparently as I can. Nor do any of my characters "represent" a certain viewpoint or some kind of agenda. None of them, in other words, are mere mouthpieces for some particular point of view. Again, there are writers who "create" characters this way, but I am not one of them. It violates the integrity of the character to make him or her a "representative" of some agenda or other. To the extent that my talent allows it, I work to create well-rounded and fully-developed characters, characters who look, think, walk and talk a lot like real human beings.

I should hedge even saying that I work to "create" characters at all: the fact of the matter is that my characters pretty much appear in

V

my consciousness already formed. This is not a process I can adequately describe. But to give you an idea of it, Kendra, the lead in this book, is agnostic. Why isn't Kendra Catholic? a reader might ask. Because Kendra is agnostic, is my answer. Why is she agnostic? Because she's Kendra. How do I know why Kendra is not a believer? I just know that she isn't. I have known it as long as I have known Kendra; I have known it since 1980. It's the same with every other member of the cast, right down to the characters who make only cameo appearances. Each of them came to me already formed; I am much more in the business of letting my characters reveal themselves than of creating them.

It follows that my characters are the real authors of their story. They know themselves and each other; they know their situation and the plot gets worked out through and among them far more than is it "directed" by me. If I allow them to show me the story, they inevitably do just that, revealing it to me plot twist by plot twist. My job is to report accurately on what they are doing. I am often surprised by my characters; that is part of the fun for me, in writing fiction.

AND THE ANGELS SING is a thoughtful and at times even a philosophical novel. But its driving engine is the emotional interplay among the characters. The novel carries no message and supports no agenda. Again, novels driven by an agenda violate, in my view, the whole art and craft of fiction. Quite a few such books were written, in support of the socialist revolution in the first half of the twentieth century, both in the West and in the Soviet Union. No one reads these books today. For good reason: they were literary failures from the outset. Exercises in propaganda dressed up as fiction.

As is the case with all of my earlier novels, there is a certain Catholic sensibility at work in AND THE ANGELS SING. But what I mean by this is simply that the book has several Catholic characters, and the narrator takes them seriously. They are characters, not caricatures, such as one encounters in the work of

Dan Brown. The fact that my novels treat Catholic (and all religious) belief with respect is one of their distinguishing features; most "literary" novelists are decidedly agnostic, if not outright atheist in their convictions, and faith is largely absent in the stories they tell.

Finally, as I guess is clearly implied in all I have said above, my characters are not saints. I don't want anyone shocked because they commit sins. In my experience as a novelist, no sin, no plot. It is that simple. AND THE ANGELS SING could be described in several ways; one of the most direct is to call it a story of redemption. It is simply an acknowledgment of reality that we do not experience redemption without a need for it, that is, if there is going to be redemption there is first going to be sin. Some of my characters are more virtuous than others, but I love all my characters equally, and in spite of their sins. One of my former agents, Aleta Daley in New York, once commented on my "generosity" toward my characters, saying she loved them even when they were behaving badly. Aleta made that comment in 1994, but it stays with me today; I love my characters no matter what they do.

In this last respect the work of the creative artist, and perhaps especially the novelist, can offer a pale reflection of the creative work of God. Dorothy Sayers has written on this parallel in her book, THE MIND OF THE MAKER, arguing right down to the "freedom of will" of the character – a reality I experienced already with the writing of my first novel in 1979. Sayers' book, incidentally, is also one of the best works on the Trinity that I have ever read: for folks interested in the issues of art and the creative process being discussed here, or for those wanting a deeper set of insights into the Trinity, THE MIND OF THE MAKER is highly recommended.

I laughed (like Sarah, like Zechariah) when the Lord told me that He would one day resurrect me as a novelist. Twelve springs after the spring of 2002, the Lord has made good on that promise. I have greatly enjoyed keeping company with Kendra and her friends, this past spring. I hope you will enjoy your time with them, as well.

Fr. Brawn Sullivan
June 25, 2014
Brentwood

ONE

"He's seen Damien," said Linda.

She crossed from the open patio to the covered area, into the shade. This part of the patio featured a bar and a spacious seating area beneath an overhead wood lattice, covered in orange bougainvillea. She dropped her purse onto a cushioned patio chair and slipped gratefully out of her cream-colored linen jacket, for it was a blazing Los Angeles April afternoon, temperatures in the high eighties. Her white silk top had only spaghetti straps but she was done with seeing clients for the day. The shade felt nice, and Linda was happy at the prospect of spending the rest of her afternoon here, here with the people who most mattered to her.

"He's seen Damien," she repeated.

"Really?" Kendra asked.

Linda nodded, lifting her dark glasses but not taking them off. "He said Damien was standing at the door to the room for several minutes before I arrived."

"Wow," said Kendra. There was a note of resignation in the way she spoke the word.

Linda laid her jacket over the back of the chair and looked at her friend. Kendra was sitting in one of the reclining wooden deck chairs, her legs pulled up on a matching wooden ottoman. She wore a filmy and transparent white beach caftan over a maroon one-piece. Despite the bougainvillea, sunlight filtered through the overhead lattice here and there, catching flame-red highlights in Kendra's almost-black hair, left loose today so that it hung to just above her shoulders.

"You look very MOGAMBO, girlfriend," said Linda, "with all that sunlit tropical foliage as a backdrop." She was referring to the screen of palms, tree ferns and brightly blooming birds of paradise beyond the patio bar. "Very Ava Gardner does the Zambezi, or whatever river they were on."

"You're thinking of THE AFRICAN QUEEN," said Matt. He was lying on his back on a chaise, in full sun, just beyond the shaded area.

"Hello Matt," said Linda, turning to him. "And no way. Nobody's ever compared Kendra to Katharine Hepburn. For that matter, no one has ever compared her to Audrey Hepburn," she added. "We're talking Gardner here, we're talking MOGAMBO."

Matt, wearing a pale blue Speedo square-cut and a pair of pricey shades, ran a hand through his dark curls, shrugged and went back to the business of lying in the sun.

"Ava Gardner, Liz Taylor, yes," Linda went on, replacing her sunglasses for beyond the shade the afternoon was very bright. "Either one of the Hepburns, no. Kendra's too glamorous for Kate and too intellectual for Audrey."

"She's too intellectual for any other actress period," said Matt.

"I'm still here, you two," said Kendra, with a smile.

"You are," Linda agreed, turning back to Kendra. "And looking radiant. If I'd been a brunette of your stripe, I'd have stayed a brunette." Linda's hair was an expensive shade of blonde.

"But he saw Damien," Kendra said. "David saw Damien just now."

"Just a few minutes ago," Linda said, throwing her hair back from her artificially tanned shoulders. "Just before I arrived, I guess."

"Did they talk?" Kendra asked. "Did Damien speak to him?"

"Evidently not. I mean, okay, I didn't actually ask. But I had the distinct impression, from the way David talked, that he only saw Damien. Sort of like a vision, I guess. But it wasn't some momentary flash kind of thing, you know? David saw Damien, for several minutes, standing in the doorway, smiling. I guess Damien disappeared when I showed up."

"You scared Damien away?" asked Matt. "It's usually the ghosts that scare us."

Linda laughed. She crossed toward the bar.

"Damien's ghost," said Kendra, "is not one I would be afraid of." She lifted her iced tea from an adjacent table. "David, in any event, has been getting visitors from the other side for several days now. He saw his parents over the weekend."

"Really?" said Linda.

Kendra nodded, sipped her iced tea. "Solange says it is a sure sign. She says we're very close. No more than a few days."

Before Linda could respond she found herself in a bare-armed and bare-chested hug from a young man with smooth golden-brown skin and black hair. His smile was bright. He wore dark glasses and a pair of board shorts, a black-and-red hibiscus print. He had just crossed out from the house.

"Tino!" Linda smiled.

"I didn't know you were here," Tino said. His name was Celestino, but everyone had called him Tino since he was little.

"I just got here," Linda said. "I've been with your uncle. I've just come from his room. He is better today," she went on, to all of them. "Or so it seems to me. David is more himself today. A lot more alert."

"Very much so," agreed Kendra. "Responsive and talkative."

"More so than he has been in a week," said Matt.

Tino had taken up position meanwhile behind the bar. "What'll it be?" he asked Linda.

"This kid," Linda said to Kendra, and shook her head.

Kendra smiled. "He was born to the business," she said.

"Bartending?" Linda scoffed. "I think David was right about you years ago, Tino. You shoulda been in pictures."

"I think my aunt was referring to the family business," said Tino.

"And I'm not?" asked Linda. "The family business isn't movies?"

"Oh that," said Kendra, and returning her iced tea to the end table, sat back in her seat.

"If you have a Sauvignon blanc," Linda said, "I'll have that. If not, any Chardonnay."

Tino made a quick survey of the bar's stock. "Damn! Tia," he said, turning to Kendra. "A Sauvignon blanc?"

Kendra shrugged. "In the house," she said.

4

"No!" Linda said, placing a hand on Tino's shoulder and so arresting his impulse to go inside to find the right bottle. "Chardonnay. Riva Ranch is fine. And really, Tino, I could have got it myself. But I guess you've got to put these shoulders to some use."

Tino smiled. "It's the family business," he said. "Besides, I like waiting on you." He brought the bottle up and began to pour.

"I hope you are not expecting a tip. All I have is plastic."

Tino blew Linda a kiss.

"But tell me," Kendra continued, sitting forward again and putting up her sunglasses, as if to better concentrate on what Linda might report. "David saw Damien but there was no communication?"

"Nobody said anything, as nearly as I can gather," Linda replied, crossing with her glass toward the edge of the shade, where Matt lay. "It was all – spiritual communication. Don't mean to crowd you, writerboy," Linda said, and took a seat still in the shade but close to the chaise longue on which Matt was stretched. "I want to sit right on the edge of the shade because I like the view from here."

"Thank you," said Matt from behind his sunglasses.

"I was talking about the pool," Linda said, "and the flower beds."

"Aw shucks," said Matt. "And I sent my autograph book to the cleaners."

Linda laughed. It was a private joke. Then, looking out across the pool and toward the extensive and brightly blooming beds, "My

5

gosh, Kendra, the azaleas are spectacular, front and back. You'd think we really were in the Deep South, Miz Scarlett and all."

"Nobody's ever compared Kendra to Vivien Leigh, either," said Matt.

"No, but people have compared this house to the GONE WITH THE WIND set, and with all these azaleas just now, easy to see why."

"Kendra's questions interest me," Matt said. "I want to hear more about David seeing Damien. It's not every day you have an encounter with someone who is dead."

"I should hope not," Linda agreed. She took a sip of her chardonnay. "I asked David. I said, 'Really? Damien was here?' I gave him no reason to doubt that I believed him – or at least, so help me, I trust I gave him no such reason. I mean, the idea that his older brother is with him right now, has crossed from the other side to be with him, is very comforting to David. So I said, 'Really, Damien was just here?' And David just smiled.

"Oh! What a smile he still has, Kendra!" Linda went on, her voice suddenly choking back a sob. "What a beautiful smile." She was all at once so overcome that she had to put her hand to her mouth, had to take in a deep, calming breath. Really, even now, she had trouble believing this was real. David! David dying.

Kendra had replaced her dark glasses. From behind their protective coloring, tears started in her hazel eyes. But they did not fall. She had not cried for weeks. And it had begun to occur to her why: she feared that if she started, she would not be able to stop. Perhaps precisely because of that fact, she was grateful to Linda for her unguardedness with her feelings.

"He said Damien was waiting," Linda continued, gathering her composure once more. "Damien was standing there at the door to the room and he was smiling. David felt his love, felt such peace. David knows that Damien is waiting. That's what he told me."

"He felt the same way after seeing his parents," Kendra said. "He saw his mother on Friday, and then both his mother and his father, yesterday."

"He said he needed to go to Mass with them," added Tino, now seated next to Kendra. "He knew it was Sunday yesterday. That was unusual in itself, him knowing what day it was. He was a little more alert yesterday, a little more there, yesterday. But he's really there, today. Awake and responsive. This is a good day for Uncle David."

Linda shook her head, looking at her glass. "I go back and forth," she said, "between acceptance and rebellion. It's just so – so unreal. And so unfair."

Matt roused himself enough to glance through his dark glasses at Kendra. "How long has it been?" he asked. "Since he was rejected for the experimental protocol?"

"That was September," Kendra said. "It's been since September." She shifted in her seat and the caftan fell open, revealing her bare legs and the maroon one-piece. Though in good shape, Kendra had abandoned two-piece swimsuits almost twenty years earlier; around about the time, in fact, that she'd married David. She had suddenly gone from being an up-and-coming young film star to being the step-mother of three young children. Kendra had been accustomed to dress for parts. The part of new wife and step-mother of young children, it had seemed to her, eliminated the possibility of cavorting in bikinis, even in places, such as the patio of her own Brentwood home, where she was not likely to be photographed.

7

She had kicked off her sandals and sat with her legs drawn up on the ottoman. She pulled the caftan up and over her legs.

"September," she repeated. "That's when we found out he didn't qualify for the new drug. His numbers were off. What's that? Seven, eight months ago? The doctors told us he probably would not make Christmas."

"He was still strong at Christmas," Linda said.

"Like you would not have known he was sick," agreed Tino.

"He wanted to be here for one more holiday season," said Kendra. "For the kids, you know."

"For the kids," said Linda, and stared out over the pool.

TWO

Two years before, in February, David de la Fuente, the Hollywood producer and director, then sixty-three, had been diagnosed with a rare form of liver cancer. The cancer had already metastasized and the doctors gave him a year; at the outside, eighteen months.

"That's with the chemo," one of the specialists called in on the case had told them, told David and Kendra, the afternoon that they had definitive lab results. The cancer was inoperable; the chemo course would retard its progress, nothing more. But reactions to the chemo combination the doctors were recommending tended to be mild, and for what it was worth, David might spend the last year of his life relatively comfortably, he might have, in fact, a good year, an almost-normal year, before going into irreversible -- and rapid -- decline.

David had listened to all of this in silence; it was Kendra who had asked the questions, Kendra who had taken the notes. They got home that bright afternoon and at David's request, went out to the patio bar, where he poured Kendra a glass of wine and himself a Glenlivet neat.

"Quiet afternoon," David said.

The houses on this street were far enough away from each other so that most afternoons were quiet, but Kendra said, "Yeah. Well, February. How many people are going to be swimming, even though it is certainly warm enough?"

"Funny how that works, isn't it?" David said, and sipped his scotch, leaning against the bar. He was, that afternoon, still strong and stocky, with thick grey hair; he was, that afternoon, still very much the man he had always been. "Funny. It can be warmer here in January than in June, but who uses the pool in January?"

"I love the L.A. notion of winter," Kendra said, relaxing back into her seat. She was, as usual, in one of the wooden deck chairs. "I think it was Joan Didion who once observed that winter in California is generally conceived of as contiguous with the Christmas season. Even up north," she went on, for Kendra had grown up in the Bay Area, "by now, by February, temperatures are back in the seventies, and everything is blooming."

David grinned. "How do people in Chicago do it?"

"Ask Linda."

David laughed. "Why do you think Linda is here?"

Kendra laughed. "You're right," she said. "And her visits home are always timed April to October. She may have been born in Chicago, but she is a California girl now."

They were silent a moment. The light breeze rustled through the overhead bougainvillea and the sunlight sparkled amid the palms. Isis, one of their several cats, named for the Egyptian goddess, appeared from the shrubbery and rubbed herself against David's jean-clad legs. He looked down at the cat, smiled, and looked back out over the pool, not really seeing the pool, however, nor the bordering patio, nor the brightly blooming flower beds, nor the stands of palms, the hedges of hibiscus, nor the orange and lemon trees, nor the remote seating areas, nor the guest house, nor the stand of eucalyptus at the far property line.

"Maybe the three most shocking words you can ever hear in your life," David said, "are 'you have cancer.'"

Kendra said nothing, waiting.

10

"And not just any cancer," David said. "Rare and metastasized liver cancer." He held up his glass and looked at it. He laughed a short, ironic laugh. "Liver cancer. You don't suppose this is helping it, darling?"

Before Kendra could respond, David added, "This is going to be tough on the family. Especially coming now, so soon after Damien."

David's older brother Damien had died of a stroke right after New Year's.

"Just six weeks since we buried Damien," David said. "This is going to be hard on the family."

"We need to talk to other experts," Kendra said, setting her glass aside. "We need to examine non-Western options."

David smiled. "Oh Kendra," he said. He shook his head, smiling. "Kendra."

She looked at him. "We do, David. These doctors have told you their incapacity. They've told you what they cannot do. We need to go to alternative therapies and procedures – all the while, going ahead with the protocol here. We can't leave ourselves at the mercy of Western medicine. It fails to take in half the picture. We've got to advocate for ourselves because these doctors have told us, in no uncertain terms, what they cannot do. Well, what they cannot do will not do for us. Their limitations are not ours. We need to go online, we need to research our options, we need to talk to other experts."

Kendra had been prepared to say more but she stopped, noticing the solitary tear streaking her husband's cheek.

THREE

"Strong through Christmas," Linda said, and sipped her chardonnay. "Actually, through his birthday, huh, Kendra? Mid-January. When is his birthday?"

"The seventeenth," Kendra said, and nodded. "He started getting bad the following week." She smiled ironically. "My birthday," for Kendra had been born January twenty-third, fifty-three years earlier. "We were at the ER the day after my birthday. We were there again the following week, and then came the first of the hospital stays, what?" She looked at her nephew. "Around Valentine's Day?"

"Ten days mid-February," Tino said. "He came home right after Presidents' Day."

"Ten days mid-February. We thought we were going to lose him. At that point, we were two years past the initial diagnosis. He beat the odds."

"Of course he did," Linda said, smiling. "Sixty-five," she went on, and swirled the wine in her glass. "From where we sit it doesn't seem as old as it used to."

"The new fifty?" Matt smiled from the chaise, still on his back and with his arms folded behind his head.

"Oh let's not go there," said Linda. "Remember all that nonsense a few years back about fifty being the new thirty-five? I never once heard a thirty-five year old say that."

"The new fifty or no, sixty-five's not old," said Tino, who was thirty-two. "Not these days. Not in North America. And especially not for a man like David. It's only the late middle of life. Uncle David had great plans."

Kendra smiled. "He did. I guess those films will never be made now."

"Interesting to think about the art that has not come into the world," said Matt, "because of the premature death of the artist. Bizet, Gerschwin – what music have we never heard because they died in their thirties?"

"He might have gone strong another fifteen years," Linda said. "Who knows when David would have said, 'I'm through'?"

"I don't think he ever would have," said Matt. "He was a visionary before, during and after everything else. I don't think he'd have known what to do with himself in retirement. What do you say, Kendra?"

Kendra just smiled. "No," she said after a moment. "I never imagined him retiring, either."

"Damien aged all of us," Linda said. "None of us saw that coming. Strokes are so sudden, and they can be so devastating. All of a sudden Damien went from strength and vibrance and apparent health to --" She did not finish the sentence. "And his struggle, his weakness, his suddenly being old, that aged all of us."

"It's true," said Matt.

"Until Damien's first stroke," Linda continued, "all of us may as well have been thirty-five, or well, make it forty for the sake of argument and ineffective wrinkle creams."

"It's true," Matt agreed. "Everything was still as it had always been, and all of us were as we had always been. And then, suddenly, Damien was old and weak and dependent."

"We sort of lived in defiance," Linda said. "I mean defiance of reality."

"Well, after all," said Matt. "Plenty of folks much older than David or Damien are still strong and vital. Look at my parents. And Polly," he said, turning to Kendra.

"Eighty-three," said Kendra, of her mother. "And going strong."

"How old was Damien?" Linda asked.

"Seventy-two," Matt, Tino and Kendra answered together, so that, instantaneously, they all laughed.

Kendra sipped her iced tea, set it on the table beside her. "I remember the first time I met Damien," she said. "I remember it well because it was the first time I met the whole family. David and Lana took me to a graduation party at the restaurant."

"I remember that," said Matt.

"How could you? You weren't there."

"No, but you told me all about it the next day. You fell in love that night."

Kendra smiled. "I did," she said.

Matt smiled. "But not with David."

"No, not with David," Kendra agreed.

14

"Was I there?" Tino asked.

"You were seven or eight," said Kendra. "You were part of the reason I fell in love. Everyone was. It was an awesome night. If I'd had any idea then –"

"That this was your own future?" Linda asked.

"My own family," Kendra said. She frowned slightly, as if trying to bring into focus a night that was now twenty-four years past.

FOUR

The de la Fuente family operated a large and successful restaurant near Mission San Gabriel, Casa de la Fuente. Kendra had heard of the restaurant from David, who alone among the six de la Fuente siblings had not tied his fortunes to those of the restaurant. Kendra and David had met through his first wife, Lana, a couple of years before. Lana and Kendra had known each other from the music circuit, for in her twenties, Kendra had been a singer. At the time that she met the family, Kendra was twenty-nine and just breaking into film as an actress, a development she had not sought, rather, it had sought her.

Among those directors who wanted to work with her was David de la Fuente. They had not yet worked together, but the prospect seemed likely, and they were friendly in their professional association with one another. One of David's many nephews, Carlos, had seen each of the three films Kendra had at that time appeared in and he was an ardent fan. He was graduating from high school that June and having a big party at the restaurant. David and Lana thought it would be a great graduation gift for Carlos, to bring Kendra as a surprise guest to the party.

"Carlos is just crazy about you," Lana had told Kendra, extending the invitation to the graduation party. "David and I will take you out and bring you back. It's San Gabriel -- a bit of a drive; that way you can relax and not worry about the next glass of wine.

"Anyway, Carlos. He's a great kid," Lana had gone on, taking a drag on her Marlboro and then with the hand that held the cigarette pushing her bright blonde curls back as she exhaled, a gesture Kendra had come to associate with Lana. "Headed to Stanford in the fall; wants to study Near Eastern archaeology or something.

Brainy kid, but fun, you know. Soccer player, class officer. Wonderful kid. Great sense of humor, and, in the right company, way irreverent! Big fan of Soul Circus and its blonde lead singer, or so I am told," Lana went on, referring to her own band. "But he's an even bigger fan of a certain beautiful brunette just now making her way in the film business. Oh my God, Kendra, what it will mean to Carlos to have you at his party!

"And you'll like David's family. They won't like you but don't worry, they will never show it, because they're too proud to let anyone see how jealous and bitchy they can be. This is mostly David's sisters, I am talking about. They don't like anybody from the West Side, and if you're in the business, well, that's two strikes against you. If you're younger, and I might add, better-looking – though they are hardly ugly – strike three, kid, head for the showers. But like I say, they'll never show it. And the nieces and nephews!" Lana finished with a great good-natured laugh. "Oh, they will be at your feet! Can I get you something to drink?"

Kendra asked Lana what she should get Carlos as a gift. "An autographed photo," was Lana's immediate reply. Kendra had the photo framed and gift-wrapped and then placed a one hundred dollar bill in the card, and on the appointed evening she arrived at the house in Brentwood – the house which one day would become her home – and found her hosts in disagreement about the evening's plan.

Lana had greeted her at the door. She was dressed in orange silk and a genuine fur stole, such as Kendra had not seen since the days of her great aunts in Oakland. It was silver-grey. Kendra could not guess the species, she had no personal acquaintance with furs.

"Some righteous throwback to Puritanism once asked me what this thing was," Lana laughed, displaying the stole as if walking on a runway. "I told him it was dead."

17

Kendra gasped. Lana laughed, adding "I support a woman's right to choose -- to wear fur! And I don't need anybody trying to impose their morality on me about it! We all need to be tolerant, don't we?"

"Stop proselytizing," David said, coming up behind his wife. "Kendra is a Berkeley grad, and immune to your contagions."

Now Kendra laughed. David extended his hand to Kendra.

"So I guess I'll take the Porsche," Lana said, lighting a cigarette. "And you can meet me there after you've brought Kendra back."

David looked confused. "The Porsche? There isn't room --"

"That's what I'm saying. You take Kendra to and from San Gabriel, and then meet me at Meno's afterward. Well, unless of course, Kendra, you're up for two parties tonight. You're more than welcome at Meno's."

Meno's was a swank restaurant/music venue in West Hollywood.

"Two parties?" said Kendra.

"Wait a minute," David said, laying a hand on his wife's arm.

"Soul Circus is having an album launch party tonight," Lana explained to Kendra, and took a deep drag on her Marlboro.

"Darling," David said, "It's not an album launch --"

"Close enough. The album is in stores in three weeks."

"It's a party," David said now, to Kendra. The look in his deep brown eyes left Kendra a little uneasy for him. He ran a hand

18

through his thick, prematurely grey hair. "We discussed this, Lana --"

"We did," she agreed, exhaling a long grey plume of smoke. "Kendra, are you up for Meno's with the band tonight and – I don't know, maybe a hundred other people – after the party with the family?"

Before Kendra could answer, David made her response unnecessary. "Lana. I told you I have a meeting with backers tomorrow at ten in the morning. I can't get there bleary-eyed from a late night with the band. I am not going to Meno's."

Lana hardly missed a beat. "That's fine," she shrugged. "I guess we miscommunicated. I thought you wanted to go. I have to go. It's a big night for the band. This album," she said, looking at Kendra imploringly. "You should be grateful none of the bands you played with ever made it out," Lana went on. "Music was fun, before it became a business."

"Take the Porsche," said David, sounding resigned. "I'll drive Kendra out and back."

At the restaurant, Kendra met the star-struck Carlos, a bright-eyed eighteen year old with spikey black hair and a diamond stud in one ear. She liked him. She also met the allegedly fearsome de la Fuente sisters, Carmen, Ana and Raquel, and she met David's two brothers, Damien and Ramon. Just as Lana had promised, she loved the family, especially the nephews and nieces, the majority of whom at that time were already teens and twenty-somethings. David was the last of the de la Fuente siblings and his three children, all very young at that time, brought up the rear among the younger generation. A cousin near them in age, however, was Damien's boy, Celestino.

"What a beautiful name," Kendra said, when introduced to the eight year old. Tino smiled bashfully and looked at the floor. "And what a beautiful child," Kendra thought. Delicate features and simply soulful eyes, huge and brown, long-lashed; they fairly defined his face.

She also had an instinctive liking for Tino's father, Damien, the eldest of the siblings. "He is reserved and polite," she would tell Matt the next day. "With a slow smile, a careful smile, I might even say a care-worn smile." For she had heard from several guests at the party that Damien carried the weight of responsibility for the family; he was the paterfamilias, even though the elder de la Fuentes were alive and well, and in fact, still working, at that time. "Damien's taken over all the real work of the restaurant," a guest assured Kendra that bright evening, "and his parents now can relax and play host to northeastern Los Angeles, which they are very good at."

At some point Damien offered to show Kendra around the restaurant, which had five dining rooms, plus a banquet room upstairs, all of them that evening placed at the disposal of Carlos and his party. "My parents built the original restaurant on this site," Damien told her, "almost fifty years ago. They built a second, larger restaurant about ten years after that. This structure went up fifteen years ago, and as you can see, we have pretty much overwhelmed the lot. We have to leave a certain number of parking spaces, after all, city ordinance. So we are not getting any bigger than this."

At another moment, Kendra saw Damien, not quite tall, hefty but firm, in good shape, just beginning to go grey, in his role as father: Tino had gotten into a shoving match with a cousin, and his mother, Isabel, was ready to take him home. The boy appealed to his father.

20

"Okay," Damien said, knees bent so that he could be eye-to-eye with his son. "You want to stay?"

Tino indicated an affirmative answer with an emphatic nod.

"Then I need you to be on your gentleman's behavior," Damien said, evidently referencing a discussion he and the child had had before. "I need you to behave in a manner that is appropriate to attendance at a nice party with a lot of nice people. Shoving and shouting and blaming and accusing are not part of that, Tino. Right?"

Again, the boy nodded.

"Okay," said Damien. "Then be my little gentleman. Not just for me, but for everybody. Do we have a deal?" And Damien extended his hand.

Kendra watched as the child extended his. She smiled.

About ten, with the party in full swing, Kendra was with David and several other guests when Lana swept in among them and announced that "the nephews" were taking her to the party at Meno's. "Rico will bring the Porsche back tomorrow."

David stopped talking and looked with what seemed to Kendra to be alarm in his eyes, at his wife. "The nephews?" he said.

"Rico!" Lana called. "Javier!"

Not just Rico and Javier, but Julian too, materialized at Lana's side. The young men were all in their early twenties.

"They'll bring the Porsche back tomorrow," Lana said. "Meanwhile, we're off to Meno's."

21

David seemed momentarily at a loss. He actually turned to Kendra for an instant, but encountering her surprise, he realized no one could help him in this matter.

"Rico will drive me the rest of the night," Lana said. And turning to the young men she added, "And if you need to stay with us in Brentwood tonight, guys, we have plenty of room." She turned back to David. "Rico will bring the Porsche back manana, baby! We're leaving it here, of course, since there's four of us. Don't get worried, angel," she said, a hand to David's cheek, which she followed with a kiss. "I'll be late."

David seemed to have frozen in place. He much later told Kendra how he'd known Lana was already drunk, and had probably done a couple of lines as well, because she was repeating herself, for instance, about Rico and the Porsche.

"Rico," David said, turning to his nephew.

The young man stepped forward, clear-eyed and certain. "Don't worry, Tio," he said. "We'll go to West Hollywood, we'll all stay together; it will be fine. Tomorrow, I will bring the Porsche back over."

David looked at his nephew as if begging him for something. Rico squeezed David's shoulder. "I am fine," Rico assured him. "And I'm going to stay that way."

"Come on sobrinos!" Lana called, turning away with a sort of sashay from David and his conversational circle. "It's party time! Whose car are we taking? I vote the Lexus!"

Driving back to Brentwood together, David said to Kendra, "I guess I should have given this band party tonight more consideration. I really did think Lana had agreed not to go. It's

22

just a party. There really isn't anything special going on with the band tonight."

Kendra felt awkward, being privy to a clear and deep family disagreement. But she also felt so badly for David that she wanted to respond in a way that reassured him, if she could. While she was trying to formulate a response, David obviated the need for her to do so.

"You know what it's like, in music," he said.

"I do," Kendra agreed.

"They start the party at eleven PM."

"Why do you think I left it?" Kendra said.

David laughed. Kendra was glad that he laughed.

"Of course I'm glad she has a three-nephew escort," David added. "A little surprised that my sisters were cool with it, but after all the boys are over twenty-one." He sighed, hit the turn signal and began to look for the chance to get over toward the exits. "I don't know, Kendra," he said. "I don't know. I'm forty-one." He shook his head. "We have a brand new baby, you know."

"I know," Kendra said, for Jeffrey, the last of David's and Lana's children, had been born only the previous autumn.

"It's tough, trying to have it all," David said, and said it in such a way that Kendra could not help but feel that, at this point, he was trying to cover a little for Lana, doing what he could to put the best face on things.

"I'm sure," Kendra said.

23

"What about you?" David asked now, as they switched lanes, preparatory to switching freeways. "How is Kendra Collins managing, in the effort to have it all?"

Kendra laughed. Her laugh was so informative that she did not need to elaborate with words.

David grinned. "Sensible Kendra," he said. "Career first. Anything else…"

"Pretty much," Kendra said.

"What about marriage?"

"What about it?"

David laughed. "You ever going to do it?"

"You make it sound like I'm fifty."

David smiled. "Just wondering," he said. "As, I am sure, are an untold number of other men in this town. Will Kendra marry, and when, and whom? Carlos is probably asking those questions."

Kendra laughed. "He's adorable. Love his hair. And Stanford! You guys can be proud of him."

"Good kid," David agreed. "Well, if you ever do marry, I hope to God the guy is worthy of you."

The next day, telling Matt about the party, Kendra was not at all focused on Lana.

"What a family David's got!" she told Matt. "All those siblings, all those in-laws, all those nephews and nieces! I was introduced to so many I lost count. It was a huge party. Lot of young people, friends you know; Carlos is a popular boy."

Matt smiled. "I'll bet they were thrilled. Not just their famous Auntie Lana, but Kendra Collins, too!"

"I was thrilled," Kendra said. "The honor last night was all mine. What a wonderful family."

"I'm glad to hear it, for David's sake," Matt said. "The family is his anchor. They're the reason he can still walk on the wild side at forty. Of course, Lana's never walked anywhere else, so I guess he has no choice. By the bye," Matt went on. "You gonna take David up on that offer? To do the title track?"

Kendra shook her head. "I'm done singing," she said.

"Never say never," said Matt.

FIVE

The rush of the cool water about his arms, his chest, his back, his legs, made Matt smile. He loved swimming. Always had, all the way back to lessons at the Salinas municipal plunge his sixth and seventh summers. He loved the feeling of being in another medium, another element, cool, wet, supportive, above all, freeing – "If I could do the little mermaid thing in reverse," he had once told Kendra, "I'd be very tempted."

"You'd be very tempting," Kendra said, "as a merman."

"Maybe we should write a script about that," Matt grinned.

"You gonna play the lead?"

"Not hardly," Matt answered.

This conversation had been very early in their friendship. Almost thirty years ago. It came forward from the recesses of memory now, as Matt dove into the water.

Coursing with easy but powerful strokes, Matt opened his eyes underwater and saw the other end of the pool, far enough off so that he decided to surface then and there. He didn't want to get to the shallow end, anyway. He loved the deep end of a swimming pool, loved the feeling of nothing but water below his feet.

He came to the surface and looked toward the patio, toward the shaded bar area with its chaises and deck chairs and side tables, the overhead lattice flowing with the orange bougainvillea.

"A little kitschy," Linda had said of the patio arrangement, a few years ago, at some party or other, when she and Matt had been seated under the bougainvillea. "A little too GILLIGAN'S ISLAND, for my taste. All we need are the tiki torches. But David did not want to bother with a re-model, because it would have taken the patio away from the family for most of a season. That's David and Kendra. Always thinking of the kids."

"Children have a way of redirecting our priorities," Matt said.

"Got that right," said Linda. "Why do you think I never had any?"

Matt had known Linda almost as long as he had known Kendra; Linda had become, if it were possible for anyone to do so, as close a friend to him as Kendra. Neither he nor Linda was family to Kendra and David, but they had been taken in as if they were. And in any event Matt cherished his female friendships. The youngest of four brothers, he had never had a sister.

He lightly treaded water there in the middle of the pool, looking at the women and Tino in their island of shade amid a sea of light. The sun danced across the surface of the water and glared off the patio. It lit the back of the house a lustrous creamy near-white, and accentuated the wrought-iron balconies of the second floor, meant to give the house a New Orleans-like look. It lit up the banana trees and the jacaranda at the back of the house. Best of all, the sun shone on him. It was light and warm on his wet shoulders, a cosmic caress, and Matt, smiling, let himself luxuriate in it for a moment.

Then he turned toward the deep end and dove back under. He dove deep, feeling the strength of his shoulders, his chest, his arms, as he swam at an angle to the floor of the pool. He touched the bottom with both hands and then shot back upward in a rush of sun-dazzled waves and bubbles. He surfaced, threw his head back, face upward to the sun, exhaled, took a deep breath and then dove again, free as a dolphin and almost as much at home in the element.

Another long-ago conversation; this one with David, a few weeks after Lana's funeral. Lana had died in a suite at a Las Vegas hotel after performing at a charity event. The coroner ruled it an accidental drug overdose. She was thirty-seven.

"I never expected us to grow old together," David had said to Matt. This conversation had taken place right here, in the house, the room that now was David's sick room but which then and until this winter had been his office. "I mean, think about it. Did you ever imagine Lana old?"

The comment surprised Matt and he was unsure how to respond. Unsure, in part, because, no, now that David brought it up, he never had thought of Lana as someday being an old woman. In his mind he had never seen Lana anyway but that which she was: blonde and voluptuous, intelligent, racy and provocative, always ready to lend a devastating critique or a smiling -- and not infrequently condescending -- reassurance, a star-spangled rock and roll diva, but you could not help but love her. And yes. Yes. He had seen her trouble. He had worried about it. Everyone had.

"No one ever thought of Lana the grandmother," David said. "It was not a future image she projected to anyone, including herself. To be honest with you, she did not want to grow old."

"But the children," Matt started. Jessica, Justin and Jeffrey were at that time under ten.

David sighed, ran the hand on which he wore his wedding ring through his hair. "Yeah," he said, looking out the windows toward the patio, toward the pool. "Yeah, the kids," and Matt heard him choke back a sob. David shook his head. "She couldn't pull out,"

28

he said. "She couldn't pull out for her band, she couldn't pull out for me, and she couldn't pull out for the kids."

They were silent a long moment. Then David took a deep breath and exhaled with a sigh. He turned back to Matt.

"I want you to talk to Kendra about the part of Betsy," David said. "For heaven's sake, it could have been written for her, and properly cast, this picture could go over big. I mean it, Matt, it could give Kendra the break-through she needs, the role all Hollywood is waiting for her to find. She's going to be big, Matt. Big."

"She doesn't give a damn about being big," Matt said. "Every time she takes a part in a film she says it is going to be her last. She really is a writer, you know."

Kendra had left music not to act, but to write screenplays. Matt was her partner in that ambition.

"Big, Matt," David repeated. "Kendra is going to be big. Huge. She's got what it takes. But she needs to commit herself, and she needs to do it now."

"I'll talk with her," Matt promised, and smiled for his friend, who after all, was in deep grief, and needed all the support he could get. "I'll tell her what you think."

"Tell her what you think," David urged. "You have influence with her."

"Which is precisely why," Matt said, with an arched eye brow, "if you want her in this picture, you do not want me telling her what I think."

Matt surfaced at the deep end of the pool. The memory of this last conversation had damped down his spirits a little. He supposed that was only appropriate. His sunny serenity of a few minutes before, enjoying his swim, matched the day, matched the setting, but defied the context. After all, just a few hundred feet away, one of his lifelong friends lay almost unrecognizable, his once thick hair gone, his once chunky frame wasted away to near-skeletal proportions. Hooked up to morphine, almost unable to eat, uncomplainingly submitting to all the little indignities necessitated by his round-the-clock care, David slept most of most days and when awake, was given to receiving visits from the dead. Considering David's reality, Matt might have wondered at his callousness, enjoying his swim.

But he didn't. He was here for David, as much "here" as any of them could be. And after all, the pool was also here. So was the sun.

David's time had come. Astonishing all of them, it had come. And for sure, one day Matt's time would come. This was not that day.

SIX

"I can take you out to see it tomorrow," Linda was saying to a client via her iPhone. "It's spectacular. Three levels above the beach but a fourth, down a set of steps built right into the slope, that is actually on the beach…Not private, no, but access across the highway is difficult, and you won't see many non-residents there…Hm hmm…Yeah…No – huge. Simply huge, and all open because of the windows overlooking the beach. I'm telling you, you look up the coast all the way to Santa Barbara. Just gorgeous. Okay…Okay…No, later in the week is fine. Call. We'll set it up and we'll go out."

Linda worked in real estate, mostly high-end commercial, but her firm also handled a certain type of residential property, a type beyond the reach of ninety-seven point-five per cent of the population of Los Angeles. Many of her residential clients were foreigners. Their money and their hunger to spend it on California real estate had been something of an advanced lesson in international relations, for Linda.

"They're going to wind up owning the state capitol, Disneyland and the Golden Gate Bridge, the way things are going," Linda would say of her foreign-born clients. "And who can blame them? When the dollar finally tanks and they're left holding all those t-bills that suddenly have junk-bond status, they're going to want something firm, something real, on their investment."

"House in Malibu?" Kendra now asked, as Linda got off the phone.

"Near Zuma," Linda said. "Dreadful place. All stucco angles and glass. So sixties. But nine thousand square feet and on the beach,

31

and the views are unrivalled. Who knows? These guys might want it for a tear down. It's a Shanghai investment group."

"I was in Shanghai," Kendra said.

"I remember," said Linda, thinking of a business trip David and Kendra had made to East Asia just three or four years earlier.

"No, I mean yes," Kendra said. "I was there with David not long ago. But what I was thinking about was my first trip. The one I took two years after I graduated from Cal."

SEVEN

Kendra had been born in Oakland, and grew up there. Her father was a professor of history at Mills College and her mother a dance teacher. She had two brothers, both now long married, with children, and working and living in Silicon Valley. The siblings were close in age and had all gone to Berkeley, their terms there overlapping. Kendra had studied political science – "Of all things," she would say later, meeting people at music parties around the bay or in Los Angeles. But given her priorities, the major had made sense. She liked the subject; her family was active in Bay Area politics and Kendra and her brothers had grown up hearing political and economic discussions at parties and over dinner as a matter of course. She wrote well, an important factor in any social science major; she was good at organizing her thoughts and quite good at guessing the bias of the instructor. Kendra sailed along with remarkably little effort, pulling honor student grades at a top public university, all the while putting the greater part of her energies, mental and physical, into the pursuit of rock music.

She played piano and guitar, but above all, she sang, sang with a rich contralto with which she could make "Do Re Mi" sound suggestive. She could write lyrics, but not the melodies themselves, an incapacity that eventually led her out of music altogether, but not before she had played and above all, sung, with several bands in both the Bay Area and L.A., and not before she had begun to make friends with other young artists living on the scuffle and in their dreams. One of these young artists was a twenty-five year old would-be screenwriter who would eventually see his name listed in the credits of many films, Matthew Chase Trevino.

To Kendra, of course, he was just Matt. They met late one September evening at a rock club in Hollywood, a club where Kendra's band had just performed a sort of musical comedy, had told a story, complete with costumes, props and deliberately farcical acting, linking the songs of their set together. It was something unusual, something extra, something suggesting talent beyond the ordinary, and Matt, taken not just with Kendra's voice, but with her compelling stage presence, her breezy confidence, her exquisite comic timing, stood in line to talk with her after the gig.

"Have you got someone who can videotape your gigs?" Matt had asked. (This was before YouTube.) "Because I think you should document what you are doing. There's no way you can describe it to an agent or a producer --"

"I agree," said Kendra, twenty-four at the time of this conversation. "But the clubs are so dark. To get decent video you really need a professional and they cost too much."

"Either that," said Matt, "or you could rent studio space and shoot a video in proper lighting."

"Oh, we could shoot it at Jerzy's loft downtown," Kendra said. "But again, if it's amateur, it won't do us any good. What did you think of the music itself?"

Matt shrugged. "Uh – how about 'I didn't hear a single?'"

Kendra laughed. She liked his honesty. "That's because we don't have one," she said. "None of us can write music."

"No, but somebody can write dialogue," Matt said. "I was busting up. The whole place was. You guys are hilarious. Who's your head writer?"

Kendra smiled. "I'm actually our only writer," she said.

34

Matt sat back, impressed. "Can I get you something to drink?" he asked.

Before the night was over, Matt and Kendra had agreed to get together the next evening, to see a foreign film, a French comedy Matt had heard was very good. When Kendra met him at the theatre she was struck all over again with his good looks: tall, skinny but with muscles, dark eyes and dark curls. His smile was quick and lasting; suggestive to Kendra of a deeply good nature, a naturally happy heart. He had a pretty blonde girlfriend, a would-be model, or Kendra herself would have been interested in him. She at the time was between romances.

They met for lunch the following week and then again, at the weekend. They began to e-mail each other. Matt showed Kendra some of his in-progress film scripts. Kendra told Matt about some of the story-lines she had in mind for future gigs with the rock band. She asked Matt about finding an agent, for he had one.

Then came Shanghai. For two years since graduating from college, Kendra had worked, largely at waiting tables, both to support her musical ambitions and to save money, to save money to travel, which she had all her young life had a hunger to do. In college she had spent a semester at sea, visiting four continents. The summer after she graduated, she spent travelling around western Europe. "Not backpacking!" she assured Matt, in one of their first conversations. "I took the train except for those few times when I had to take a bus. I'm not into roughing it." Matt had been charmed.

Kendra had been saving for two years when she met Matt. She and two friends had the Asian trip planned and the air tickets paid for. She left for six weeks in mid-October, getting home two days before Thanksgiving. She visited Shanghai, Hong Kong, Macao,

Bangkok, Phuket and Bali. After two years of expectation, her spirits for the adventure had been high.

But two weeks into the trip something unexpected happened. She found herself distracted, a little anxious, a little restless. She surprised herself at wanting to be somewhere else than Southeast Asia – not necessarily California, but to be settled in one place. To be settled in one place and to be writing, and – to be writing with Matt. She e-mailed him when she was able to do so. She wrote him several hand-written letters, a couple of which arrived months after her return. These they both read with some real fascination, later that winter.

"You've been through a sea change," Matt said to her, one bright January afternoon, as they lunched at an outdoor table at a Carl's Jr. just below Sunset Boulevard. "You've shed a skin. And best of all, as the writer that you are," and he held up the letter they were reading, "you've kept a record of it. I love your letters. I wish we had not let e-mail so enfeeble us. There was a time, not that long ago, when letter writing was something everybody did. It is rapidly becoming a lost art."

Kendra did not entirely grasp it at the time, because after all, she had more than one talent, but she deeply intuited it: in her association with Matt, in her focus now on the written word, rather than on music, on instruments, lights, amps, costumes and stages, she had discovered her true vocation. She was a writer. She could sing, but she was a writer. She could play piano and guitar, but she was a writer. She could act, but she was a writer. She always had been. It was, after all, precisely on the strength of her writing that she had scored A after A in her classes at Cal. Looking back, Kendra realized that, in one form or another, she had always written: poems to her parents on their birthdays, a junior high school diary, reporting for her class in the high school student newspaper. She had always written because she was, at heart and most deeply, a writer. No doubt at some point she would have

36

come to this realization on her own, but her arriving at it that fall of her twenty-fourth year was facilitated by her teaming up with a bright new friend, a friend who would become her major professional partner over the next three decades, Matt Trevino.

"I'm so glad to be back," she said to Matt, who met her at LAX.

Matt grinned, taking her bags. "When you told me you wanted to be in L.A., at your keyboard or even with paper and pen," he said, "and I considered that you were in Bali," Matt threw his head back, laughing. "Born to the breed," he said. "I'd like to see the world eventually, too," he went on, as they walked toward the glass exits. "But first things first. And I'm a writer first, an adventurer second."

Kendra beamed. She had perhaps never before enjoyed such clarity, such a sense of ownership where her own future was concerned.

EIGHT

Matt was still at the deep end of the pool, his arms on the edge, idly swinging his legs in the water. He lifted his face toward the sun, eyes closed, and smiled. He was in the light and the warmth as much as he was in the water. He lifted one arm, extending it full stretch as if reaching for the sun itself. He looked at his arm, illumined and shadowed by the light so that the muscles showed. He had always been an athlete. Not just football, basketball and soccer in his school days, but later, in college and after, tennis and working out, racquetball and beach volleyball and skiing, both water- and downhill. Friends had taken him to the slopes for the first time when he was a freshman at UCLA. He astounded them by paralleling his first afternoon. He had never been anything but in great shape.

"Fifty-four," he said quietly. "Fifty-four. And frankly, better than you were in your twenties," for he had been too skinny in his twenties, despite his overall athleticism. He brought his arm down and looked at his shoulders, looked at his chest above the water. "How long?" he wondered. "How long before it will be your time?"

"I hope I go quick," he'd said once, to Kendra, when they were both about thirty. Wide-ranging conversation had always been characteristic of their friendship. "When it's my time, I hope I go quickly," he repeated, correcting his grammar.

They were working on a script. It was someone else's script, not theirs. It had been given to them by the producers for a re-write. The money was good; the work only marginally satisfying, for neither one of them thought much of the story, though as it happened, the film when released made a ton at the box office.

"I don't want to be one of those poor helpless old folks drooling into his bib at some dreadful skilled nursing facility, waiting to die, warehoused like defective human merchandise."

"No one wants that," said Kendra.

"Then why do we have it?" Matt asked. "Why are so many enfeebled old folks in nursing homes instead of at home, or anyway, in small-group homes, where they can be attended to with some dignity?"

Kendra shrugged. "Isn't it obvious?"

"It's only obvious how screwed up our values are," said Matt. "That that's what we do with mom and pop, old Auntie Thelma and crazy cousin George when they become too much of a bother to us. We've organized our lives, and through that organization we have organized society, in such a way as to make efficient and convenient storage of the old, the weak, the enfeebled our priority, rather than their tender care and loving comfort."

"Did we organize our lives on such principles, or has society done it for us?"

"I believe in individual responsibility," said Matt. "If we organized our lives according to humane values, society would reflect those values."

Kendra was doubtful. "I suppose there is some interplay, some trading and mixing of influences," she said. "But I think we've pretty much inherited the situation and that there is little most of us can do about it. The rich needn't worry. The rest of us have to manage with mom and pop and Auntie Thelma as best we can. There are times when that means a skilled nursing facility. It doesn't imply lack of love for the person who is placed there."

"Do you know what most of the workers in care homes get paid?" Matt asked.

Kendra did not know.

"Barely minimum wage," Matt said. "What does that tell you?"

"The monthly cost to the families, though, is huge, if they can't get MediCal," said Kendra. "I agree the staff in these places are doing important work and deserve better pay. But again, it's rather global, isn't it? I mean, how do we make a difference, individually?"

"Neither one of my folks is ever going into a rest home," said Matt, deciding not to pursue his side of the debate. "If I have to move back to Salinas to take care of them, I will." He laughed. "'Rest home!'" he said. "What a euphemism."

Kendra smiled. "The writer in you is offended," she said.

"I do like to see words used honestly," Matt agreed. "And I don't want to die a slow death. I don't need to 'rest' in any home before I go. I hope I go, literally, in a heartbeat."

"I suppose falling asleep one night and not waking in the morning would be the way most of us would choose," said Kendra. "But," she added, with an air of getting back to work, "we don't get to choose."

We don't get to choose. Kendra's words echoed through Matt's mind. No. Certainly David would not have chosen the cancer. Nor Damien the strokes.

When Matt had in fact begun to travel, begun to see the world, in his mid-thirties and a successful screenwriter, he'd seen the statue of Milo of Croton at the Louvre. He had not known the story; he'd only read the Greek myths in school, and Milo had really lived. The visceral image of the lion sinking its fangs into the man's living flesh had sent Matt searching through the guidebook, where he read a thumbnail description, providing the broad outlines of the tale. Matt had then been twenty years younger, but even so he had felt a resonance with the tragic hero. Strong and fit though long past youth, Milo proudly and manfully tested his strength in the open, never guessing that when it came to it, strength and health would matter not at all – or indeed, given that a lion might be imagined to deliberately choose attractive prey, that these very attributes might have facilitated his sudden and violent death. The lion chose Milo precisely because he was strong and fit.

Matt gathered that the moral interpretation of the story typically ran along the lines of Milo being punished for his pride. He'd defied time, he'd maintained a youthful strength and appearance well into middle age, he'd aped the Olympians, the gods themselves, and the gods were not going to have that.

"Hell," Matt said to himself, looking down at his legs, swinging lightly in the water. "That's all of us today. All of us out here in La-La-Land, anyway."

Never mind L.A.'s, that is Hollywood's, particular obsessions, never mind all the injections, all the suctions and peels, never mind the variety of surgical options. One needn't have 'had work done' to buy into the mindset, to buy into the illusion, to defy, as Linda had just put it, reality itself. Ponce de Leon might be this town's patron saint, and the fountain of youth its holy grail. Nobody got old in L.A.

"We all bought into it," Matt thought, of himself and his friends. "We lived as if illness and death were for others, for the folks in the rest homes, maybe. We were all Milo of Croton, all of us, until

Damien's first stroke. That stroke was the lion. And the lion has been with us since."

He turned from the edge of the pool and gazed across the water to the patio bar. The sound of Linda's laughter floated across the water. He slipped beneath the surface and swam to the shallow end.

NINE

"No, he's awake and alert today," Linda was saying, the phone to her ear. "A lot more energy than yesterday or the day before." She was talking to her husband. "No pain that we know of, but I mean he has a morphine drip...Just me, Tino and Matt right now..." She looked across the short space to Kendra. "How are you? Sammy's asking."

Kendra shrugged. "Tell him to come. David's got energy today."

"That's what I was saying," Linda said, both to Kendra and into the phone. "Yes...Come this afternoon...Oh that's right. Well, tonight, then. I'm here 'til late. It's my turn to make dinner...Actually I was thinking Chinese, as in take-out."

Kendra and Tino heard Sam's laugh.

Linda was married to a producer. That is, she was married to a former portfolio funds manager who had come from wealth to begin with and who, while still living and working in Chicago, had begun to invest in films. When, about twenty-five years ago, one of those films grossed three hundred million, Sam Stefani decided that the time was right, and he "loaded up the Lexus," as Linda would put it, singing the theme song from THE BEVERLY HILLBILLIES, "and moved to Beverly. All right, all right," Linda would concede. "We moved to Bel Air. It's close enough for government work."

"Nothing Hollywood loves more," David had once joked with Sam, "than a Midwesterner with money."

43

Sam, modest and self-effacing despite his success, laughed. He had put quite a bit of money, over the years, into David's films. Sam was twenty years older than Linda, who was his second wife.

"Yes, come tonight," Linda was saying to Sam. "And if I decide on Chinese, you can pick it up on your way over. Love you, baby!" She made a double-kiss sound into the phone, then locked it and dropped it back into her purse. "When it's my turn for dinner," she said to Kendra and Tino, "all I have to do is make sure we eat. No obligation to make a mess in the kitchen."

"Chinese might be a good idea, actually," Kendra said. "I don't know what we've got in the house."

Linda rolled grey-green eyes toward the bougainvillea. "Tino, tell your tia what we've got in the house."

Tino grinned. He and Linda had carted in several bags of groceries just yesterday afternoon. "We're good," he said to Kendra. Then, "Beer, Matt?" he asked, as Matt came up from the pool.

Matt shook his head. "Too early. Another iced tea would be great, though," and stretching out on the chaise as Tino got up, Matt smiled at Linda. "I have no problem with the boy waiting on me," Matt said. "We have an obligation to the young, after all. We want them to come to know the joys of service, the pleasures of giving."

"The young learn by example," Linda replied.

Matt laughed. Tino crossed out of the shade to the chaise and handed Matt the iced tea.

"Matt," Kendra said. "Put some of this on," and she handed Tino a plastic bottle of sunblock.

Tino handed it to Matt, who set it aside, and made himself comfortable on the chaise.

"It's a death wish," said Linda, shaking her head.

"Sunlight's natural," said Matt.

"So are tornadoes," said Linda.

"So are cobras," said Kendra. "So is strychnine. So are earthquakes."

Matt appealed to Tino with a look. Tino broke up.

"Women," Matt said.

"They're a whole other sex," said Tino.

One of the several glass doors that gave access to the patio opened and a dark-haired and pregnant young woman, followed by a balding young man, stepped through it.

Linda fairly hooted. "Jessica!" she said.

TEN

Lana's death had left David with three young children: Jessica, six, Justin, five, and Jeffrey, two. ("Lana liked 'J' names," David would later explain to Kendra. "There is no one on her side or mine, with any of those names.") David's huge family had of course responded with alacrity to the children's needs. But these needs were entirely emotional; they had been tended all along by a series of au pairs. Despite this fact, Carmen, Ana and Raquel, David's sisters, had arranged a schedule of daily visits to Brentwood, to make sure that the children were properly attended to – the de la Fuentes were not in the habit of raising their children by proxy.

"The girl is lovely," Carmen, the oldest of the sisters, said to David, of Anneke, the blonde Norwegian au pair who happened to be employed at the time of Lana's death. "But you cannot delegate parenting, David. In the absence of their mother, the children will have their aunts."

David was cool with that. He was cool with any help at all his family could give him, since as a rising young director and producer, he could not be a stay-at-home dad. Not, of course, that Lana had ever been a stay-at-home mom. The whole au pair thing had been her idea, to keep her free for rock gigs, free for studio sessions, and well, as David would readily admit because everyone knew it anyway, free for parties.

Had Lana loved her children? David did not doubt it. But she loved them the way she loved him – after her own fashion.

"It's like, Lana had this life," David would later tell Kendra. "She had this big life that was hers, that was Lana's. Multi-platinum

46

albums, shows and concerts, though never, after the kids started coming, tours. She quit the tour circuit the spring Jess was born. She had studio sessions, she had video shoots, she had publicity shoots, she had charity events and red-carpet nights and – well, you know the drill. And oh yeah, she was married – to me! – and we had first one and then two and then three children. She fit us in where she could, and honestly, Kendra, she loved us. She just...loved us in her own way. Who knows what drove her? She needed all that, all those trappings of success, and the word 'trapping' seems kind of sinister now, doesn't it? She needed all that – and she needed the parties. She was nothing like you."

"I liked Lana," Kendra said.

"I loved her," David said.

The de la Fuente sisters, then in their late forties and with their own children largely raised, drove across the city on a day-to-day rotation, to spend time at the Brentwood house with David and the children. This was the dynamic in place when David and Kendra began to see each other on a more than merely-social-or-professional level, a year after Lana's death.

Kendra was at first very circumspect with the children. She did not know where her romance with David might lead, and if in fact she and David were to break up, the last thing these children needed was more trauma. But she was reserved with the children for a second reason, one harder to articulate but every bit as important to her. She had recognized within a few weeks of dating David that things between them might become serious. That being the case, she might well find herself the step-mother of these three children. She was alert to the mix of emotions such a development might provoke in the young psyches of Jessica, Justin and Jeffrey. If she were to become their step-mother, she could only do it by slow and carefully measured degrees. The fact of the children significantly altered her romantic interaction with David. She took

47

a slow and considered approach with him when she might otherwise have been breezy and relaxed. David saw this change in her, recognized its cause and secretly treasured it: "Kendra can mother my children!" he thought.

ELEVEN

"Solange told us that they are attending to Dad right now," Jessica said, crossing into the shade.

"When did you get in?" Linda asked, hugging her.

"Late last night," Jessica answered. She turned to the young man accompanying her. "Almost midnight, Brett?"

"Past it," Brett answered. "It was almost two when we got to the beach house. I was worried about us waking Justin and Jeffrey."

"Which is why we are so late getting here, this afternoon. I slept 'til past eleven. Chicago to L.A. should not be so exhausting."

"Well, if you are going to consider price," Brett said. "Which we did! Starving law students, you know. We got a great price, but you pay for it in other ways, I guess."

"It's barely two," said Kendra, getting up to greet them. "Not so late." She thought of, but left unmentioned, her standing offer to fly both of them out, business class, anytime, any day that they wanted to come. For heaven's sake, she and David did not lack for money. But Jessica was adamant that she and Brett could and would handle their own expenses.

"The boys were gone when we got up this morning," Jessica said, of her brothers.

"They were here a couple hours ago," Kendra said, accepting Brett's hug.

"How's my beautiful mom-in-law?" Brett asked, sort of rocking Kendra in his embrace.

Kendra pulled back enough to look into Brett's blue eyes. "I've been better," she said, and smiled.

Brett renewed the hug. He was about thirty, over six feet and certainly two hundred pounds. He and Jessica had married the previous September.

Matt, meanwhile, on his feet to greet them, said, "Justin and Jeffrey will be back soon. I gave them passes to my club. I think they wanted to play racquetball. Monique went, too, of course." He was referring to Justin's wife.

"I can't wait to see Monique," said Jessica. "I'm six months with little David," she went on, meaning the baby in her womb, "but she's eight months now. How I wish Dad could live to see at least one of his grandchildren."

Kendra smiled a sad smile at this comment.

Linda patted Jessica's shoulder. "No fear," she said. "David knows the babies are on their way. That is a great joy to him. Meanwhile you picked the best possible day to see your father. He's wide awake and talkative."

"Yes," said Jessica. "Solange said that."

Brett still had his arm around Kendra. He let go as Jessica stepped forward.

"Kendra," Jessica said, giving her a light hug.

Kendra responded to the non-embrace in kind, wanting to respect her step-daughter's space.

"All these flights out to L.A.," Jessica went on, turning away from Kendra and toward the others. "I almost feel like I am living here again. And we've got finals in three weeks."

"It's so good to be seeing so much of you," Brett said, squeezing Kendra's hand. "We want to be here for you, Kendra."

Brett's words, and the reassuring gesture, came in under Kendra's radar. She was suddenly on the verge of tears. She squeezed Brett's hand in grateful return.

"What'll you have?" Tino asked.

"Oh, I'll get it myself," Jessica answered, turning toward the bar. And Tino, smiling and resuming his seat, let her do so.

"Only us old folks you insist on waiting on?" asked Linda, who had resumed her seat.

Tino grinned. "This is Jessica's house," he said, "not mine."

"So Dad's alert," Jessica said, looking over the bottles of wine at the bar. "Last week he was so sleepy I was not sure I would still find him with us, coming back today."

"The most awake he has been in several days," said Linda.

"He's been having visitors, though," said Kendra, resuming her seat. "His parents, over the weekend. Now this afternoon Linda tells us he saw Damien."

Jessica put down the bottle she had been examining. "Really?"

Kendra nodded.

Linda said, "I saw him an hour ago. He told me that Damien had been there, standing at the door to the room, smiling and happy. It evidently gave him a huge peace."

"Then it's near the end," Jessica said. She looked at Brett. "I'm so glad we said, 'Screw it' about the inconvenient flights, and got out here."

"Well me, too," Brett said.

"And he's seen abuella and abuellito, too?" Jessica asked, looking at Kendra, meaning, David's parents, who had died years before.

"Over the weekend," Kendra nodded.

Jessica put a hand to her mouth. She turned to the house, as if wondering how much longer the nursing team would be.

Linda got up and crossed to the bar. "What'll you have, darling?" she asked.

Jessica let Linda pour her a glass of the Riva Ranch chardonnay she was drinking. Brett wanted Calistoga water. Linda placed the drinks on the bar; then took Jessica in her arms. And suddenly Jessica was sobbing.

Kendra watched in silence. Tino and Matt both glanced at Kendra, but she only smiled a slow and small smile. In fact, her step-daughter's closeness to Linda was something for which Kendra had long been grateful.

"Kind of amazing, isn't it?" asked Jessica, a few moments later, as she and Brett took seat next to Linda. "I mean, the way the brain works. It produces morphine at times of deep physical stress, to alleviate the pain. And it produces images of our loved ones, as

52

we are approaching death, to alleviate the fear and the pain of dying. What the dying brain can do is really pretty remarkable."

Linda picked up her glass and studied it, not wanting to look elsewhere. For surely a reply would be forthcoming. That was the thing with this family, a startling mix of Catholic and atheist with a few peace-loving agnostics in-between. No matter which side of your mouth you were talking out of you were bound to be dismissed by half of them.

"Need not be a dying brain," said Matt, once again stretched in the sun on the chaise. "Isabel also saw Damien, you know. Three days after the funeral."

"I didn't know that," said Kendra, looking toward Matt.

"Yeah," Matt said. "Three days after the funeral." Isabel was Tino's mother.

"She told me about it," said Tino. "It gave her a lot of comfort."

"Tell us about it," said Jessica.

Tino shrugged. "Mom said that Dad was sort of radiant. Light all around him, wearing white, that he somehow communicated with her without words, and that she knew he was safe. Safe and happy."

"That sounds like what David saw, just now," said Linda.

"How long did it last?" Jessica asked. "With Aunt Isabel? How long did she see Uncle Damien?"

"It was just a flash," Tino answered.

"Isabel said it was over almost before she realized it had happened," Matt added. "But she was very clear about it; it was mid-morning, she was wide awake, and it felt absolutely real to her. So, it need not be a dying brain to receive such an image."

"Wow," said Jessica, and was quiet a moment, as if for thought. "You say the brain 'receives' the image, Matt, and I say it 'produces' it, and I'll admit, in those two verbs there are two profoundly different world views. But in the end, if the effect is the same, it doesn't matter who's right. Whichever verb applies, I am happy for Aunt Isabel. And happy for Dad. I can't imagine what it must be, to be Dad right now, to be standing at that boundary; the boundary between being and – not being. I think of it as an abyss, but then I realize that that's inaccurate, because after all an abyss is still an abyss, it is something. It's not nothing. It's nothingness that we can't imagine."

"There may be a reason for that," Matt suggested, and shot Jessica a wink.

"I believe in mystical experiences," said Tino. "But I've never had one. Well," he grinned, and turned to Kendra. "Except maybe seeing Tia Kendra dressed for the Oscars."

TWELVE

When Kendra heard the news of Lana's death, she sent David a card, and she attended the funeral. She and David were not really friends, at that point, more like friendly business associates. Even that description probably overstated their relationship, for as yet they had done no business together.

That was not David's fault. With the first of three films in an action-adventure trilogy immediately behind him, the film's worldwide gross more than a third of a billion dollars, David was establishing himself as a hot new director. His ambitions were large; they went well beyond mere box-office considerations. With partners who included Sam Stefani, David set up an independent production company, through which he hoped to work on film projects of real quality. As Kendra was known for by-passing parts she thought cheap and commercial, regardless of their box office potential, David had thought of her for a couple of his more artistically ambitious projects. Two years before Lana died, the very summer, in fact, of Carlos' party, David approached Kendra with a two-picture deal. Kendra resisted the offer. And "resist" was the word she used, to describe her response.

"I think there is more in the offer than a couple of admittedly good film roles," she told Matt, one breezy August night, dining amid palms, fountains and floodlights outdoors in Hollywood.

"What?" Matt asked. "You think he has romantic designs?"

Kendra shrugged. But she shrugged in such a way as to say, effectively, "Yes, that's what I think."

"He's got a rather sexy wife, girlfriend."

Kendra shrugged again. "There's just something in the air between me and him," Kendra said. "I don't trust it. Maybe I would, if Lana were not in the picture."

Matt nodded, considering it. "I think he's right," he said, "that these two roles could launch you."

"'Launch me?'" Kendra laughed. "I already am launched, with you. I write screenplays. And television pilots. And I sell them. And I make good money. And I am happy with the work and happy with the money. I don't give a damn about acting."

"Maybe not," Matt said, "but you've appeared in three films, and there has been a response to you. And I understand that response, because I share it. I saw your abilities five years ago in the clubs. I saw that, appealing as you were as a singer, your real talent was comic acting."

"You saw that my real talent was writing," Kendra protested.

Matt nodded. "Yeah, I did. After I discovered that you had scripted that gig."

"So let's keep focused," said Kendra. "I write. I can sing. I can act. But I write. That's what I do. David has this notion that he can build me up into a real star. Good God, Matt! I couldn't care less. You know that."

"Do you like singing?"

Kendra gave him a smiling frown. "What do you mean? I love singing."

"Do you enjoy acting?"

Kendra hesitated before responding. "I enjoy doing intelligent comedy," she said.

"And what are these parts that David is offering you? What kind of films are they?"

Kendra chuckled, pleased with Matt's persistence, for he knew the answer already. "They are intelligent comedies," she said, smiling, as if to say, "your point." "Well, one is. The other really is drama, but it is very witty. I showed you samples from the script."

Matt nodded. "I was almost jealous, the writing was so good." He downed what was left of his Pacifico, and signaled the waiter for another. "So the only reason you won't sign with David is that you think he wants to have an affair?"

Having it put like that, Kendra wanted to backtrack a bit. "I have no idea what his real situation is, with Lana," she said. "I just know a charged atmosphere when I am breathing in one. And I don't need the aggravation. I mean, Matt. It's not as if I wanted to become a film star. I don't need to sleep with anybody, to get what I want. I've got what I want. I did GIRL THURSDAY because Braxton is a friend of mine. And after all, it was a small part. I had no idea it was going to lead to other offers – or that they would lead to this idea that David has, that I might become, Lord help me, a movie star."

"David's not the only one with that idea."

"I don't care if the whole world's got that idea," said Kendra. "My idea is the one that matters. I'm not interested in being any kind of star."

THIRTEEN

Kendra did not do the films with David. But they worked and socialized in overlapping circles, and she saw him with some regularity, those two years between Carlos' party and Lana's death. At Lana's funeral, held at Mission San Gabriel, Kendra watched David and the children as they placed roses on the casket, and her heart ached. The little one, Jeffrey, was two and one-half.

She attended the burial after the Mass, and then went to the reception, held at the restaurant, and which was a mob scene. Then, at David's request, she went to the family gathering, at Carmen's house. She was warmly greeted by many members of the family, most of whom had not seen her since Carlos' graduation party, two summers before.

"We appreciate so much your being here," Damien said to her. "This is very hard. We need our friends."

Kendra could have wept. "Your family is strong, Damien," she said. "You will pull together, and get through this."

Carlos, the enchanted nephew, was of course also there. He was circumspect when he saw Kendra arrive at the church, and the reception at the restaurant was so huge that he never got near her. But at the house he hugged her. Without a word. Hugged her. Long and hard.

"Thank you so much for being here for us," he said, pulling back from the embrace.

Kendra's eyes were clouded by tears. After Carlos left her, she moved into the crowded main rooms of the house. She looked for David, she looked for his little ones.

FOURTEEN

For a year after Lana's funeral, David and Kendra were only occasionally in touch. He had made yet another film offer to her, the second lead in the last of the three action films. It was an over-the-top comic villainess sort of role and the success of this series guaranteed Kendra a huge new audience. Kendra turned the part down without a thought. She was committed to two other pictures at that time, filming almost back-to-back that summer and fall, and in any event, as she was always telling Matt, and telling her mother Polly and her brothers in the Bay Area, "I am done with acting; it was never meant to become a career."

For a year after the funeral, David and Kendra saw each other sporadically, almost accidentally, when for instance, they might both be at the same red carpet event, an awards show, perhaps, or the premiere of a film, or when they might be in attendance at the same script meeting, for in fact, during that year, she and Matt were writing a script for David's production company.

This haphazard set of arrangements, however, did not actually reflect Kendra's heart, on the matter of seeing David de la Fuente and his children. The thought of the children's anguish, their incomprehension, their hurting hearts, hurt Kendra's heart. She found herself thinking of Jessica, Justin and Jeffrey, whom she had only met a couple of times, every single day.

And she thought of David. She thought of his consternation, the evening of Carlos' party, as Lana had announced that she was leaving with three of the nephews for the party in West Hollywood. David a few months after the funeral told Kendra that Lana had not come home until the next day, about two in the afternoon.

"And then she slept," David said, "'til almost nine that evening. I ordered pizza for me and the kids for dinner, and told them mommy was sick. Kendra, I told them many times that mommy was sick. Many times."

It was the first time since Carlos' party that he had opened up with her on the troubles in his marriage. It would not be the last. Kendra recognized that the "charged atmosphere" of her relationship with him had two sources: his heart and hers. She was falling in love with him.

But she could not allow herself to give any sort of freedom to these feelings, during that first year after Lana's death. It would have been wrong, to take advantage of David in his shock and his grief. Kendra bided her time, and meanwhile, ached in her heart for both David and the children.

FIFTEEN

Ten months after Lana's death, Kendra and David ran into each other at a party in Beverly Hills. It was a garden affair with assigned seating and they were not at the same table, but when the dancing started around nine-thirty, David crossed to Kendra and asked if she would accompany him to the floor.

Kendra, rising from her table and turning to him, smiled. "Honestly, I'd rather accompany you to the bar," she said. She'd never been big on dancing. "Funny," she'd tell friends, "considering Mom was a dance teacher for half a century."

At the bar, set against several fairy-lit trellises of roses, Kendra asked David about the children.

"They are changed," he said. "They will never be the same. Not even Jeffrey, the baby. You have to think," David went on, "Manhattan," he said to the young man in the tux on the other side of the bar. "Kendra?"

Kendra asked for white wine.

"You have to think about what this has done to them, think about the children, the teens, the people they will now be, because they lost their mother. They are changed, Kendra. And I am everything to them now."

Kendra smiled a relaxed but deliberate smile. "They are very fortunate to have David de la Fuente as their father. To have the whole family."

"My sisters have been our lifeline," he answered. "I do not know how we'd have made it this far without them. Anneke's been wonderful, too," he said of the Norwegian au pair. "But she is young and single and, well, there is a difference. My sisters are moms."

Kendra's smile was now almost radiant. "They certainly are," she said. "I'm glad they live close enough to be there for all of you."

Their drinks arrived. David lifted his and looked out over the candle-lit tables, the big rented dance floor, the patio, the floodlit pool. The garden was romantically lit and lively with bright conversation and music, it was one of the big swing bands playing twentieth century standards such as STARDUST. Just at the moment, the band struck up CORCOVADO.

"I love this song," David said, smiling. "Quiet nights of quiet stars," he sang, his voice just above a whisper.

"Quiet chords from my guitar," Kendra sang almost breathlessly back.

"And a view of Corcovado," David said, with a grin. "Ever been to Rio?" he asked.

"Never," said Kendra, and sipped her wine. "Never to South America, in fact."

"That surprises me. I mean, from the world traveler that Matt says you were, in your youth."

Kendra smiled. "Life intervened."

"If that means life kept you here in L.A.," David said, "I call it a most fortuitous intervention."

He looked again around the glamorous scene. "No view of Corcovado from a garden in Beverly Hills, and not exactly a quiet night for us, but," and he looked skyward, "I do see a few stars up there."

Kendra looked up, too.

SIXTEEN

Their courtship lasted two years. Kendra approached it almost strategically: she never once lost sight of the children. Anything she said or did with David was always said or done with the realization that he was the father of three young children who had suffered a tragedy. Kendra's own interests in all of it thus went well beyond the familiar parameters of romantic love. If she were to marry David, the children had to accept her, and if they were to accept her, they had to like and trust her. Winning their hearts was as much a part of Kendra's goal as was winning David's.

There was also the family to consider. Lana had been loved despite her failings, and the family had felt something like betrayal, at her death. Among the de la Fuentes the family was a given. The family was not one's first consideration because one does not need to "consider the family" as though it were simply one priority among others. The family had priority, had it a priori, so to speak. The claims of the family were unquestioned. They were axiomatic. They were not "thought of" or "considered." They were met.

Much as they had loved and accepted Lana, David's parents and siblings could clearly see that her understanding of family was deficient, resulting in her disordered set of priorities. David and Lana were married ten years, the first four of which they did not have children. When the children started to arrive, the family assumed that there would be a re-ordering of Lana's priorities. When this did not happen right away, the family assumed it would happen over time, as Lana got used to motherhood. When that did not appear to be happening, either, the family talked a lot among themselves, about David and Lana, and the children, and what might, should or could be done. The general consensus was that David needed to persuade his wife to be less a rock star and more a mother. These conversations with his parents and siblings wearied David, who loved Lana passionately, but could not control her. Although everyone saw the trouble in the marriage, not trouble between David and Lana so much as between Lana and her responsibilities, the family had in fact by a sort of natural instinct taken Lana in as one of their own, and had by no means given up on her. Quite the opposite, they genuinely loved her.

Her death was like something from outer space. The de la Fuentes had no reference points for such an unimaginable event. Their overall conclusion was that "Hollywood" was to blame; Lana, though by no means entirely absolved, was nonetheless in the end perceived almost as much a victim as David and the children. "Hollywood" killed Lana; "Hollywood" brought tragedy to the family. This conclusion, Kendra knew, would mitigate against the family's acceptance of her as David's new wife and the children's new mother.

Kendra had some advantages over Lana, however, and over the course of her courtship with David, she played them well, like a veteran at poker.

In the first place, Kendra was not a rock star. She was a screenwriter and an occasional actress. That she enjoyed a certain degree of celebrity was not in and of itself damning, in the family's collective mind. Her film roles were mostly supporting, often requiring her to sing, which was an admirable talent; she never took her clothes off and what's more, with a couple of exceptions, her films were not hits. And Kendra didn't care. Unlike Lana, Kendra was not determined to reach the top, however that goal might be defined. Kendra's evident lack of drive, where acting and singing both were concerned, reassured the de la Fuentes.

But they were yet more reassured by Kendra's quietly winning personal style. They had met her on several occasions at large family events, well before she and David went public with their romance. They had first-hand experience of Kendra's breezy and relaxed style, of her tendency to stand off on the side somewhere and wait for others to draw her into the party; nothing at all like Lana, who from the moment she entered the room was the center of attention.

Kendra's own family background recommended her to the de la Fuentes. But for David, no one in the family had met Polly, Kendra's mother, or Terry and Richard, Kendra's brothers, until the engagement party held at the restaurant six months before the wedding. But David was able to tell his family that Kendra's mother and brothers, her sisters-in-law and nephews and nieces in the Bay Area were down-to-earth, reliable, hard-working, fun-loving and above all, family-oriented people. Kendra had come from a solid and stable family; Lana, her father in and out of jail all his life, and her mother, stormily married three times between an ongoing and equally stormy series of lovers, had not.

There was finally Kendra's reception with David's children. She was a great hit with Jessica, who idolized her and wanted to look, dress, talk and act "just like Kendra." The boys also clearly loved her; they loved her above all because Kendra had so carefully, so determinedly, set out to love them. She never once came to the house without spending time with them. She measured this time out carefully, only minutes at first, when the children were just beginning to know her; much much more than minutes, a year into the courtship. Gradually, the children came to be at home in her presence, and that, after all, had been Kendra's goal. The family saw this and approved.

So it was, by deliberate and considered steps, that Kendra overcame the very real initial doubts which the de la Fuentes entertained, about the prospect of David marrying yet another woman from Hollywood.

SEVENTEEN

David and Kendra were married at Mission San Gabriel on the third Saturday in May, just family and close friends at the wedding Mass itself, but the reception at the restaurant overflowed with guests – there were several hundred.

"This is so so so unreal!" said Carlos, now a graduate student in Eastern Mediterranean Archaeology at Berkeley, hugging his new aunt, at the reception.

Kendra laughed. "We're family!" she said. "On top of being Old Blues together."

"Go Bears!" said Carlos.

Kendra frowned.

"What?" he asked.

"Where's your stud?" she asked, looking at his ear.

David had wanted a long and exotic honeymoon. Kendra had actually wanted a family vacation with the children.

"Baby," David said, "we have the next forty years for family vacations. This time is our time."

"All right," Kendra conceded. "But not long, David. It sends the wrong message to the children."

David said, "Okay, how about two weeks?"

Kendra said, "How about five days?"

David said, "How about twelve days?"

Kendra said, "How about ten?"

That is what they decided on. As to where they were going, they were all along agreed on that.

"You can see Corcovado from Ipanema," David said, "but not from Copacabana."

"Well I guess that settles it," said Kendra. "We stay at Ipanema."

And so Kendra saw Rio for the first time.

EIGHTEEN

"The yard is lovely, Kendra," Jessica said. "The birds of paradise are spectacular."

Kendra smiled. "You father planted those," she said.

"Had them planted," Jessica corrected, and the others laughed. She looked at Tino. "Funny, the way these things shift from generation to generation. Dad loved gardening, but would not go near it, except to give orders to a crew. You --"

"It would be my profession," Tino said, "but for the restaurants."

"Most of what you see in the garden here this spring you can thank your cousin for," Kendra said, and smiled at Tino. "He's taken the time to attend to the yard. I haven't."

Tino did not live with Kendra and David, but since his uncle's serious decline had set in, three months before, he had been at the house almost every day, and he often spent nights. A natural at gardening, he'd taken over supervision of the yard crew, who came in once a week.

"Seriously," Jessica asked her cousin. "You would work as a gardener, but for the restaurants?"

"Happily," Tino replied. "I think it's just about the most rewarding work on earth. In exchange for a little loving attention on your part, the roses bloom, the oranges ripen and the jasmine scents the air. Find me more satisfying work."

"I've tried to steal him away on several occasions," Linda said, "to attend to my back forty."

Tino grinned. "I've told you what you need to do," he said. "Fill plants with showy blooms, like hydrangea and oleander, backed by palms. Maybe tree ferns. And you could drape some flowering climbers, like trumpetvine or bougainvillea, along that stretch of bare stone wall. It would really pick things up."

Linda waved her hand as if she could not be bothered. "Gardening is a talent like any other," she said. "I haven't got it. But though I may not know anything about gardening, I know what I like," she went on, and surveyed the overall scene from her shaded seat. "And I like this." She hesitated, and then added, "Well, not this," and indicated the shaded patio area, and everyone laughed, for her GILLIGAN'S ISLAND comments were widely reported. "But the rest of it, yes. Big time yes. When you live in the subtropics you should take advantage of it, and you have, Kendra. I love this yard."

"Well, a lot of it is David," Kendra said, "and of late, a lot of it is Tino."

A silky grey cat crossed out from behind the bar, spied Kendra, and jumped onto her lap. "Cleo," Kendra said, smiling, and started to pet the animal, which settled down quickly, purring. All of Kendra's and David's cats had Egyptian names, though some were ironic; Cleo, for instance, was short not for Cleopatra but for Cleocatra.

"Would you really work as a gardener," Jessica pressed Tino, "but for the restaurants?"

"Why not?" Tino smiled.

"Well, if nothing else," Jessica said, "your photography."

70

Tino had been serious about taking pictures since his teens.

"I mean, a lot of our family is artistic," Jessica went on. "Why not pursue your photography professionally?"

Tino shrugged. "Why not pursue gardening?" he asked. "I love both."

"And the restaurants?"

Tino grinned. "The restaurants are the family," he said, brushing back a lock of black hair. "And only a few of us – our generation, I mean – have any commitment to them. And too," he added, "it's a way to honor Dad."

"Photography would honor Uncle Damien," Jessica said. Damien, too, had been an avid amateur photographer. "You inherited the talent from your dad, I'm sure."

Tino shrugged. "Did I mention?" he asked. "I love running the restaurants."

"If it keeps him here in L.A.," said Linda, "that works for me," and she shot Tino a wink. "Not that it does my garden any good."

Tino grinned and indicated the house, that is, David. "I've been a little preoccupied," he said. "I'll be happy to help with your garden, Linda, as soon as I am able to do so."

"I love the way you love your uncle," said Linda. "Heaven help me. I wish my family was like this."

"Hey look," said Matt. "It's the boys."

71

NINETEEN

From the same glass door through which some minutes before Jessica and Brett had stepped there now appeared two young men, dark-haired, medium height and with chunky-muscular builds.

"Man oh man, they look like David," Linda said.

A young woman followed the boys out; she was African-American, slender and graceful with a bright smile and just at the moment, showing all eight months of her pregnancy.

"Solange and crew are with Dad," Justin, the older of the brothers, said, crossing toward the patio. "She said just a few minutes."

"How was the work-out?" asked Jessica, rising and hugging her brothers, one after the other.

"Awesome!" said Jeffrey, and shot Matt a thumbs-up. "When I come back, I'm joining that club, dude."

Matt grinned, and returned the thumbs up. "What did you do, Monique," he asked, "while they were playing racquet ball?"

Monique smiled and closed her eyes as if to underscore her answer, "I had a heavenly loofah scrub and massage. I know the baby enjoyed it, too. Thank you, Matt."

"No change from this morning?" Justin asked Kendra.

"No," Kendra said. "He's the same. Bright and alert and talkative." She did not get up, and neither did Tino. They had been with Monique and the brothers just earlier in the day.

"I so want Dad to hold on," Jessica was saying, still holding Jeffrey's arms, but looking at Monique. "I want him to see your baby."

Monique smiled. "Oh I wish that could happen, too," she said. She was carrying a girl, but she and Justin had not yet decided on a name.

"He could make it," Justin said. "We're due in just over three weeks. And Dad's already beat the odds more than once. He was not supposed to be there for our weddings. He was supposed to be gone by last summer. Right, Kendra?"

Kendra, stroking Cleo, who was looking up at the newcomers, nodded. "According to the MDs, Dad should have been gone last summer, and that was at the outside. Here it is late April of the following year."

"It's all the voo-doo medicine Mom got for him," said Jeffrey, and laughed. "All that gin-shin stuff, all that gingko biloco or whatever it is called."

Everyone laughed, including Kendra. In fact, she was personally inclined to believe that their wide-ranging searches among alternative therapies and medicines had prolonged David's immunity and strength. But she would never be able to prove it, and in any event, in the end they, too, had failed him.

"Hey Mom," Jeffrey said. "Whatcha drinking here?" He lifted her glass, which held only ice and a lemon wedge. "Iced tea?"

Kendra smiled.

"Kisses to Cleo," Jeffrey said, patting the cat's head. "I'll get you some more," he said, and crossed to the bar.

TWENTY

Although Kendra never actually said outright that she was giving up acting for the children, that in fact is precisely what she did. At the time she and David were engaged she had appeared in eight films, two of which were only released after their wedding, and she had been considering another couple of offers. Then David proposed and, though she made no announcement about it, that was that, as far as Kendra was concerned.

She would always have screenwriting. She had only gotten into acting through an almost accidental set of developments, and now she was leaving it just as inobtrusively. She let the directors in question know that she could not take the parts because she was about to assume a new role – wife and mother to three young children – and she needed time to learn it. The first couple years after the wedding she continued to receive offers, not many, but then there had never been a flood of them, and she turned them all away, always saying the same thing: she had to learn her new part, her real-life part. After a while word got around that Kendra Collins, who had until recently seemed poised for real stardom, had turned her back on acting, and the offers dried up. And that was just fine with Kendra.

Becoming a mother had never been first on Kendra's list of priorities. All the more surprising, then, what a "natural" she was at it. At the time of the wedding, Jessica was nine, Justin eight and Jeffrey five. They'd gotten to know Kendra gradually over the previous two years, the years of the courtship, during which time they had called her, at Kendra's insistence, Kendra. When she and David told the children of their engagement, Jeffrey waited until his older siblings, full of happy talk and future plans with Kendra, left the room. Then he asked her, "So you are going to be my new mother?"

"Lana will always be your mother," Kendra told him. "I can never take her place. But I can be the best step-mother I know how to be for you, Jeffrey."

The child looked at the floor and took a minute to ask the next question. "Can I call you Mom?" he asked.

Kendra's breath caught and for an instant she could not respond. Tears came into her eyes. Then, with a radiant smile, "Yes! Yes, Jeffrey! You can call me mom! It would make me very happy."

Jeffrey ran to embrace her.

TWENTY-ONE

Being a mother had never been one of her chief goals, so all the more surprising at how good Kendra was at it. She understood her responsibilities as if by a set of natural intuitions. Of course she would be at home when the children came in from school. If she and Matt were writing at his place, or if there were a script meeting at one of the studios, or if she had a meeting with a producer, Kendra made sure that her professional schedule did not overlap her time with the children. There were occasional meetings she had to attend while the children were at home, but she met by far the majority of her professional commitments during school hours.

David and Lana had been out sometimes as often as three or four nights a week, both socially and professionally, a schedule which, by the last couple of years before Lana's death, David had begun to resent. David and Kendra were out for such affairs, parties, charity events, premieres and so on, several times a month, not several times a week.

When Jessica went out for a part in the school play, Kendra was there to coach her with her lines. When Justin wiped out on his roller blades and came limping home with bloodied knees and scraped hands and arms, Kendra was there to clean him up, get the disinfectant and band-aids in place, and above all, to let him show his tears – more from humiliation, than pain.

As for Jeffrey, there was one incident from his childhood that rose brightly in Kendra's memory, each year, on his birthday, which was near Thanksgiving. The first birthday that he celebrated with his "new mom" was Jeffrey's sixth. He wanted a Saturday pool party with his friends. Kendra hoped for dry weather, which they got. She invited not just Jeffrey's friends, but the family, as well, and a large contingent of the de la Fuentes was in attendance that bright afternoon. David and Kendra had gone to the usual effort to create a kid-friendly environment on the patio and near the pool, a bounce house, popcorn and cotton candy and snow-cone machines, hot dogs and burgers on the barbecue. It was a lovely autumn day, temperatures well into the seventies, quite warm enough for the pool, which the children were using, several de la Fuente nephews acting as life guards.

At Jeffrey's request, Kendra had worn a light and filmy canary-yellow designer dress, a dress she'd bought for a film premiere, and of which Jeffrey was particularly fond. He thought his new mother looked more beautiful in that dress than in anything else from her wardrobe.

When it came time for the cake, the de la Fuente nephews were all over it: Rico lit the candles, Javier got everyone gathered to sing, and the two of them together cut the pieces, Rico working from one side, Javier the other. Julian, Angelo and Santino handed the cake out. It was a white and dark chocolate bakery confection, with milk chocolate frosting.

"Cake's for the kids," said Rico as Julian and Angelo both helped themselves to a piece, while distributing it to the children.

"We're kids," said Angelo.

"I'm barely old enough to drink," agreed Santino.

All the children had been served when Jeffrey came back and asked for a second piece. His older cousins razzed him about it, but Jeffrey upbraided them.

"Not for me!" he said. "For my mom!"

"Whoa, dude!" laughed Rico. "Shut us up!"

77

Javier handed Jeffrey a second piece of cake, on a paper plate, with a napkin.

Kendra was standing near the pool, watching the several children who, having finished their cake, had already gotten back in. Jeffrey was in board shorts and flip flops. He hurried across the patio to Kendra, carrying the cake in both hands. When he reached the wet part of the patio nearest the pool, one of his flip-flops buckled, and he tripped. He careened forward toward Kendra, who at once reached out toward him, catching him in his fall. The cake hit Kendra's dress.

"Are you all right?" Kendra asked, bending down to meet him at eye level, her hands on his arms.

Jeffrey blinked, as if trying to bring into focus what had just happened. He looked back toward the table where his older cousins stood with the cake. "Oh, bummer, dude!" said Rico. "Come back for more, Jeffy," said Javier. "You okay, Jeff-Jeff?" said Julian. Jeffrey seemed not to hear them. He turned back to his step-mother, blinking more. He looked at her dress, with the smashed-up cake. He looked into Kendra's eyes, still blinking, and blinking back, Kendra now saw, tears.

"My little boy!" Kendra cried softly to him, not wanting to embarrass him but determined to comfort him. "My darling little boy!"

"Mommy, I'm sorry!" Jeffrey cried, loudly, not caring at all who heard. "I'm sorry I ruined your dress! I'm sorry I ruined your dress!"

Kendra drew him close, running her fingers through his hair.

A few minutes later they were up in the dressing room off the master bedroom, selecting her replacement dress.

So it was that the children taught Kendra her new role.

TWENTY-TWO

Solange, with coffee-and-cream colored skin and tightly-coiffed pale orange curls, stepped through the glass door. "Daddy is waiting!" she called, with a big smile.

"Don't you just adore the accents and cadences of the French Caribbean?" Linda asked, for Solange hailed from Martinique.

"Yeah, especially when they are speaking English," said Matt. "Such a rich mix of sounds."

Solange was the housekeeper. Since David's illness, she had been busy with considerably more than merely keeping house, but officially, that was her title.

Jessica and Brett had risen to go inside. "Aren't you coming?" said Jessica, adjusting her sunglasses and turning to her brothers, who had not moved.

"We saw Dad this morning," said Justin. "We don't want to crowd your visit."

"Don't be ridiculous," said Jessica. "Come on, he can see all his kids at once. And his kids-in-law," and she indicated Monique, who'd been talking with Kendra. "And his grandchildren. After all, the babies are here!" and she patted her belly.

Justin and Jeffrey looked one to another and shrugged. They got up.

"In a minute," Monique said, in response to a gesture from Justin. "Mom and I are talking."

The others went inside.

"Such a wonderful thing for them," Monique said, resuming her conversation with Kendra, "to be able to come back home, by which I mean not just southern California, not just Brentwood, but to come home to this house. This beautiful house and yard, so full of memories for them. I urged Justin to stay here this week, but he said you had other guests expected, so we are out at the beach."

"Well, yes," Kendra said, "my brother Richard is coming down from the Bay Area the day after tomorrow, with my mom and my sister-in-law. They are only staying a couple of days, and there would have been room for you and Justin."

In fact, Jessica, learning that all three siblings would be in Brentwood this week, had suggested the beach house as a sort of "sibling reunion," and Justin and Jeffrey had agreed to the plan.

"There is actually room for all of us right here," Monique went on.

"Oh, we'd be a little crowded," said Kendra. "I mean, I think that's how the kids would see it."

"Not at all," said Monique. "I have six brothers and sisters and we grew up in a four bedroom house in the Ninth Ward." Monique was from New Orleans. "It would be nice, to have the whole family here together."

Kendra would have been happiest with that arrangement as well, but she had not been in charge of the siblings' accommodations. Jessica had.

"Funny about the beach house," she said now, to her daughter-in-law. "I never wanted it. It was David's idea."

TWENTY-THREE

It was one of their first real disagreements. In the second year of their marriage, David told Kendra that they were going to move.

"We can afford a bigger place," he said to Kendra, arranging chicken breasts on a platter, for they had decided to barbecue that evening. "And we should have it. I am thinking Bel Air or Beverly Hills, though I am open to a couple other possibilities."

Kendra handed him the first of several cut lemons, which he proceeded to squeeze over the breasts. David, when home, enjoyed cooking and did quite a bit more of it than did Kendra.

"We need to be able to entertain properly," David went on. "You know the sort of place I mean. We don't have even one decent reception room here, nothing close."

Kendra knew very well the sort of house he was talking about, and yes, Bel Air and Beverly Hills were full of them.

"With your career simply in orbit," David went on, for this was while Kendra's film appearances were still fresh in the public imagination, "and several prospects for me with the right groups of people, we need a bigger place."

"We have sixteen rooms," Kendra said, handing him a second lemon. "We actually live in half of them."

"The number of rooms is irrelevant," David said, squeezing the lemon, back and forth over the breasts. "Well, all right," he said, tossing the lemon and reaching the next from Kendra's hands.

"Obviously not irrelevant. But what I am talking about is the kind of rooms, the kind of house, the kind of acreage."

The Brentwood home sat on a full two-acre lot. Kendra thought of this but did not say it; after all, David knew it.

"You remember the garden party at Mort and Celia's," David went on, shaking salt onto the breasts. "Where the band played CORCOVADO, the evening we linked up. Four and a quarter acres, huge reception rooms, twenty foot ceilings --"

"Lovely place," Kendra said.

David smiled, thinking he was winning her over. "Beautiful place. Well, that's the kind of place we need now, Kendra, a hot new film star and her up-and-coming director-producer husband. That's the kind of place we need now."

"I'm not hot," Kendra said, "I'm not new, and I'm not a star – never was."

"That's not my fault!" David laughed, now shaking lemon pepper onto the chicken.

"You're talking about buying a showplace," Kendra said.

"Why not? We can afford it. And we need it."

"That we can afford it is neither here nor there," Kendra replied, handing him the platter of wings and drumsticks, the pieces the kids liked. "But we certainly do not 'need' it, David, not if the word 'need' is to be allowed any actual reference point to reality."

David looked up from the chicken. "You know what I am talking about, Kendra."

"Of course I do."

"We need to have the right address. Brentwood is for our agents and our attorneys, not us."

Kendra laughed.

"Laugh all you want, you know it is true."

"There are lots of film stars in Brentwood," Kendra countered. "Directors and producers, too."

"Not like us," David said, turning back to the chicken, and holding his hand out for another cut lemon.

Kendra handed him a lemon. "These are from our trees," she said.

"They have lemon trees in Beverly Hills," David said, missing neither a beat nor her implication. "They have backyard barbecues and sandboxes and swing sets. It will be a home for the children."

"No it won't," Kendra said. "It will be a showplace for your deal-making."

"And yours."

"I don't need a showplace to make deals," Kendra said. "I'm a writer. We can live anywhere, and we make deals in restaurants."

"You'll make more deals and better," David said, "at home in Beverly Hills."

Kendra shook her head. "You surprise me."

He looked at her, holding the lemon still over the chicken. "Why?"

She shrugged. "I did not think you would be – susceptible -- to this kind of thing."

"'This kind of thing?'"

"Keeping up with Joneses."

David scoffed. "Please, Kendra."

"That is what it amounts to. It's such a shallow, stupid insecurity, this business of where you live on the West Side," Kendra said. "I wouldn't have thought you susceptible to it. You're David de la Fuente, the trailblazing Mexican American director and producer, the proud native Angeleno in this city full of people who were born elsewhere, the smash-hit commercial genius behind a trilogy of teen action flicks that did a billion worldwide and who with the other side of his brain has created an independent film production company which is responsible for several intelligent and engaging films, films which have swept the indie awards circuit and racked up half a dozen Oscar nominations."

David cocked his head slightly to one side, as if considering this assessment, and finding it adequate. "I didn't realize you'd paid such close attention to my successes," he added with a grin, and turned back to the chicken. "It's eight Oscar nominations, so far, incidentally, but who's counting? I guess we'll start counting when we start winning."

"You don't need to conform to any set of preconceptions in this town," Kendra said, "including the preconception that to be taken seriously, you need to have forty rooms on five acres in the right zip code. You're hot no matter where you live, and anyway, you should be above such considerations. It's a stupid prejudice and not one you should be influenced by."

"Kendra, you know as well as I do the importance of image in this town."

"I do," Kendra agreed.

David gestured palms up, as if to say, "Well?"

"I've never confused my image with who I am."

David's response was entirely in the upward movement of his eyebrows.

"You want to really make an impression?" she said. "Buy a place east of La Cienega. Imagine it. One of the hottest of the new generation of directors living in Fairfax! That would make them sit up and think for a minute. Not much more than a minute, I am sure, because thought can be painful activity, especially when it causes one to examine one's underlying prejudices. But you'd sure make an impression. Who knows, given the herd-instinct, you might just provoke a wholesale reassessment of property values on the West Side. Wasn't it Lady Bracknell who said that either side of Belgrave Square could be made the more fashionable, to fit her needs?"

"Oscar Wilde," David said, "often made us laugh at the truth. But it's the truth all the same. And in any event I think it was Portman Square."

Kendra smiled.

David returned his attention to the chicken. "I am gathering you don't like the idea of moving."

"If you'd come to me and said you wanted to move because you wanted a house in Beverly Hills because you wanted to live in Beverly Hills because you like it in Beverly Hills, that would be one thing," Kendra said. "I still would be resistant to a move, but the point is, you don't want to move to Beverly Hills or Bel Air because you particularly like it there. You want to move there because you perceive that that is where other people think you should be. And that's crap."

She handed him the chopped cilantro. "Not too much," she said. "Jessica's not crazy about it."

"I'm leaving it off two wings and two drumsticks," David said, "just for her."

"David," Kendra began again. "We have by any but the standards of maybe Newport and Mayfair, a magnificent home. We have a resort-like garden, a lovely pool and patio, a guest house, and a garage that would hold five cars if we had them. And we have something more than all of that: we have memories, we have family history here. This is the only home the children have ever known, and it is a home, not a showplace. They remember Lana here, and that is important. You can't pretend that isn't important."

David scattered the cilantro over the chicken.

"The children are all in school now," Kendra continued.

"Private school," David said. "Not like they'd have to change."

"But here in Brentwood," Kendra argued. "Are they going to keep going to school here, if we are living in Beverly Hills? I don't think so."

"There's nothing to prevent it," David said.

"Their friends are here," Kendra went on.

87

"They would make new friends," David said, "anywhere. And seriously, Kendra, when they see some of these homes – well, the kids themselves just might surprise you with their readiness to move."

Kendra drew in a deep breath. "David, I don't want to move. Not for myself. Not for the children."

David reached the vegetable platter, for he was going to grill zucchini, bell peppers and tomatoes as well. "This all ready?" he asked.

"Unless there is something else you want."

"No yellow squash?"

Kendra shook her head.

"Asparagus?"

Kendra went to the refrigerator and returned with a bunch of asparagus, which David proceeded to wash and lay out, neither of them for that moment saying anything.

"This is good." He drew himself up and stepped back from the counter, looking at the platters. Then he took a deep breath and when he exhaled, it was with a sigh.

"Kendra," he said, and raised his hands toward her shoulders but stopped, seeing as his hands were smeared with lemon, cilantro and asparagus. He grinned. "I want you to trust me. We are going to find a great new house, the right new house, and it will be a home for the children. How could it not be? You will be there."

In the end, David did something that astounded Kendra. He kept the Brentwood house for them to live in. And he bought a second home, a house built along the lines of what he was looking for, in Malibu.

"Well, after all," David's realtor said to Kendra, after she'd shown him some places in Malibu, "if you already have a house in town, you don't need a second one there. Brentwood's fine for the kids. Malibu works for the professional considerations. More than works. Works very very well. Wait'll you see these places I am showing David."

The realtor was Linda Stefani.

"I mean, when he came to me and said you were going to buy in Malibu," Linda went on, "I thought, 'What the hell?' I think I know Kendra. I think I know she does not want a beach house. Well, maybe if it were in Monterey County."

Kendra smiled.

"But then I understand David's motivation," Linda said. "And I mean, you are not going to be the only couple in the film colony to have two domiciles within twenty miles of each other. If anything, that looks damned good. And Brentwood more than holds up its end of the equation. You can't argue with someone who has sixteen rooms on two acres in Brentwood and an eleven million dollar home in Malibu."

Kendra gasped. "Is that what David is going to spend?" she asked.

Linda shrugged. "That's mid-range," she said. "He can't get what he wants for less than eight or nine, and as his realtor and his friend, and knowing what's behind this, I am urging him toward the pricier properties. I mean, if this is business, let's get it right."

The thought of Linda's commission flashed through Kendra's mind, but she dismissed it. She had no objection whatever to her friend making money on her hard-earned deals. Kendra objected, from someplace deep within, to the idea of spending several million dollars simply to conform to a prejudice. She was surprised at David. She chalked it up to some unexamined insecurity on his part. She only hoped he would be satisfied to own two beautiful homes, and not five or six, not suddenly have to have a place in Manhattan and another in Mexico and still another on Maui. The excesses she encountered every day in the film world had always left Kendra dispirited.

"When I think of what else could be done with the money," she'd said at the time, to Matt, who shared her views on the matter. "I just shake my head."

Kendra had never had to deal directly with Hollywood excess her first dozen years in L.A. She saw it all the time, and walked right past it. It was only when she married David that it became an issue in her own life.

TWENTY-FOUR

David had bought higher, rather than lower, in Malibu, but not as high as he might have. The house was only a little larger, in terms of square feet, than the Brentwood house. The difference was in lay-out and design, the difference was in the reasons for the house's existence. "No family ever grew up here," thought Kendra, the first time Linda took her through it. She was impressed with the ocean views, with the beach access, with the banana trees and hibiscus along the property line, but on the whole, yes, frankly, she would have preferred a beach house in Monterey County. This house felt sterile to her. It felt empty.

Oddly enough, Kendra had come over the years to feel – of all things – a family connection, where the Malibu house was concerned. Though it had, indeed, served as the desired venue for David to entertain wealthy backers and potential investors, to party with his stars and writers and set crew, the Malibu house had become, in the seventeen years since David bought it, a huge favorite with the family, with the siblings and the nephews and nieces alike.

"Hola Tia," Rico said, calling Kendra from San Gabriel one morning in early summer, a couple years after David had bought the house. "I am wondering if Malibu is available the second weekend in October? Santino's getting married you know --"

"Yes, I know," Kendra smiled, always pleased with the breezy trust the de la Fuente nephews and nieces placed in her. Santino was one of the nephews.

"Well, we have a big bachelor party planned. Me, Javier, Julian, Angelo, Carlos, all the guy cousins, plus about ten friends. The second Thursday in October. It's all on the West Side, all the trendy places --"

"You need a place to crash?" Kendra asked.

"It's all limos, Tia," Rico said. "None of us are driving. But we may be pretty drunk before the night is over, and the last clubs on the itinerary are in Santa Monica. We were thinking that if Malibu was available, we could all dry out on the beach the next day."

Kendra was trying to imagine it. "The limos aren't overnight, are they?"

"No."

"How are you going to get home on Friday?"

Rico laughed. "Our girlfriends will come and get us," he said.

Kendra laughed. "Let me talk to your uncle," she said, and in fact, the young men had crashed at Malibu the night of the bachelor party.

"Kendra," Carmen said, just days after the call from Rico, over the phone from the restaurant, where she was that afternoon working as hostess. "Maria's eighteenth birthday is this fall," Carmen said, of her youngest daughter. "She wants to have a birthday on the beach. It will be November, and I was thinking that maybe the house would be available."

The family came to love Malibu. To Kendra's very great surprise, she found the beach house feeling like a home, after all. But it was entirely because of the larger family's frequent use of it.

TWENTY-FIVE

Monique had joined the other young people with David. Linda was on the phone to yet another client, rolling her eyes toward the bougainvillea while all the same reassuring the person on the other end of the line how completely she understood his outrage at some alleged infraction on the part of the owner of a property this client was interested in buying. Matt and Tino were talking about the Dodgers. Kendra stroked Cleo's silver fur, listened to the cat's contented purr and felt a certain contentment herself. Linda hung up, exasperated.

"Why do I work?" she asked, asked, as it might be, the bougainvillea. "I mean, seriously. These prima donnas who think the world owes them strawberry Jello with bananas and whipped cream on top!"

"Huh?" said Tino, laughing, his conversation with Matt disrupted.

"You're too young," Linda said. "I mean, I do not need to work," she went on. "Not like I'd be on food stamps tomorrow, if I quit this afternoon, and oh!, I can't tell you how many afternoons I have said to myself, 'Quit. Quit, girlfriend. Be the trophy wife that Sammy married.' After all, what's wrong with being a trophy wife – especially after twenty-seven years of marriage?"

"I'm sorry, Linda," said Tino.

"Oh, to Hell with it," said Linda. "I'm not going to quit. I like having my own money too much."

"I imagine we can all relate to that," said Matt.

"We are so damned privileged," said Linda, and sipped her chardonnay. "I mean, leave aside GILLIGAN'S ISLAND, here we sit in a virtual paradise, and what have we done to deserve it?"

"Nothing," said Matt.

"You two work hard," Tino objected.

"Migrant farm laborers work hard, too," said Matt.

"Amen," said Linda.

"And what have they got to show for their efforts?" Matt went on, from the chaise, where he had taken off his sunglasses because "I don't want to look like a raccoon," he'd said. "I'd venture that no one in this country works harder than a migrant farm laborer," Matt now said. "And what have they got to show for their honest and at times back-breaking efforts?"

"Nada," said Linda.

"I mean, I hope we can all agree that the work that migrant farm laborers do is important work," Matt said. "Without them, we would have to go into the fields ourselves, to pick our food. I would say that bringing food in from the fields is pretty important work."

"I would agree with that," said Tino.

"Amen," said Linda.

Kendra, still stroking Cleo, said nothing. But she was gazing at Matt. Gazing at him and smiling.

"But what do farm laborers get paid for their efforts?" Matt asked. "What respect do they get, what recognition, what accolades? We readily reward executives on Wall Street, entrepreneurs in Silicon Valley and all of us in Hollywood, to say nothing of the sports world, and act as if our inflated salaries were somehow justified because we are 'special,' because we are doing such important and rarefied work. Well, left to ourselves to go out and pick the lettuce, pick the carrots and the new potatoes, pick the oranges and the grapefruit, I have a feeling most of us would rather quickly assign a higher priority to the work of the migrant farm laborer than to that of even the most gloriously talented film or sports-world superstar."

"Amen," said Linda. "Couldn't have said it better myself. Couldn't have said it at all, in fact, but that's beside the point."

"Viva la revolucion," said Tino.

Matt laughed. "You and your generation," he said. "Don't think cynicism hasn't been tried. It pre-dates my generation, by several generations."

"By several millennia," said Kendra. "It goes back at least to the pre-Socratics. But this boy's not cynical," she said, and patted her nephew's arm. "He's very idealistic."

"I think it's wonderful to have ideals," said Linda. "I wouldn't know, since I've never had any. But the overall concept – that there are things out there worth giving it all for – must be rather comforting."

"You've got ideals," said Matt. "We all do. All of us have dreams, and if you've got a dream, you've got an ideal."

"Not buying it," said Linda. "I dream of looking thirty-five 'til I'm seventy, but I don't call that idealism. I call it idolatry."

Matt laughed. "Right there at the altar with you," he said. "On my knees, yet. But I'd be satisfied to look fifty at seventy. My idols are among the lesser gods, I guess."

"If you are going to go to the trouble of worshipping an idol," Linda said, "worship it well."

Matt turned and looked at her, smiling. "If you're gonna go to Hell --"

"At least enjoy the ride," said Linda, and sipped her chardonnay.

"Speaking of the devil," said Matt, looking toward the house.

"Braxton!" cried Linda.

TWENTY-SIX

Kendra and Matt had started writing together within a few weeks of their first meeting, that long-ago September evening at the Hollywood rock club. When Kendra returned from Shanghai that autumn, she and Matt set up regular working hours, hours scheduled around her shifts at the Santa Monica restaurant at which she was then waiting tables, and his schedule at the Westwood health club where he worked as a trainer. Because they both worked only part time, they had a lot of time for writing. They sometimes put in as many as thirty hours a week together, in pursuit of their mutual dream.

Their time was not all spent writing. They rented movies they loved, movies they would have been glad to have written themselves, and watched them. More than watched them; studied them. They counted scenes. They counted lines of dialogue within scenes. They took note of non-verbal clues, non-verbal action which moved the plot forward. They paid attention to the cinematography, to the way the camera was used, to help advance the storyline. They read books on screenwriting; they took a course on it together through UCLA Extension, they attended screenwriting workshops.

And they wrote. They wrote and wrote and wrote some more, and then they re-wrote.

"Didn't somebody say 'writing is re-writing?'" Kendra once asked.

"Yeah, I think somebody did say that," Matt answered. "But since neither one of us can remember his name, maybe we shouldn't attach too much importance to it."

They wrote original material, working together on several screenplay ideas of Matt's, and developing some of Kendra's stage-scripts for the band, which she continued to perform with, during this time. They also worked on non-original material; in particular, they worked on film adaptations of several twentieth-century novels that Matt felt should be brought to the screen.

"Rights and permissions can be worked out later," Matt said of the adaptations. "It takes money to option a novel. I haven't got any – yet – but I do have the talent to translate these great stories for the screen."

At the time that he met Kendra, Matt had several screenplays in progress, but not yet one completed. Despite this not-entirely-promising fact, Matt had an agent, largely courtesy of the strong recommendation of a friend.

"Friends are everything in this business," Matt said. "Raw talent will only get you so far. And frankly, the reason why is that there is a whole lot of raw talent out there. What you and I can do, Kendra? It's not that incredibly special. A lot of other people can do it. But half of the people who could write for film will never even bother to give it a shot; they'll go to work in advertising or for a magazine, instead. The other half includes us, and it's a highly populated half. But you can eliminate half of them on the basis of persistence – successive rejections wear most people out. And you can eliminate maybe half of those still left on the basis of distractions – it takes a laser-like focus to succeed at what we want to do. If your real focus is your lover or your bank account or having fun, you are not going to make it in screenwriting."

He stopped, ran a hand through his dark curls, and smiled. "As if I would know what it takes to make it in screenwriting!" he said, and laughed.

But what he said made sense to Kendra. "It's the same in music," she said. "I have played with four or five bands in the last five years, both here and in the Bay Area. I can't tell you the frustration I have felt, with musicians who can't stay the course. If it is not personal infighting within the group itself, then it is outside distractions. Of the six of us who made up the first band I played with, up north, five years ago, I am the last one standing. Everyone else has abandoned music for – gee, it's depressing to think about what they left it for. Nine-to-five security and law school."

"Nothing wrong with nine-to-five security or law school, in any objective sense," said Matt. "And in any event, that's the process. That's how the field gets narrowed. Meanwhile, those of us who stay in the race need every break we can get, and friends in the business are the easiest way to the breaks."

The friend who had introduced Matt to his agent was an ambitious young television writer who had recently had several successes. His name was Alan Braxton. Matt spoke often of Alan to Kendra. "I want you two to meet," he said.

TWENTY-SEVEN

"He doesn't eat," Matt said to Kendra, of Alan, the day the three of them got together for lunch in West L.A. "He drinks. And he works. I assume he sleeps, though I don't know when, given his schedule at Parker-Ford Productions --"

"Parker-Ford," Alan said, "is to be a thing of the past as of this spring."

"Really?" said Matt. "Why? What's happened?"

"It's all good," Alan assured him. Then he assured Kendra, "I do eat, actually."

He was seated across the table from them. He was a little older than Matt and Kendra, early thirties. His general appearance was not too different from Matt's: tall and slim, almost aquiline features. His hair was dark and he kept it short, not wild curls like Matt's. His eyes were, in Matt's description, "shocking blue." He had a bright smile and a confident manner, but what most struck Kendra about Alan that first meeting was the intensity she sensed behind those piercingly blue eyes.

Alan was looking at Kendra. "I eat once a day," he said. "I appreciate Matt's concern, but as I'm sure you've noticed, he can exaggerate."

"You don't get hungry more than that?" Kendra asked.

"I don't get hungry at all," Alan said.

"Seriously?" asked Matt.

"Seriously," said Alan. "I just – don't get hungry. Oh, maybe, once a month."

"Once a month!" Matt laughed, and Kendra, too, was incredulous.

Alan shrugged. "I eat once a day because I know I need to," he said. "That's enough, and no, I do not get hungry."

"Is it a particular meal?" Kendra asked, intrigued.

Alan shook his head. "It's usually dinner, but that is not because dinner is when I 'want' to eat. I don't ever want to eat. It could be breakfast, brunch, lunch or happy hour hors d'ouvres. Makes no difference to me. Once a day, I remember to eat."

Kendra sat back, looking at him, smiling and frowning at the same time.

"Lucky you," she said finally. Alan and Matt laughed.

"What is going on with Parker-Ford?" asked Matt.

Alan smiled a beaming smile. "Remember I told you I'd found some backers for independent production?"

"You've done it?"

"I've done it. Starting this upcoming season."

"You've got a series?"

Alan grinned. "I've got two," he said.

"No way!"

"Way. We're in development on a third. Should be on the air with the first two in the winter. It's all just come together since late last month."

Matt was so genuinely surprised that he had no immediate response, so Alan said, "Amigo, I have been working on this for five years."

"Damn!" Matt said, and high-fived his friend across the table.

Alan turned to Kendra. "I have written for Parker-Ford for five years, written across their shows, written for all their shows – you familiar with their shows?"

Kendra shook her head. "I don't watch television," she said.

Alan laughed. "Wow! I can see why you are so crazy about her!" he said to Matt. "What an awesome thing to say to a tv writer."

"I understand that you are more than a tv writer," said Kendra.

"Okay," Alan said, nodding, smiling, and glancing from Kendra to Matt. "Okay. I can see that you've been talking to Kendra about me the way you've been talking to me about Kendra."

"He is much more than a television writer," Matt said.

"Television is where I am right now," Alan said. "And given recent developments, it is not a bad place to be. But yeah," he said, and fixed Kendra in that blue gaze. "I want more. Much more."

TWENTY-EIGHT

"The kids are with David," said Alan, as he crossed in under the lattice and bougainvillea. "Family time. All three of them here, Kendra?"

Kendra smiled. "Just as of yesterday. This is the first time since he was hospitalized in February that all three of them are here at the same time."

Alan nodded. "Stay put, Tino," he said. "I know this bar."

Tino grinned. Kendra smiled.

"He's way awake today, Alan," Linda said. "You'll be amazed."

Alan was looking at scotches. "That is what Solange said," he answered. "This," he said, holding up a bottle of Glenlivet, "was David's preference. I'll make it mine today, in his honor." He reached up a tumbler and filled it with ice. "I'm a wimp, of course, compared to David. I have to have it ice cold."

"You should fix yourself a martini," Matt said from the chaise. "For the nutritional value of the olive."

Alan smirked. He looked across the short stretch of shaded patio to where Matt lay stretched, bronzed and bronzing, in the southern California sun. "Matt, there's a portrait in an attic someplace, probably in Salinas, that is aging, instead of you."

"I know," said Matt. "I paid the artist myself."

"Not with your soul, I hope," said Linda. "For the price of your soul you should have held out for two portraits. The second one could have been of me. I could have gotten eternal youth at no cost."

Matt grinned. "We were just talking about the devil," he said, "when you arrived, Braxton."

Alan poured the scotch over the ice. "Sorry to disappoint you."

"Amigo," Matt said. "Aren't you hot in that jacket? I mean, speaking of Hell."

"I was going to say the same thing," said Linda. "Relax. Take your coat off. You're among friends. Nobody to impress here."

"Aren't you hot," Alan asked Matt, "lying almost naked in the sun of an L.A. April afternoon?"

"Feels like Heaven's own embrace," said Matt.

"May be closer to reality than you want to imagine," said Alan. He stepped out from behind the bar. "When you die of a metastasized malignant melanoma, Matthew Chase, Kendra and I will sing at your funeral."

"Good grief!" laughed Kendra.

"You should follow it up by dancing on my grave," said Matt. "Except that, given that I am going to be cremated, there will not be a whole lot of room."

Alan sat down next to Kendra.

TWENTY-NINE

"I want to do much more," Alan Braxton had told Kendra, that first time they met over lunch in West L.A.

That "much more" involved film-making; writing, directing and producing. It was a set of ambitions stretching far into the future, and Alan was at once anxious to bring these goals into reality, and deeply, even glacially patient with their accomplishment. He needed that patience, for he was determined to make quality entertainment; he had no patience in reserve whatever for what he termed "the standard Hollywood product."

"There will never be a car chase in any Alan Braxton film," he liked to say. "I'm compromised enough as it is," he would say at other times, "writing for television. At least it's good tv, and yes, there is such a thing." He spoke this way while writing for Parker-Ford; once he'd formed his own production company and was launching his own shows, he could make that claim with even greater assurance. His television work, however, was all in service of a longer-range set of goals; the money in television was so good that, with time, he would be able to branch into film on his own, as an independent writer-director-producer. He could see no other way to achieve his vision, the studios answered to corporate judgment calls; per force, they played to the lowest common denominator. Alan was not interested in the lowest common denominator.

"Braxton's already written the screenplays for his first four films," Matt told Kendra, one afternoon while they were counting scenes in DEATH BECOMES HER, at Matt's sunny studio apartment in

West L.A. "Two of them are comedies, one's a legal drama and one's a tragedy. He's got a lot of range as a writer."

"I guess so," Kendra agreed. "I mean, his tv work alone is impressive." Since meeting Alan, Kendra had actually watched an episode or two of a couple of the series for which he wrote. She was looking forward to seeing him again, so that she could tell him as much.

The next time they got together, however, it was Kendra's, not Alan's talent, that was on display. Matt had several times invited Alan to attend one of the music gigs of Kendra's band. "You've got to see this girl," Matt assured his friend. "She's awesome on the stage. The storylines she comes up with, stringing the songs together, making it really a kind of musical theater – well, you just gotta see for yourself, dude. She's amazing."

One way and another, Alan had never found the time on a weekend evening to come to one of Kendra's gigs. Then he met Kendra. She had a gig two weeks later. Alan was there.

"Well?" Matt asked, glancing from the stage to Alan, as the patrons in the club burst into applause at a particularly good punchline, delivered not by Kendra herself, but the bass player.

Alan, intent on the action onstage, did not respond.

"Kendra's very generous," Matt went on. "She writes all of it and she gives the other members of the band a lot of the best lines."

The banter ceased and the band began to play. The song, a love-lament, was not especially memorable, but Kendra's voice was. So was her dramatic stage persona – the raven hair, highlighted red in the stage lights, the shimmery costume, beaded and silver, the red lips and "Mata Hari eyes," as Alan would later put it. It was enough to make one forget the music.

Well, almost enough.

"She needs a better gig than this," Alan said, meaning the band.

"She's got one," Matt smiled. "With me."

"Yeah, and I agree," Alan said. "Her writing is great. Does she only write comedy?"

"So far," Matt answered.

"Well, she needn't ever do anything else, because she is damned funny. But what I mean is that as an actress, she needs a better gig."

"You mean as a singer."

"I mean as an actress," Alan said. "She's an actress, Matt," he repeated and gestured toward the stage. "She can sing, too, but what I am looking at right now, looking at the movements, the gestures, the tossed-back head, the mock-sultry glances out over the audience – I am looking at an actress. A fine comic performer. She's hella talented, bro. I would love to work with her."

Matt gave a non-committal shrug. "I'd be surprised if she agrees with you," he said. "About acting, I mean. And in any event, I can't see Kendra doing tv. She doesn't even own one. She's a professor's daughter, remember."

"Who's talking about tv?" said Alan.

THIRTY

A little more than two years after meeting Kendra, Alan was in a position to shoot his first film, an off-beat romantic comedy called GIRL THURSDAY. The story was set amid young artists on the make in Los Angeles; it was a story, in other words, right from life as experienced by Alan and his friends. He cast several of the more talented of these friends as characters in the film. One of these talented friends was Kendra Collins.

"It's just three scenes," Alan had pleaded with Kendra, while he was scouting for his actors. "And it's the singer in the cast. And she's sexy and she's intelligent and she's funny. So you won't really have to act at all, to play the part. Just show up and be Kendra on camera."

Matt had been right when two years before he'd told Alan that he thought Kendra would make, at best, a reluctant actress. "Singing is something I always wanted to do," she said to Matt, while trying to find a way to say "no" to Alan. "Writing is something I always have done. Acting? Not on my bucket list."

"No, but you did it well, in all those gigs with the band back in the day," Matt said. "You were very convincing up there in the klieg lights."

"I wrote the storylines because I wanted to write," Kendra argued. "It just happened that, as part of the band, I also had to act, when we did a storyline show."

"It's only one film," said Matt. "And a bit part, at that."

"You know Braxton," said Kendra. "If I say yes to this, he'll want me to be second lead in the next one."

Matt smiled. "So tell him no thanks."

Kendra agreed that was what she would do.

But in the end Kendra said yes. She agreed to appear in the film for several reasons. One, it did give her the chance to sing. She played a rock singer on the make, and sang in two of her three scenes. Kendra's last band had broken up about a year before and, by then experiencing her first successes as a screenwriter, she had not bothered to look for another band. Music was over; her future was set, writing. Two, Kendra owed some of her newfound success in writing to Alan. She and Matt had the previous year sold two screenplays back-to-back on their own, a success so sudden that they were months getting used to it. But they also got commissions that year for writing a television pilot and several sample scripts for a projected new legal series, a series being developed by Alan Braxton Productions. Three, Kendra took the part because, after all, it was a small part, it was only one film, and it was for Alan. She and Alan had, by that time, developed a relationship in which friendship, professional ambition, romantic interest and sexual desire vied intermittently for the upper hand. Still, at the time she took the part, she and Alan had not become lovers.

THIRTY-ONE

"How could we become lovers?" she asked Matt, of her relationship with Alan, one rainy winter morning, as they were working on a script for the legal series. Matt had said that he thought Alan had fallen in love with her.

"You summed him up pretty well the day we met," Kendra went on. "How did you put it? Doesn't eat, doesn't sleep, works a lot, drinks a little. Not enough, actually. If he drank more, maybe he'd learn how to relax. I'd call him a workaholic except he doesn't fit the classic outline. He's got friendship down."

"He does," Matt agreed. "Alan's a great friend."

"And you see that capacity in a guy and you think, well, he must have other capacities for relationship as well," Kendra said. "But the only evidence of such capacities that I see is in his professional relationships. He's a good writer. He's a great director. He's a firm but kind-hearted boss. He's a reassuring coach for anyone who works with him, he knows how to build us all up and get the best out of us, and make us feel almost like we achieved it ourselves, and that's all just awesome and…And I don't see him making time for love. You've known him what, five, six years?"

"Yeah there-about."

"Has he ever had a serious romance in that time?"

Matt did not answer immediately.

"If you have to think about it," said Kendra, "the answer is pretty clearly no. Which proves my point. You said several years ago

110

that it takes laser-like focus to succeed in this business, a willingness to sacrifice, a willingness to wait. Well, I applaud Alan on all those points, and Heaven knows, his determination is paying off. But life cannot be nothing but work, even when the work is so deeply satisfying. I'd be afraid of having a relationship with Alan. I'm afraid I'd wind up resentful of his schedule, and the very fact that I was feeling resentful would make me more resentful, because that's not me. Do you understand what I mean?"

"Of course I do," said Matt. "All the same, I think Braxton's in love with you."

Kendra said nothing. But in fact, and despite her protestations, Matt's suspicion made Kendra deeply and cautiously hopeful. For whether or not Alan was in love with her, she was in love with him.

THIRTY-TWO

Tino shot into the air off the board, giving himself the height he needed to perform a corkscrew twist, during which for just the fraction of a second he seemed to hang suspended above the water. Then he straightened out and entered the water, arms outstretched, fingertips first, the rest of him disappearing beneath the surface with scarcely a splash.

"Wow," said Matt, who had come in from the sun, and was standing in front of the bar.

"Beautiful," said Linda. "With divers like that in the family, I can see why David never took the board out."

"Another?" Matt asked, indicating Linda's empty glass.

"Sure," Linda said. "I'm driving. In about eight hours."

Matt grinned and went behind the bar.

"You're here for dinner, right?"

"Of course," said Matt, checking the labels on the wine.

"Riva Ranch," said Linda and then, turning to the pool and seeing that Tino had come to the surface. "Bravo, Celestino! Do it again!"

Tino laughed.

Alan, meanwhile, was talking quietly with Kendra.

"May twenty-third," he was saying, a look in his blue eyes that seemed part hope and part apology. "The thing is, Kendra, you don't have to be on the set the first day of shooting."

"No, but I want to be there," said Kendra, shifting slightly in the deck chair so as to face Alan more comfortably but not to disturb the sleeping Cleo. "I've seen the shooting schedule. I will be there the first day."

Alan fixed her in his gaze, intense, concerned, and – Kendra saw it – even today, not without traces of desire. She imagined the same would show in her eyes, but they were protected by her sunglasses, which she deliberately left on.

"I am worried about you," Alan said, his voice barely above a whisper.

Under the radar, Kendra thought. He'd always been good at that. She felt the warmth come into her face, felt the tears starting in her eyes. Oh! To be able to give way to them. To be able to collapse in his arms, sobbing. But not here. Not now. The actress he himself had made of her took command.

"Thank you," she said, and stroked the cat for sheer distraction. "I deeply appreciate it, Alan."

"May twenty-third," he said, and shook his head. "It's going to be very soon after, very – well, there is no other way to say it --"

"It is going to be very soon after David's death." Kendra said it for him. Her voice, too, was low and quiet.

"You can't tell me it is not going to be very hard for you," Alan said.

Kendra sighed. "Nothing will be easy next month. Or the rest of the year. But I want to work, Alan. And our plans are set. And I trust the way it is all working out. It's almost as if it had been arranged. In the weeks immediately --" She hesitated, then continued. "I will not be able to sit around here feeling the emptiness. I'll have to be on the set every day. For six weeks, maybe seven. That will be good for me."

Alan sighed. "All right," he said. "I know you know yourself. But this," and he glanced backward toward the house. "This is not something you can calculate. You have no experience with the loss of a spouse."

Kendra nodded. "True enough," she said. "But I have experience of myself. Fifty-three years of it. I want to be on the set the first day of shooting. I don't want my scenes taken out of the schedule, shot separately, whatever. I'm going to have some time here, you know, between now and the end of May, to get used to widowhood."

Alan nodded. "What do you think, for David? Ten days?"

"I think this week," Kendra said, and mentioned that David had seen his parents and his brother.

"Wow," said Alan, and the tears started in his eyes, so that they started once again in Kendra's. "I'm glad I am here today."

Kendra smiled. "So am I," she said.

THIRTY-THREE

Before GIRL THURSDAY was released, Kendra had already made a second film. The writer, director and producer was, once again, Alan Braxton. This film was also a comedy, and though it offered Kendra no opportunity to sing, she had, precisely as she had predicted to Matt, the second female lead. The part required a greater effort on Kendra's part, and her time on the set was tripled from that of GIRL THURSDAY. Perhaps precisely because she and Alan spent so much time together on this second film, by the time it was completed, they had become lovers.

There was an evening when, after finishing for the day, Alan suggested dinner in Santa Monica, "Someplace overlooking the beach."

"I'm surprised," Kendra said, as their drinks arrived, "at how much I enjoy acting."

Alan grinned. "I'm glad," he said, "because I enjoy writing for you, and Heaven knows I enjoy directing you."

Kendra laughed. "Because I am so easy to direct, I guess. I have no ideas of my own."

"Not it at all," Alan said. "It's that you get the part, you enter completely into the character almost like a chameleon. You're a great natural."

Kendra shook her head. "You've been very selective with my roles, and that's smart. I like well-written, thoughtful comedy. Don't ask me to play in HAMLET."

"Don't ask me to direct it," said Alan. "Although I do have plans to branch beyond comic films."

The restaurant's real view was of the traffic along the Pacific Coast Highway, so after dinner, Alan suggested a walk on the floodlit beach. Kendra, in low heels, suggested they stay on the palisades, instead.

"They'll give us our beach vista," she said. Their romance started with that walk above the nighttime beach.

Kendra discovered to her surprised delight that Alan was about love as he was about work – passionately committed. She had been afraid that he would not find enough time for her, should they become involved; once involved with him, she scarcely had time for herself. Alan wanted to be with her every day, and when that was not possible, he was "with" her in all the ways made possible by electronics. He was single-minded in his devotion, an ardent, thoughtful and joyful lover; while the affair lasted, there was only one woman in the world, to Alan, and her name was Kendra Collins.

Their romance lasted over a year. It was Kendra who broke it off.

THIRTY-FOUR

"Well, we had him come in February," Kendra was saying, there beneath the wood lattice and the bougainvillea. "It was when David was in the hospital. We were afraid we might lose him, and of course, the family wanted the last rites. So we called a nearby parish one afternoon, and that's how we met Father Cesar."

"Father Cesar!" Linda said. "Don't you love it. A Catholic priest named for a Roman emperor."

"Let me guess," said Alan. "He's Filipino."

"Good guess," said Matt.

"Anyway," Kendra continued, "David really liked Father Cesar, and when we got David home, he asked if we could have Father come visit him again. That was sometime last month. He's been to the house two or three times since. Always brings David the host, and I guess a couple times he has heard his confession, because they'll close the door for a few minutes. He was here last, what?" and she looked from Linda to Matt. "Thursday, Friday of last week?"

"Something like that," said Linda. "He's a doll, too. Smile that doesn't quit. Just radiates joy. Even in a sickroom. Guess that's why David is so fond of him."

"So anyway," Kendra said, getting back to the question from Alan which had started this conversation, "though of course we will have the Mass at the Mission," and she meant San Gabriel, "Father Cesar will be in charge."

"The main celebrant," said Matt.

"The family has other priest friends over there," Kendra said, "who will also participate, and of course, Ramon will be there, but David told me he wants Father Cesar."

"I'm impressed," said Alan, "with how David has come back to his faith. I guess it should not surprise me, but I have to admit it does."

"It was the same with Damien," said Linda.

"He came back like thunder," said Matt. "Though he was always closer to the Church than David was."

"I remember Gianna," Linda said, speaking of her mother-in-law, "the day the priest came. She was past ninety, hadn't been inside a church for anything but a wedding or a funeral for probably sixty years. But when she knew it was her time, oh my gosh, call the priest! It was her last real priority. And you know? After the priest left, a calm came over her that had not been there before. Her anxiety was gone. Can't explain it, but Sammy and I – the whole family – saw it. I don't know anything about the Church's rituals, but I was impressed at Gianna's peace, after she'd been with the priest. He wasn't there more than fifteen or twenty minutes. But that was enough."

"David's had no anxiety," Kendra said. "Not since September. Not since we found out that he did not qualify for the experimental drug. He surrendered then and there. Even so, it's only since February that he's had this embrace of the faith."

"Faith is mysterious," Linda said. "I mean, you've either got it or you don't, and who knows why? I've never had it."

"No, me either," said Alan. "Sometimes I've wished I had it, because of the consolations it offers. But if those consolations are mere fantasy, are not real, because the object of faith does not exist, well, I'd rather live by the cold and severe but true light of atheism."

"I don't have enough faith to be an atheist," Kendra said, as in fact she had said before, and had said before in print, with an interviewer from ROLLING STONE. The remark had been widely reported afterward, an effect Kendra had intended. "It takes faith either way, and I don't have the faith to say that God does exist or that he does not."

"Your point," said Alan. "I suppose you better color me agnostic, too, since I can no more prove God's non-existence than can any believer prove that he's there. Still, my sympathies are with the atheists."

"Mine too, I'm afraid," said Linda.

"Well, mine aren't," said Kendra. "I am actually more inclined to believe that there is something, maybe even someone, out there. But I can't guess how I could know that. And I mean, the world's religions are not much help, because really, it has to be admitted, they are not 'all saying the same thing.' They may be pointing to the same reality, and that reality may or may not be there, but it takes willful misrepresentation of their various tenets to claim that they are all saying the same thing. They say things which contradict each other. How is one to judge?"

"Ya got me," said Linda. "Not that I lay awake at night, worrying about it." She sipped her wine. "How about you, writerboy? You've got faith."

119

Matt, seated now next to Linda, grinned. "Don't ask me how," he said. "I just do. This one does, too," Matt added, as Tino came up from the water.

"This one does too what?" asked Tino.

"Believe in God."

"Hell yes," said Tino. "Matt, you want a beer yet?"

Matt grinned. Tino went to the bar and pulled up two bottles, Sapporo and Pacifico. Matt shrugged. Tino opened them both and handed the Sapporo to Matt.

"What we want to know," Linda said, as Tino resumed his seat next to Kendra. "Is where your faith comes from."

"It comes from God," said Tino, and took a long drink from the Pacifico.

"Oh well, that explains it," said Linda.

Tino laughed. "I don't know. I mean, obviously, I was raised Catholic. Received all my sacraments by the time I was fifteen."

"Ditto," said Matt.

"But there has to be more than that," said Alan. "Lots of confirmed, so to speak!, card-carrying atheists were raised Catholic. How is it you and Matt believe and they don't?"

"God knows," Tino shrugged, and everyone laughed.

"You know," said Linda, looking at Tino. "You are usually helpful. You usually want people to understand, to feel included. We are trying to understand. So help us."

Tino glanced at Matt who shot him an "Oh boy!" look. "You want to take it, or me?" Tino asked.

"Kendra," Matt said, "how many times over the years have you heard me speak of the Artist who inspires all artists?"

Kendra smiled. "I was surprised," she said, "the first time Matt and I had a discussion about God, to find out he believed. But in those early years," she added, "it was a fairly nebulous belief, despite all your sacraments. It wasn't formalized and dogmatic. You talked about the Artist responsible for sunsets over Monterey Bay and that kind of thing."

"And why not?" said Linda. "Even if there is no such Artist. The artistry of the universe does inspire us."

"Yeah," Matt agreed, "in my twenties, and beyond, I was just a believer. Not a Christian believer. And I gather that is the subject of this afternoon's poolside symposium? Belief qua belief, rather than according to creedal and doctrinal formulations?"

"Whatever," said Linda. "Why do you and Tino think there is a God and me and Alan don't?"

"Alan and I, galpal, Alan and I."

"I don't write for a living, okay?"

"Fair enough," said Matt, and kissed the tips of his fingers and blew the kiss toward Linda, who rolled her eyes toward the bougainvillea.

"The thing is," Matt said, "I know this much. I did not invent myself. I find myself in a world of other beings apparently quite similar to myself, many of whom attest to the existence of an

121

Inventor, if you will. It appears to be a trait of the species, this tendency toward belief. That in itself is an argument, but let that go for the moment.

"I see evidence of artistry – the dreaded design argument, which is actually rather cogent – throughout the world and indeed, far far beyond the world, deep into intergalactic space and beyond even that, deep into the world of the very small, the world of the quantum. That the universe appears, as even Richard Dawkins has admitted, to have been designed is another argument. But we are going to let that go, too.

"Pondering the immensity of the creation, and its unfathomable beauty, there arises in my heart a sensation of wonder, a sensation of gratitude, a sensation of connection, and somehow, born in all of that, there is the conviction that the cosmic Artist exists. Now we are getting to the place where we can start talking about why some people believe and some don't."

"I appreciate the beauty of nature!" Linda objected.

"I did not say you, or any other non-believer didn't," Matt assured her. "I said that, in the sense of wonder and gratitude that the human heart can feel, in contemplating the beauty and the grandeur of the creation, we have arrived at the point where we can begin to discuss belief and unbelief."

"And wouldn't you know it, here are the kids," said Alan, looking up, as Jessica and the others crossed back out onto the patio. "Looks as if we are going to have to put this catechetical lesson on hold for a bit." He rose to greet them.

"You've picked the right day, Alan," Jessica said to him, after their embrace. "Dad is so awake! So here and present."

"He's not too tired for another visitor?" Alan asked.

"Not at all," said Justin. "We told him we saw you on the patio – we did see you from the windows – and he smiled. He is expecting you."

"This is the best he's been in more than a week," said Linda. "Go, Alan. You won't tire him."

Alan turned to Kendra. "So, okay, Kendra, I guess I'll –"

"No!" said Linda. "You're not going to leave after seeing David? Stay. Hang with us. This is precious time, Alan."

Alan smiled. "I have a meeting with a writer at five in Playa del Rey," he said.

"Playa del Rey! He should be coming here to meet you!" protested Linda.

"She," Alan answered, smiling, "is permanently in a wheelchair and takes public transport to get anywhere. And she is one of the best young writers I have read in the last decade. I am meeting her at her home in Playa del Rey at five. I have to scoot, after seeing my boy David. I'll be back this week. Promise." He looked to Matt. "Maybe we can pick up where we've left off, on the whole God thing. It's been years since we wrestled intellectually on that particular topic. It was a subject on which I seem to remember pinning Mr. Matt to the mat regularly."

Matt laughed. "Watch out. Faith matures."

Kendra had risen and was standing next to Alan. "I'll walk you in," she said. "I want to look in on him, anyway, and also check in with Solange."

Alan and Kendra went into the house together.

123

THIRTY-FIVE

"I love you very much," Kendra said, the bright and breezy May afternoon that she and Alan actually did walk on a beach, the one at Venice. "In fact, I can honestly say you are the only man I have ever been with in whom I have seen a potential husband."

Alan said nothing, just walked alongside her, looking at the sand as they walked it. He understood, of course, that he was being turned down. He was so surprised by it that it was easiest just to keep silent.

"I love you. I love being with you. I don't want our love to stop. But I do not want to get married, Alan. It's not you. It's marriage. I don't want to get married. Not yet."

Alan looked out across the broad stretch of beach toward the sea. He supposed it had been rash, to actually put it in 'yes' or 'no' form like this, to have actually proposed to Kendra, all but on bended knee. The romantic side of his nature had gotten the better of him. Given what he knew of Kendra – her intelligence, her independence, and maybe above all, her off-handedness, her relaxed, almost haphazard approach to living – a subtler and slower strategy, it suddenly seemed, in light of this afternoon's revelation of her deepest feelings, might have achieved his goal where a simple declaration had misfired.

It wasn't as though the subject had never come up. Just that when it did, Alan now saw in retrospect, he had heard in Kendra's remarks what he wanted to hear: he heard her say that she had never before him been with a man she would have thought of marrying. He did not hear her say that marriage was not on any short list in her possession, or if he did, he had assumed that he was the exception.

He'd assumed wrongly. It hurt. He was very much in love.

They walked and talked on Venice Beach that afternoon for well over two hours. In the end, a decision that left both of them aching, they agreed to break up.

"Women marry when they fall in love," Polly, Kendra's mother had often said. "Men marry when they are ready." Kendra had never known from where her mother drew that insight, but it bore its truth out quickly enough in Alan's case. Not long after he and Kendra parted ways, he went back to a former lover; they were married within a year.

As for Kendra, this was the spring she was twenty-nine. It was the spring she was suddenly on the covers of film magazines and being interviewed by the entertainment press. It was a spring of bright new opportunities and unexpected chances. It was not a spring when she wanted anything tied down, anything set irrevocably in stone, not even her love for Alan.

It was also the spring that David and Lana invited her to attend Carlos' graduation party. It was the spring, the summer, when, missing Alan, she would nonetheless discover the "charged atmosphere" she shared with David de la Fuente.

THIRTY-SIX

It was almost four. The office – that is, David's sick room – was flooded with bright afternoon light. Though the room had been transformed to accommodate the hospital bed and the medical equipment, it was still, to Kendra, recognizably David's office. The carpet was beige, the walls white, the wainscoting dark. The bookshelves were still fully stocked with David's favorite authors. The standing globe, which lit up from within to show where the sun was across the world's time zones, was where it had always been, to one side of David's big desk, the desk itself still organized according to David's schedule and expectations. The calendar, however, was last year's.

There were gauzy white, transparent curtains at the French doors, which Kendra had opened a few minutes before. The curtains lifted and fluttered on the light breeze off the patio. From beyond, Kendra could hear voices and laughter, could hear splashings in the pool. The room's several potted palms were backlit by the sunlight streaming through the doors. It was rather serene, the room flooded with so much light; the curtains and palms gently moving with the breeze.

Alan had left. While he had been with David, Kendra had gone upstairs to shower and change. Wearing a loose-fitting white blouse, a black skirt and black heels, she came down to find Alan waiting for her in the kitchen, talking with Solange. She walked him across the gravel drive to his car, and coming back into the house she crossed to the sick room.

David was sleeping. She was glad. He needed his rest. Although the thought occurred to her, as it had before, he really did not need it, not in the sense that this was rest that would issue in some sort of improvement, a changed reality. What, at this stage, was "rest" for? Perhaps if there had been some kind of emotional upset, some kind of anxiety that rest and sleep could alleviate, there would be a reason why "he needed his rest." But David was at peace, surrendered, given over to what was happening to him, and had been, for months. He was very close to death. It wasn't rest, in any usual sense of the term, that David was either needing or getting now. It was the exhaustion of a body that was gradually letting go of life.

"Sometimes I think things through too much," she'd once years before said to Matt.

They had been counting scenes while watching DANGEROUS LIAISONS.

"How can anyone think too much?" Matt asked. "Thinking is rapidly going the way of the steam locomotive, but unlike the steam locomotive, thinking is something still very much needed."

"Just sometimes," Kendra said. "Not a general rule with me, but now and then. I think I start analyzing situations that really do not bear analysis. I probe for depth and meaning when perhaps neither can be grasped. Better just to accept what we see, to let what is on the surface pass for what is true and real."

Matt smiled, shaking his head. "In the very fact that you acknowledge truth and reality, girlfriend, you're over-thinking, as far as contemporary America is concerned." He waited for a rejoinder from Kendra, and when it didn't come he looked at her and asked, "Do you want to talk about this?"

"No," Kendra said, and smiled. "It would only involve yet more thinking."

Matt laughed. He re-started the video. "Watch this!" he said. "Watch how Close advances the plot here, without uttering a word of dialogue. She does it all with her expression, the fading smile, the change in her eyes. She goes from a sort of malicious glee to a sudden alarm, a realization that Malkovich may be in love with Pfeiffer, and as he speaks, this suspicion deepens into a dreadful certainty, a certainty laced with sadness and a sense of loss. Her character being as proud as she is, she moves finally to a self-protective and jealous mockery – and all of that within the interval of just a few seconds and without saying a word. Our work would be a lot easier, if every performer were as talented as Glenn Close. She was robbed of the Oscar that year."

THIRTY-SEVEN

There was a serenity to the room, the brilliant light from the patio flooding through the tall windows and the open French doors. Kendra sat next to David's bed, watching him while he slept. His sleep was quiet and untroubled; she was grateful. She looked at his face, at the taut and smooth skin pulled over the bones. David had always been strong and solid, even stocky, a little hefty, in his build. He'd had the vanity to avoid getting fat, but only just that. She thought of how he'd looked only at the holidays, only over the winter. Slim, his hair gone, all that wonderful, thick grey hair, gone. But still, he had been David, recognizably so.

And yet, he remained recognizably David this afternoon, lying here asleep with the sunlight pouring through the glass, so gaunt, so thin, so wasted. In a way, it was almost as if his face had been revealed for the first time, its essential features, here in this hospital bed in the blazing light. He was still, in spite of all of it, beautiful in his extremity, in his ultimate weakness and decline. The facial lines were accentuated, the high forehead, the prominent cheekbones and strong jaw. And his eyes seemed deeper, larger, more revealing, almost as if in the wasting away of his body his soul were closer to the surface.

She looked from her husband's face to his frame, to his body, beneath the light covers. Did he weigh even one hundred pounds at this point? His withered arms were atop the covers. She looked at them and she remembered them otherwise; she remembered them strong and vital and wrapped around her, loving her, hugging her close, exulting in her, pleading with her, holding her as if for dear life itself.

129

And again, the mental exercises, again, Kendra the thinker: he was as he was; he is as he is. Very soon, he will no longer be. If she could prolong this late afternoon, seated at his bedside, watching him protectively while he slept, what would she give, to keep him here, out of pain, even if asleep, with her indefinitely?

"While he is here, he is here," she had said to Matt, to Linda, to Alan, to the nephews and nieces, to his children. "While he is here, he is here, and I am with him." Although she could speak of near-term plans, as she had done just now with Alan, plans that would come into play after David's death, the fact of his death itself was another matter. The prospect of David gone, gone forever, was not clearly articulated in her mind. Only rarely, in unbidden flashes and with a force almost of shock, did she envision this house, the family, her life, without him.

Voices beyond the room brought her back into the present moment. She glanced at the clock on his desk and was surprised to see that it was after four. She'd sat here silently watching him sleep for more than half an hour. Kendra recognized the voices: Solange, and at least two of David's three sisters. She rose and crossed toward the door, noticing once again the lit-from-within standing globe. Darkness was advancing across the Atlantic, it would soon be dusk on the East Coast. But the West Coast was still bright with light, just as the room itself was. After all, it was only late afternoon. She glanced one last time at David sleeping quietly, peacefully in the special bed, the light blazing all around him. This was not the time when the sun should be setting.

THIRTY-EIGHT

"Oh, I knew the afternoon was going too smoothly," said Linda, in an aside to Matt, and then gestured with her head toward the house, through which now Kendra appeared with three women. "The CAR Show's here."

Matt shook his head, laughing in spite of himself. "They are friends of mine, you know," he said. "Almost like sisters. But speaking of whom," he added, "I better put some clothes on," for he was still in just his light blue swimsuit.

He had left a duffle bag on an adjacent chair, when he'd first come out on the patio, hours ago. In it he carried a pair of sweats and a t-shirt, a pair of sandals, his wallet, keys, and a Dodgers cap. He had gotten into the sweats and the cap, as the new guests reached the shaded area. The ladies, all late middle age, nicely dressed and with hair and make-up that suggested a long attachment to glamour, made a bee-line for Matt, who was already standing up.

"Look at you!" said Carmen as she reached to embrace Matt. "Muy bronzeado!"

Matt grinned. Linda rolled her eyes, thinking as she did so that her eyes were getting quite the work-out this afternoon.

"The CAR Show" was how Linda had come, some good number of years before, to refer to the de la Fuente sisters, the moniker deriving from the first letter of each of their names. Carmen was the eldest, Ana the middle and Raquel the youngest. Linda's disaffection for them was entirely a reaction on behalf of her friendship with Kendra: she thought them bossy and overbearing.

131

They were all older than David – at this point, somewhere late sixties to early seventies. Linda had never bothered to keep track.

Matt, bare-chested and barefoot, was lost to the several embraces of the sisters, and so Linda checked her texts. Good grief. There was that impossible Armenian couple who wanted the place on Robertson and to whom, the owner had assured her, he would never sell, plus that devastatingly handsome Brit producer who was hoping to do business with Alan Braxton, and Linda had begun to suspect, was just using her as a way to meet him, plus yet again the Shanghai investment group who wanted the property near Zuma Beach. Linda sighed and dropped the phone back into her purse. She really made herself just too available to her clients. Well, for the rest of this afternoon, they could all wait. She watched as the sisters embraced Tino and the others, exclaiming with wonder and delight over the extent of Monique's belly. Linda plastered a smile on her face and rose, crossed into the crowd, and both initiated and accepted hugs as if no one on the patio that afternoon were more delighted than she, to be greeting the CAR Show. "I just hope they don't stay for dinner," she breathed almost silently to Matt, as she resumed her seat; Matt, too, taking his seat next to her.

"I liked you better in the Speedo," she said, glancing at the baggy blue sweats and the Dodgers cap.

"Know your audience, girlfriend," Matt said.

"I don't have an audience."

"I really do love them," said Matt. He watched Carmen, Ana and Raquel as they continued to hug and greet, and he smiled. "You should see them at the care homes over in San Gabriel. So maternal and gentle. They have hearts of gold."

"If they can reduce Matthew Chase Trevino to clichés," Linda said, "my hat's off to them. Just remember where gold is found. Beneath tons of granite."

"I like granite."

"I'm so happy you're happy."

Matt caught the clue.

"I can't believe you're making this up," he said. "It sounds like something out of an old Clyde Fitch play."

"Clyde Fitch," Linda shot back, "though you may not think so, was considerably before my time."

"I've always denied the legend that you were in OUR AMERICAN COUSIN the night Lincoln was shot."

Linda broke up. "I wasn't," she laughed. "But the CAR Show was!"

They were quoting lines to one another, as they often enough did, from a favorite film, in this case, ALL ABOUT EVE. They had whole swaths of dialogue memorized between them, from that film and a number of others, from BLADE RUNNER to YOUNG FRANKENSTEIN, from CASABLANCA to DR. ZHIVAGO, from DIRTY HARRY to THE TEN COMMANDMENTS. Their range was broad and deep, and they could slip into a conversation, inaccessible to all but themselves, quoting film dialogue as easily as they might have slipped into speaking a foreign language. It was a unique feature of their long friendship, a sort of coded exercise between them, a mutual invitation to private amusement.

THIRTY-NINE

Kendra took seat on one of the dozen high chairs that lined the patio bar. The sisters had no sooner greeted everyone on the patio than they were off to their car, where they had loaded up on appetizers from the restaurant. As they came back in, assisted by several of the young people, Kendra and others marveled at the bounty – taquitos, empenadas, flautas, guacamole, salsa, chips and more. They spread the food across the bar and over several side tables, and Kendra watched smiling as her guests began to help themselves. It occurred to her how much David had loved moments such this, impromptu gatherings of family and friends, food brought in from Casa de la Fuente or ordered in from somewhere else, conversations happening across the patio, laughter, light-heartedness, simple enjoyment of life and its blessings. He would have loved being here with them all, right now. He would have reveled in the simple joy of it.

The sisters had largely converged on Monique, full of questions about the baby, about plans for maternity leave – "Five years," Kendra heard Ana say, "five years, Monique, is what your children need. Just quit your job. Justin can support you." This comment gave rise to others in a similar vein, Justin laughing and assuring his aunts that Monique, a para-legal, would be off 'til after the New Year.

Jessica was talking with Matt. Talking with him about an upcoming charity event. The event was to raise money for programs in the arts for disadvantaged Los Angeles teens; Matt was co-chair of the event, which was to be held at Casa de la Fuente. Not the restaurant in San Gabriel. Not the original Casa de la Fuente. The second restaurant. The one on the West Side, the Casa de la Fuente in Century City.

Damien had built it some seventeen years before. It was a spectacular restaurant. Kendra remembered its gala opening. She remembered, too, the evening's unanticipated consequences.

FORTY

Casa de la Fuente, Century City, had opened on a mild and breezy January evening seventeen years before. The second restaurant had been Damien's brainchild, predicated on his conviction that the city's West Side was just as fond of Mexican food and a rich and comfortable hacienda ambience as were people in the San Gabriel Valley. That his brother and sister-in-law were in the entertainment business and had many connections and friends on the West Side was only a further enticement to build the restaurant. Damien scouted possible locales for many months before deciding on the Century City venue. During the actual construction phase he was spending so much time on the West Side that he purchased a condo in a high-rise on Wilshire Boulevard in Westwood.

Damien wanted to launch the new restaurant with a gala opening, and he asked David and Kendra for help in attracting some of their famous friends to the event. The nearly two hundred-fifty guests included several dozen well-known Hollywood personalities, many of whom were photographed that evening by Damien himself, an avid photographer, who later dedicated one wall of the restaurant's extensive bar to photos from the opening night.

Kendra and David, married less than two years at the time, arrived early and with the children, for the opening was a family event. The children stayed til nine and then were taken home by Anneke, the au pair, who continued to work for David and Kendra the first couple years of their marriage. A salsa band played in the bar; there was mariachi on the patio. Guests sipped their drinks, sampled appetizers from a sumptuous buffet and mingled in any of four spacious dining rooms. They also congregated on the patio, with its fountains and tropical flowers, and in the bar, which included both indoor and outdoor seating. It was late January, a couple of days after Kendra's birthday and more than a week after David's, but Damien had ordered cake and it was duly rolled out and lit with candles that formed two question marks. After being serenaded in English and Spanish, Kendra and David blew the candles out to raucous applause and a blitz of photographers' flashes, for the event had drawn local media.

As he had done on her first visit to the San Gabriel restaurant, Damien, dapper in his tux, offered Kendra a tour. She had been sitting at a table in the patio section of the bar with Matt and a friend, Jean Marc Giroux, a French-Canadian ski instructor with Hollywood ambitions. All three of them took the tour, seeing the huge kitchen, the upstairs banquet areas and each of the main dining rooms, three on the ground level and one upstairs, overlooking the others. Damien provided his guests with details about the décor, the materials used, the wood and the tile, the carpets, the fabrics and colors so carefully thought about and chosen.

"The patios are not done yet," Damien explained, adding that two more outdoor seating areas were to be completed by the spring. "When we are finished," he said, "our capacity will be just above three hundred."

"The bar alone must seat one hundred," said Jean Marc. He had wavy blonde hair, brown eyes and was in his early thirties, several years younger than Kendra, who had just turned thirty-six.

Damien smiled. "Bar and tables together it seats eighty-two," he said. "It's actually a fifth dining room, as of course people will be able to order dinner there."

"I love the ambience on the patio," said Kendra. "Very Mexican Riviera."

"All you need out there are parrots," Matt said. "Or maybe iguanas."

"The flowers are gorgeous," Jean Marc said. "And I love the fountains." He laughed. "Fountains playing outdoors, at night, at the end of January! In Quebec they would be frozen! Ice sculptures. I love Los Angeles."

"You are from Montreal?" Damien asked Jean Marc.

"Quebec City," Jean Marc answered. "But I went to college in Montreal."

"I understand it is a beautiful city," said Damien.

"Both of them," Jean Marc agreed. "Like no place else in the Americas."

"Tell me, where does one ski in Quebec?" asked Damien.

"The Laurentians," Jean Marc replied. "They are our principal range, though there are others."

"But are they high enough for skiing?" asked Damien.

"Well," Jean Marc laughed. "Not by California standards. They are foothills compared to the Sierras. But yes, we have some fine ski areas. Le Massif, Mont Blanc, Mont Tremblant – some of them have vertical drops of half a mile."

"Are you skiing here in California?"

"Every chance I get," said Jean Marc. "This guy's shown me some great slopes," and he patted Matt's shoulder. "Mammoth, Tahoe. But," he added, perhaps wistfully, "I did not come to California to ski."

FORTY-ONE

"Yeah, we're eight-one right now," the fifteen year-old Tino was saying to Kendra and Matt. "We're on track to go to the championships." He was talking about his high school basketball team. He was starting center.

They were in the upstairs dining room at the Century City restaurant, standing at the railing and looking out over the opening night festivities below. Tino was taking random photos with his father's Leica.

"And you're in the student senate, too, I hear," Kendra said.

"Sophomore slate," Tino said. "I like it. I like the way the administration takes us seriously – or anyway, goes to the trouble of making it appear that they take us seriously. It may not be the real thing, but while the illusion lasts, it is very pleasant."

Matt and Kendra laughed. "Good grief!" said Kendra. "You could have a career in politics!"

"I'm enjoying high school," Tino said. He was dressed in a tux like the other de la Fuente men. His hair was very short and – like his cousin Carlos several years before – he wore a stud in one ear.

"Hey look," said Matt. "There's Mom and Dad."

Kendra and Tino looked over the balustrade where, below them, Damien and Isabel came into view. Isabel, her dark hair swept up, wore cream-colored silk with pearls. Tino snapped several pictures, one right after the other.

"Your mother is beautiful," Matt said.

Tino smiled. "Everyone says I look like her."

Matt and Kendra laughed. In fact, Tino took after his mother's side of the family. He was tall and slim and had Isabel's delicacy of feature.

"Hey," Matt said. "Speaking of a career in politics. That's Gayle Swainston." He meant the woman Damien and Isabel were talking to. She was a candidate that year for the L.A. city council.

"There's a lot of West Side politicos here tonight," Kendra said. "I guess word about the opening got around."

"Your parents themselves ought to be in politics," Matt said, to Tino.

"Oh no!" said Kendra. "Damien's much too serious for politics. And Isabel's much too honest."

Matt glanced at Tino, who grinned. "Your folks are an amazing couple, all the same," Matt said.

"How long have they been married?" Kendra asked.

"Thirty-five years," said Tino.

"They married young," said Matt.

"That they did," Tino agreed. He shot a couple of candids of Matt and Kendra. Then he said, "Let's go down. It's pretty sparse up here. The real party is downstairs."

FORTY-TWO

A few days after the opening, Matt found himself in Century City
for a late lunch, with the specific purpose of talking to Damien
about doing a fundraiser at the restaurant. Several years before
with the help of some good friends including Sam and Linda
Stefani, David de la Fuente, Alan Braxton and Kendra Collins,
Matt had founded a non-profit organization committed to partner
with youth organizations in Los Angeles to provide funding for
sports opportunities for local teens in low-income areas. Matt
called the non-profit LA Futures. Though the organization had
substantial private backing, with Matt himself some years donating
up to half his income to it, a high-profile fundraising event was
part of Matt's overall strategy with the non-profit, and he needed a
venue for that event. Following the opening of Casa de la Fuente,
Century City, Matt was convinced he'd found the venue.

"It's a win-win, bro," he'd said to Damien, sitting amid the tropical
foliage of the patio that bright winter afternoon. "You get
Hollywood here at the restaurant, and lots of free and excellent
publicity. LA Futures gets that publicity, too. And we get money.
Money to partner with inner city youth leagues and CYO programs
and Boys and Girls Clubs and so on. Our at-risk teens get chances
they would not have had otherwise, and Hollywood gets a chance
to party for a good cause. I mean, look at this place! It's 'our
kind' of place," Matt said, and he meant that the restaurant was
Hollywood's kind of place.

Damien, flattered and enthused, was on board from that first
meeting. The inaugural LA Futures gala was held late that spring,
raising several hundred thousand dollars. Two dozen celebrities
attended that first year; the number grew to a couple hundred
within a few years, receipts doubled and then tripled and the time

came when getting an invitation to the gala was considered an achievement. The restaurant played host to the event every year and benefitted from the sidelight publicity. Casa de la Fuente, Century City, was not just a great restaurant; it came to be associated with a star-studded charity event, a charity event that all Los Angeles could get behind. The long-term development of the LA Futures gala at Casa de la Fuente was, as Matt had predicted, win-win.

"Rumor has it," Matt said, that day on the patio, "that you are thinking of moving permanently to the West Side."

Damien laughed. "Oh! Rumors. Don't believe them. Isabel would never leave Arcadia. I have my condo. I need it, because I am here late a lot, and do not want to drive back across town some nights. I figure, too, who knows? The condo is in Westwood. Tino is thinking he will go to UCLA; it would be convenient for him."

"The view from up there must be spectacular," Matt said. Damien's condo was on the twenty-second floor.

"Isabel says you can see the curvature of the earth," Damien joked. "But in fact, you can see Catalina, on a clear day."

"Isabel looked smashing, the other night."

"Didn't she?" Damien agreed. "Sometimes I have to stop and remind myself that we are in our fifties. The de la Fuentes are aging, Matt. Even baby David is forty-eight. He is fortunate to have married Kendra. A wife twelve years your junior will help keep you young."

"I have to manage that on my own," Matt said, and grinned.

"Sometimes I envy you," Damien said. "You are what? Thirty-five?"

"Thirty-seven, but who's counting?"

"Thirty-seven," said Damien. "I had been married fifteen years, at thirty-seven. My oldest was already a teen."

"I can't imagine it," said Matt. "I'm scarcely able to take responsibility for myself, at this point, let alone a kid."

"You don't want children?" Damien asked.

"I have my nephews and nieces."

"But children of your own," Damien pressed. "You do not want your own children?"

"I'm not opposed to the idea on principle," Matt shrugged. "But no, just at the moment. No, I don't want children. I am too busy having screenplays to have kids. Talk with me again after I've put an Oscar on my mantle."

Damien grinned. "What about just settling down?" he asked. "Just you and the right lady, never mind the question of children. You have had some lovely girlfriends."

Matt shrugged. "I like my freedom," he said.

"There's something to be said for your approach," Damien said. "It gives you time to know yourself."

"From what I can tell of myself," Matt said, "that's an over-rated advantage."

FORTY-THREE

Kendra sipped her iced tea and watched through her dark glasses as Jessica continued to press Matt for information about his new charity. Matt had nephews and nieces of his own, in Salinas, but over the years he had become extended family and had played very much an uncle-type of role, in the lives of Jessica, Justin and Jeffrey; also of Tino, for Matt had become good friends with Damien and Isabel, as well.

"For kids with acting ambitions, yes," Matt was saying, in answer to Jessica's question, as they together moved in the direction of the bar. "But also for kids who dream of doing costumes or sets, for kids who hope to become announcers or broadcasters --"

"Even future screenwriters may apply," smiled Kendra.

"Even future screenwriters," Matt agreed. He and Jessica reached the bar, Matt leaning against it and Jessica taking a seat. Carmen and Tino, working the bar from the other side, slid appetizers their way.

"We want to help kids who hope for any kind of career in film, music, television, radio, the theatre or online media work," Matt explained. "It's a direct counterpart to the athletic program, but it targets a new group of teens. Frankly, I'm surprised it took me this long to think of doing it."

"It just sounds wonderful," said Jessica. "When Brett and I are done with the books, and that is just a month off, when we are working attorneys, I want you to come to Chicago and brainstorm with us, help us launch a charity for the teens there."

"We'll do all your paperwork!" Brett promised. He was standing at the bar, for the proximity to guacamole and chips.

"I just think how different the world would be," said Jessica, "if everybody thought the way you do. I mean, Matt, your attitude about your own money --"

"That's just it," said Linda, crossing in to the bar for a bottled water. "Matt doesn't think of his money as his own. To writerboy here, money is like water or air – a communal resource."

"There's only so much you can spend on yourself," said Matt.

"Oh no!" said Linda, and laughed, and so did everyone else.

"Well, anyway," said Jessica. "I love the whole idea, Matt. You're literally creating hope."

"It is a beautiful thing," said Carmen, and turned a beaming gaze on Matt.

"All right, enough, you guys," said Matt. "Change the conversation or I'm going back in the pool."

"I'll go back in with you," said Tino. "I'll race you. Three laps."

Matt grinned. "You're on."

FORTY-FOUR

"Oh, it's no fun, getting old," said Matt, flopping down on the chaise, as he came up from the pool, where he had just finished almost half a lap behind Tino.

"What do you mean?" asked Jessica. "You held pace with Tino 'til the last lap. I'm sure I couldn't have done as well."

"Me either," laughed Brett.

"I could have!" said Jeffrey, and Tino, dripping wet and reaching for the towel Kendra offered him at the bar, laughed.

"Come on then, cuz," Tino said. "Put your board shorts where your mouth is!"

"Left 'em in Malibu," said Jeffrey.

"Lucky for you!" said Tino, and crossing behind the bar, opened the refrigerator.

"Have some taquitos, Mateo," Carmen said, crossing toward Matt from the bar, where she had prepared a plate for him.

"And come in from the sun," commanded Linda.

"I need to dry off," said Matt.

"Somewhere back around the time of the founding of Jericho they invented a thing called the towel," Linda retorted. "Ever heard of it?"

Matt laughed, kept his place on the chaise and accepted the plate from Carmen.

"Enough guacamole?" Carmen asked.

"More than enough," Matt assured her, setting up with an end table Linda had pushed his way with her foot. "If it were left to you, Carmen, I would weigh three hundred pounds."

"That's my motherly affection, Matthew," said Carmen, while Tino handed Matt another beer, already open.

"Thanks, punk," Matt said, and shot him a look.

Tino laughed. Then, addressing no one in particular and everyone at once, he said, "Well, it's almost five. I need to get moving."

"What?" said Jessica.

"Dinner shift at Century City," shrugged Tino.

"No, Tino," said Linda. "Not tonight. Your cousins are here. The restaurant can handle itself."

Tino shook his head. "I have not arranged coverage --"

"You're the boss!" cried Linda. "You don't need to arrange anything. Just call and let them know you're not coming in this evening."

"Is Maribel working tonight?" asked Kendra, with a smile.

Tino smiled. Maribel was his long-time girlfriend. She was a hostess at the restaurant.

"We understand," Kendra said.

"I don't," said Jessica. "You can see Maribel any night of the week, cousin. But Justin and Monique go back to Atlanta the day after tomorrow, and Brett and I leave Thursday. Linda's right. The restaurant will do the same business this evening whether you are there or not. Please stay."

While Jessica was speaking, Matt's iPhone lit up with a text. "Hey," he said, looking at it. "It's Isabel."

"She's at the restaurant tonight, too," Tino said now, of his mother. "That's one of the reasons I need to go to Century City."

"Not anymore you don't," Matt said, reading the text. "She's on her way here. With Ramon and Sandra."

Ramon was David's other brother and Sandra was his wife.

"She says she sent you this text, too," Matt went on, to Tino.

"My phone's in the house," said Tino.

"Well, your mom is headed here," said Matt.

"And that settles it!" said Linda. "Just call Maribel and tell her to take the night off, come here instead, and we'll all be happy."

Tino laughed. "If I am taking the night off," he said, "Maribel can't."

"You're staying then?" said Jessica.

Tino grinned, shrugged. "Mom's on her way. I'm staying."

"When you gonna make an honest man of yourself," said Linda. "With Maribel, I mean?"

"She wants to get married, cousin," said Jessica.

"I know," said Tino, and crossed back to the bar where he took seat alongside Kendra, with whom he exchanged a knowing smile.

"Well?" said Linda.

"Maribel wants to get married," said Tino, with a playful grin. "What's that got to do with me?"

"You better be careful," said Jessica. "Maribel's twenty-eight. You've been together – how long?"

"Four years," said Tino.

"She's ready for children, Tino," Jessica persisted. "She's told me so."

"Oh hell," said Tino. "I'm ready for children. Thanks, cousin," he said to Jeffrey, who, from the other side of the bar, handed him a Heineken. "I'm ready for kids. Being a dad – no problem. It's being a husband that I'm not ready for."

"Good grief!" cried Jessica, while Linda laughed out loud.

"Maribel might bolt, dude," said Jeffrey.

Tino shrugged, and downed a good gulp of his Heineken.

"My nephew's judgment needs to be respected here," said Kendra. "Tino will marry when he's ready to do so."

"Thanks, Tia!" said Tino.

"De nada," said Kendra and shot him a wink. "I'm glad Isabel's coming," she added.

Although Kendra loved all her in-laws, it was Tino's mother she was closest to.

FORTY-FIVE

It was a lunch that had happened fifteen years before.

"Tino is starting at UCLA in the fall, you know," Isabel said, as the waiter delivered the appetizers, maguro, flying fish roe and crab-and-avocado California rolls.

"Yes, I know," Kendra replied. "He told me of his acceptance when he got it. I'm thrilled for him. Perfect school for a young photographer with film world ambitions."

Isabel smiled. "Those are his uncle's ambitions," she said, meaning David. "It's your husband who thinks Tino should act. Tino has no interest in it."

"Funny," Kendra said. "David wanted me to act, too. I mean, he wanted me to really pursue it."

"Well, he's a director," said Isabel. "It's his job. Tino isn't interested," Isabel went on, then saying to the waiter, "Could we have the yakitori, after all? I'm thinking with a couple more appetizers," she went on, turning back to Kendra, "we'll have lunch."

"Works for me," said Kendra.

"Tino is not interested in acting. He loves photography. And he'll take courses in video and cinematography for his major. But I don't think we will ever see him on the big screen."

It was a sunny spring afternoon in West L.A., two years after the opening of the Century City restaurant. Isabel had phoned Kendra the day before asking if they could meet for lunch. "I need your help with something," Isabel had said. "Some of it involves Tino," she added. "All of it involves the family."

"When and where?" said Kendra.

Isabel said she would come to the West Side. She left the choice of restaurant to Kendra, only, "Not Century City. Not Casa de la Fuente. You'll understand why when we meet."

Isabel sipped white wine. Her dark hair was cut that year in a "Jackie-Kennedy-at-the-beach" style, as she herself put it, two or three waves about her face. "Too young a style for me," Isabel would say, "but so retro people might think I've always had it like this." She wore a striped black-and-cream dress, black belt and pumps and shiny ebony bracelets. Kendra had always admired Isabel for her subtle elegance.

"I mentioned on the phone," Isabel said now, "that this involves Tino."

Kendra nodded.

Isabel drew in a deep breath. She looked at the table between them, as if seeing something else, seeing the "scene" which she was about to describe.

"Let's start here," she said, and looked directly at Kendra. "Damien and I are separating."

Kendra's jaw dropped. She had lifted her iced tea for a sip, but now replaced it. She sat back in her seat, saying nothing, just gazing at Isabel.

"We are not divorcing," Isabel said. "That has always been understood between us. There is no reason for a divorce. It would only make the lawyers happy. But we are --" She hesitated, then went on. "We are publicly acknowledging the private reality we have experienced virtually our entire married life, back to when the girls were little."

Damien and Isabel had three daughters, born early in their marriage. Tino had been born more than ten years after the youngest of the girls.

"We'd been married several years," Isabel went on, "when we first grappled with this. From the outset, I was determined that our marriage survive. Damien seemed relieved. I think he was very afraid, then, when he was young, of what might happen in the family, if he and I were to divorce, if this were to be known."

"'This?'" asked Kendra.

"Damien is gay."

Kendra's shock registered only in a slight widening of her eyes. She said nothing.

"You're not surprised?"

Kendra laughed a short, hard laugh. "I'm stunned. Stunned speechless."

Isabel nodded. "The family will be, too. That is why I need your help. I love Damien. We have been married thirty-seven years. And we were together for four, before that. Since I was fourteen. He is the only man I have ever loved. And I love this family. And I do not want the family hurt by this."

Kendra nodded, and reached once more for her iced tea.

153

"People are not going to understand our attitude," Isabel said. "They are going to tell us what the Church says, as though we haven't always known. What am I to say? This is the reality, I am dealing with it. I will say this much: Jesus was not known for hanging out with the holy people, or the self-righteous. The family is going to ask why we aren't simply getting a divorce. They are not going to understand that we love each other, or well, at least, they are not going to understand what love means, to me and Damien. In a perfect world, Kendra, I would not have asked for this, but then, neither would Damien. We live in a broken world. Damien experiences that reality every day, just in being who he is and where he is. He has lived at war with himself since we were young. I want people to understand that.

"And I want them to believe me when I tell them that I will be fine on my own. Because, of course, I won't really be on my own: Damien is my best friend. And I am his. We will still run the restaurants together. We will still be with the children together. If he needs me, I will be there; if I need him, he will be there. We love each other. But the family is not going to understand, even though all I am doing in this is being true to my marriage vows. Call me quaint, Kendra, but when I said 'til death do us part,' do you know what I meant? I meant until either Damien or I died. I meant it then. I mean it now. I will always love Damien."

Kendra now stared at the table between them, trying to take it all in.

"I need your help, Kendra. I need you to talk with David. If you and David are supportive, the rest of the family will be."

Kendra frowned, and looked up. "Isabel, why – why 'go public,' as you say, if you and Damien have worked this all out? I mean, if you are not divorcing --"

"I started in the middle," Isabel said. "I didn't give you the story as it has developed. The remote aspects of it, years and years ago, the occasional affairs, my initial shock and grief, Damien's anguish and contrition, all that, all that is over. We have dealt with it. We chose marriage and family and we chose it together, despite his lapses. I have to tell you: after my initial near-despair, Kendra, I came to a new understanding. I had a break-through. I saw that Damien wanted to be the best husband he could be to me, and the best father he could be, to the children. And I saw as well that his sexual desires were compelling and really, almost beyond his control. I took a certain comfort in this. I was consoled, in a way, that it really had nothing to do with me, with some failure on my part. I recognized how much Damien valued what we had. I recognized that he really did love me, even as he felt a compulsion, a compulsion which, really, Kendra, only occasionally got the better of him. He fought it and fought it hard. As I say, he was at war with himself for decades.

"We worked it out. We even continued, through the years and off and on, as man and wife, if you understand me. Tino," Isabel said, and her smile lit her face, "Tino was the result of one of those interludes. We had tried, when we were young, for a boy. We had the girls, but kept trying for a boy. Only years later did Tino come. Long after I had adjusted myself to the reality of our situation, and to the certainty that there would be no more children, the Lord gave us Tino. That is why I named him as I did, and it was my decision to name him Celestino. Heaven's gift. That is what he was to us. He revived our love, Kendra. For years.

"But now, there is a new situation. Damien has found someone he is truly in love with. For the first time in his life – and remember, Kendra, we are well into our fifties – Damien has a steady and reliable relationship with another man. He wants the freedom to be in love, in love out in the sunshine, the way all the rest of us experience it, not kept hidden away in fear. This is the simple reality. I accept that this is the reality, and I still love Damien.

155

"We planned to 'go public' next year, after Tino was safely launched at UCLA, no longer living at home, you know. Damien has been very concerned for Tino in all of this. We planned to let the family know next spring, by which time Damien would have more or less accomplished the move --"

"The move?"

"Over here," Isabel said. "To the West Side. He's been back and forth for several years, you know, with the condo in Westwood. None of this, of course, could have happened while abuellita was still with us." Isabel was referring to her mother-in-law. Both of the elder de la Fuentes were now gone.

Kendra nodded.

"We planned to let the family know a year from now," Isabel went on, "but events have overtaken us." She took a sip of her wine, stared at the appetizers lying between them. "I am so sorry that it must be this way, rather than what Damien and I had planned."

Kendra said nothing.

Isabel took a deep breath and continued. "Tino and I have keys to the condo in Westwood," Isabel said, "but we are never there. Damien has to invite us, for us to be there. We live in a thirty-five hundred square foot home in Arcadia. The condo is three rooms on the twenty-second floor of a Westwood high-rise, it is not home to either me or Tino. Damien, however, thought that it might be a home for Tino, once he starts at UCLA. I wanted and want him in the dorms, so he can meet friends, but we live close enough to the campus so that he may not get a dorm assignment. In that case, the condominium would be a very good fallback. So suddenly, the condo on Wilshire Boulevard began to have a home-like feeling, for me and Tino. Do you know what I mean?"

"Of course," said Kendra. She was thinking of the Malibu house, and the family's pleasure in it.

"We – Tino and I – have always been very respectful about showing up at the condo, because we have not felt that it was 'ours.' We have always let Damien know when we would be there, and Damien has never restricted it. Well, one afternoon the week before last, Tino was at UCLA. He was on the West Side anyway, and had some papers he had to drop off, something about his classes for the fall. He started for home around four, and the traffic was so bad he never made it to the freeway. He took Wilshire to the condo and let himself in, planning just to wait out the worst of the rush hour.

"He came in and heard the shower in the bathroom and figured his father was there. He took a Coke from the refrigerator, and sat down at the big windows looking out over the West Side – such a view, Kendra!, such a view. You can practically see Disneyland. A few minutes later the sound of the shower stopped. The door to the bedroom opened, and there was a man, not Damien."

"Okay," said Kendra.

"And this is the second reason I asked you to meet me today, Kendra. The man was your friend, and Matt's, Jean Marc."

FORTY-SIX

"Good God," said Matt, as Kendra broke the news to him, less than an hour after her lunch with Isabel. "Jean Marc?"

Kendra gave a helpless gesture, and said nothing.

"Good God," Matt said again. "He's twenty-five years younger than Damien!"

Kendra considered this response for a moment. "Is that your primary response?" she asked. "The age difference?"

Matt looked at her, gestured with his hands as if to say, "Huh?"

"What shocked me was learning that Damien is gay."

Matt laughed, a short, staccato laugh. "Sorry," he said. "Sorry." He looked out the sliding glass door of his West L.A. townhouse, a vista of palms and brightly blooming flowers around one of the complex's several pools. "Sorry. It was never my business to tell anyone that Damien likes guys."

"Got it," said Kendra. "So you knew about the situation? That he and Isabel had worked out this arrangement or accommodation or whatever?"

Matt shrugged. "Yeah, I knew. What business was it of mine? I always so admired Isabel. Still do, no matter what. I figured they were indestructible. I am in shock. And Jean Marc, of all people!"

"Isabel says it's the real thing," Kendra said. "They're in love."

Matt guffawed. "Jean Marc is in love, all right. With the mirror."

"Were you aware that they had developed a – friendship?"

Matt seemed not to hear her. "My God," he said again. "Kendra. I introduced them. Do you remember? Two years ago, at the opening of the Century City restaurant. I introduced them!"

"We introduced them," Kendra corrected. "Don't think I haven't thought of that."

"It's crazy," said Matt. "A mid-life crisis badly remedied. Damien's acting out, nothing more. I'm just glad he has the sense not to divorce Isabel. He does not deserve her."

Something in this response discouraged Kendra. She had come to Matt first, before talking with David, because she had expected him to see it more or less as she did.

"I think this is something more than a mid-life crisis," Kendra said. "Damien wants to be able to live honestly and in the open."

Matt practically snorted in response. "With a thirty-five year old? Damien's almost sixty."

"I don't see what that has to do with it."

"It has everything to do with it," Matt said. "Good grief, Kendra. You can't see that?"

"I can't see how Jean Marc's age makes any difference where the real issue is concerned. What really matters here is Damien's coming out. Damien's situation in the family is what I care about."

"I care about Damien in the family," said Matt, "and I care about him overall. He is one of my best friends. Trust me, this is a huge mistake."

"It's been two years, Matt. Almost since the night Century City opened, the night we -- you and I -- introduced them."

Matt shook his head. "I wonder when they saw each other, got together, I mean. I mean, Jean Marc and I get together, usually to hit the slopes, a couple or three times a year, but Damien! I see him all the time. And with Isabel."

"Ditto," said Kendra. "I've been wondering the same thing, but in the end, who cares? The point now is to try to help the family absorb this huge new reality."

"Is that the point?" asked Matt.

Kendra looked at him, realizing for the first time in the conversation that there was a fundamental misunderstanding between them.

"What other point would there be?" Kendra asked.

"Let me put it this way," said Matt. "If Damien were leaving Isabel for a thirty-five year old woman, how would you feel about it?"

The question caught Kendra up short. It seemed to her a good one. She waited a moment, thinking about her feelings. Then, "That is precisely my point," she said. "He is not leaving Isabel for a thirty-five year old woman."

This response caught Matt up short. It seemed to him a good one. He waited a moment, thinking about it. "Okay," he said. "Okay. I take your point."

He waited another moment, and then said, "I realize you've just come from lunch with Isabel. But if you are up for a drink and an appetizer, at Casa de la Fuente, Century City, where, as I happen to know, Damien will be on duty late this afternoon, I would be happy to treat you."

Kendra gave him a quizzical look.

Matt shook his head. "The sooner I look Damien in the eye and shake his hand," he said, "the better. He's been my friend for ten years. I love him. This is crazy. But Isabel's on board with it and I don't desert my friends. I'll be there to help him pick up the pieces afterward."

FORTY-SEVEN

"I don't know who to be more astounded with," said David, when Kendra had told him, that evening, of her lunch with Isabel. "I don't know who is the crazier here, Damien for leaving Isabel, or Isabel, for cheering him on."

"I wouldn't say she is cheering him on," said Kendra. "She understands him and she loves him."

"Loves him!" said David. "Loves him! I like that. Kendra, if you have a friend who likes walking backward, and that friend is walking backward toward a sheer cliff with a thousand foot drop into the sea, and you do not tell that friend that they need to stop walking backward because they are headed for a cliff, that is not love."

Kendra waited before responding for, of course, this was the reaction from David she had been both expecting and dreading. She knew that, pushed to it, David would admit that Isabel loved Damien. This was not a point worth arguing.

"Leave aside the whole damned question of homosexuality," David said, "because I am in such shock about it being a question with my brother that honestly, I do not know how to even approach it. You're married almost forty years, stunning wife, four kids, a man of the family, and suddenly being gay is the most important thing in your life? Leave that aside, for the moment, because I can't think my way through it. Kendra, consider this scenario rationally. I mean, on the brass-tacks, rubber-meets-road-level, consider it. This guy is thirty-five, thirty-six. And from what I know of him, he is a dilettante, a ski bum who has had two or three bit parts in films, parts he got entirely through friends in the

162

business, and in which he has in no way distinguished himself beyond his telegenic looks."

Kendra shrugged. So far as she knew, this was a fairly accurate assessment of Jean Marc's efforts to establish himself in Hollywood. "Your point being," she said.

"My point," David said, "is that this doesn't add up. I'm suspicious of Jean Marc's motives. He's young and good-looking, what does he want with a fifty-nine year-old? Damien's getting rich off Century City; Jean Marc is not getting rich off his film parts or by being a ski instructor to the stars. Damien's clearly infatuated. Well, fine. You don't break up a thirty-seven year marriage over an infatuation. Doesn't add up."

Kendra wanted to point out that no divorce was pending, but thought better of it.

They were having this conversation on the patio, at the barbecue, where David was preparing hamburgers. It was early evening, and the sun had slipped behind the shadows of the eucalypts at the far property line, casting everything in a subtle blue-grey light, the light of a spring dusk.

"It's crazy," David said again. "Why not just carry on as they have, these last however many years? As long as he and Isabel are okay with their arrangements, why not just have Jean Marc on the side, out of the way and out of sight and not trouble the whole family about it? Are we going to be expected to welcome Jean Marc at Christmas, at the kids' birthday parties? Don't even think about it, as far as this home is concerned. Why ask the whole family to get on board with something so outrageous?"

"Damien is your brother," Kendra said. "He has lived in fear and secrecy all his adult life. Think about that. He wants to be able to live and love and breathe freely and in the open like any of the rest of us. Isabel understands that desire and supports it, because Damien's happiness matters to her. He is simply acknowledging to himself and to all of us who he is."

"'Who he is?'" cried David. "Who he is, Kendra? I would say that we could any of us explain to him who he is, and do a better job of it, than he himself is doing. He is the husband for thirty-seven years of a beautiful, gracious and intelligent woman and the father of four wonderful children. For crying out loud he's got five grandkids. That is who Damien is. Answer me this, if you can: where does Damien see himself in ten, in twenty years, if not the husband of Isabel de la Fuente and the father of their four children? Does he see himself the aging lover of a middle-aged Hollywood hanger-on, which I assure you, is the destiny for which Jean Marc is headed? Is that to be preferred to his marriage, his children and his grandchildren? Just what is it that Damien seeks, to 'be himself' that is not already there, that he has not already accomplished? Who he IS, Kendra? Who IS he, if he is not the husband of Isabel, and the father of Tino and his sisters?"

Kendra sighed. She felt an injustice in David's words, but was hard-pressed to elucidate it, and reply. Because, of course, there was also deep truth in David's words.

"This isn't easy," Kendra replied.

"And what about Tino?" David asked, as if he hadn't heard her.

"What about him?"

"Well, I mean, good God, Kendra," David said. "Tino walked in on them –"

"Wait a minute," said Kendra. "Tino walked in on no one and nothing. He arrived at the condo when Jean Marc happened to be in the shower --"

"In the middle of the afternoon."

"He had been at his gym," Kendra said, feeling her anger rising, for after all, Jean Marc was a friend of hers. "He was accustomed to spending time at the condo. He and Damien were to meet later that evening. He went to the condo to shower, and to wait for Damien. So hang him for the offense."

"Is it Jean Marc or Tino you care about here?"

"Why do you think it necessary to choose one over the other? Damien loves them both, a fact you are going to need to get used to," Kendra said. "Their meeting at the condo that afternoon was an accident. No one's 'at fault,' no one's guilty of anything. Isabel tells me Jean Marc was so surprised he didn't have time to try to come up with an excuse. Not that he should have lied to Tino, in any event. The circumstances spoke for themselves."

David looked at her almost as if at a stranger. "'No one's guilty of anything?'" David said. "Damien initiates an affair with a man, a man!, half his age and gives his lover the key to the family condo so that Tino walks in and finds him there, showering and drying off around the rooms as if the place were his, and – no one is guilty of anything?"

Kendra took a deep breath. "Isabel and Tino never used the condo," she said. "They considered it Damien's, not the family's. This meeting was accidental. No one is to blame for it."

"Kendra," David said. "Tino is seventeen years old."

Kendra did not reply immediately. Rather, she turned to the prep table David had set up and handed him the barbecue sauce. "Time to slap some of this on Jeffrey's burger," she said.

David, almost forgetting that he had meat on the grill, looked quickly at the burgers. Seeing that they were fine, he took the bottle and began to brush some of the sauce on one of the hamburgers.

"I understand Damien and Tino have had a couple of good talks," said Kendra. "The plan was to address all of this a year from now, after Tino was up and out and on his own at UCLA. Damien never wanted it to come out like this."

"I'd like to have been a fly on the wall," David said, "when Jean Marc came out of the shower. Can you imagine THAT conversation?"

Kendra didn't reply.

David, handing the sauce back to Kendra, just shook his head. "I'll talk to Tino," he said, almost as if threatening it.

FORTY-EIGHT

David did talk with Tino, as did Ramon, as did Matt. But it was Kendra whom Tino himself sought out. Her cell phone rang one morning while she was at Matt's, working on a re-write.

"Tino?"

"Hi Aunt Kendra," the boy said. "You busy?"

Kendra looked at Matt. "Yes," she said. "Matt and I are at work on a script."

"I can call later."

Something in Tino's voice told Kendra not to let the moment slip. "You can do that, or we can set up a date right now, and see each other."

"Are you free for lunch?" Tino asked. "I'm here. On the West Side, I mean."

"I'm free if we go late enough," Kendra said, "like maybe one-thirty."

They met at the same Japanese restaurant in West L.A. at which Kendra had met Isabel, a couple of weeks before.

"Yeah, Dad and I have talked," Tino said, stirring his miso soup with the chopsticks. "I understand how upsetting this was to him – because of me, I mean. He has bent over backwards to make sure I understand that he never wanted me to find out this way. Jean

167

Marc's been all over it, too. So many apologies, so concerned for me. Jean Marc's a good guy."

"So you and he have talked since that day?" Kendra asked. "You and Jean Marc?"

"Oh yeah," Tino said. "Couple times. He's been to the house. We're all sort of dealing with it together, I guess. I guess that's the way to deal with it. I feel bad for my dad, because he feels so bad for me."

The waiter came with the California rolls.

"I love these babies," Tino said, taking one up with his chopsticks.

"Where'd you learn to eat with chopsticks?" Kendra asked, smiling at his dexterity.

Tino grinned. "Peggy, of course." He meant Peggy Matsumura, a cheerleader he'd dated all through junior year.

"Anyway, like I said," Tino went on. "I feel bad for Dad. And I feel bad for Jean Marc. He was mortified. He just stood there, looking at me, and well, I guess I just sat there, looking at him. If he had wanted to lie to me, he could not have brought it off. Not after that initial moment. We both knew what was what, instantaneously."

"What an enormous shock for you," said Kendra.

"Yeah. Sort of like, reality shifted all of a sudden. Sort of like an earthquake, I guess. One minute the ground is solid under your feet, the next, it is cracked open and shaking."

He waited a moment, playing with the California roll with his chopsticks. Then he looked up, looked up, Kendra thought, with the huge, deep brown and long-lashed eyes of the little boy she had first encountered at Carlos' party years before. The sad eyes of the little boy who was in trouble. "I need to see my little gentleman," Damien had told his son.

"You know what's hardest about it, Tia?" Tino asked.

Kendra said nothing, just held his gaze.

"It's not the discovery that the rest of the family is so focused on," Tino said. "It's not that Dad is gay. The hardest part about it, for me, isn't about the fact that Dad likes guys. The hardest part for me is accepting the fact that Dad would rather be with Jean Marc, or anyone else at all, anyone other than Mom."

FORTY-NINE

"We'll wait," said Isabel, to Carmen. "You go in first."

David was awake again. Isabel, Ramon and Sandra had just arrived. Solange had almost simultaneously appeared on the patio and announced that David was ready to receive visitors.

"You got here first, sisters," Ramon said, smiling. "Go see nuestro hermano and we will follow."

Carmen, Ana and Raquel headed into the house.

"My poor brother," Ramon said, to no one in particular. "I don't imagine he ever would have guessed that dying peacefully at home would be so demanding."

Tino, at the bar, was taking, rather, soliciting orders. "Mom?" he asked. "Merlot? Shiraz?"

"You choose," Isabel smiled, and took a high seat at the bar alongside Kendra. Isabel was dressed in black slacks and gold-embroidered black top, with lacy black sleeves. At seventy, she remained slim, stylish, beautiful.

Ramon, taller than his brothers, and slimmer, and with thick grey hair that looked like David's, came around the bar to give Tino a hand.

"Chardonnay, darling?" he asked his wife. Sandra, dark blonde with the help of her stylist, large-eyed and with fluorescent orange lips and nails, smiled.

"What have we got in the way of hard stuff here?" Ramon asked, after getting his wife her glass of wine.

"Whatever you want," Tino replied, serving Isabel her Shiraz.

"Kendra," Ramon said. "What is that?" He pointed at her glass, which held only ice and lemon.

"The afternoon's preference," Kendra answered. "Iced tea."

"Would you like a real drink?" Ramon asked.

Kendra smiled.

FIFTY

"Yes," Ramon said, glancing across the garden to where Damien and Isabel were talking with a couple of the nieces. "I am in shock. I suppose we all are."

It was several weeks after Kendra's lunch with Isabel; a bright and breezy Sunday in May, Mother's Day. The family was gathered at Carmen's for brunch, the new routine, now that the elder de la Fuentes had died. Carmen had prepared an indoor and outdoor reception, and Kendra and Ramon were seated at one of several umbrella tables on the patio, sipping mimosas while the nephews set up the buffet.

"I am glad you say that," said Kendra, "because I am shocked, too, but it seems overlooked in family discussions. People seem to take my empathy for Damien as approval of abandoning marriage."

Ramon nodded. "Real empathy almost always exacts a cost," he said.

Ramon, the middle of the de la Fuente brothers, was really just about the last person Kendra would have expected understanding from, where her conflicted feelings for Damien were concerned. Ramon was a Catholic deacon. Kendra did not know just what a deacon was, or how they were distinguished from priests, other than that she knew, obviously, that deacons could be married and could not say Mass. Ramon and Sandra had married late, by the standards of the family – in their mid-thirties. They had been unable to have children, and after several years of trying, adopted twins, little boys from China. As luck, fate or divine providence would have it, several months after the boys arrived, Sandra became pregnant. She had a girl. A little over a year later, she had

172

a boy. The year after that, she miscarried, and she and Ramon initiated adoption procedures for a little girl from Uganda. Ramon worked as a CPA – the restaurants were among his clients. But he worked as well for his parish in Pasadena, as a deacon, and Sandra was active there in children's faith formation and youth and young adult ministry. They were among the most 'Catholic' members of the family, and Kendra had not imagined that she would encounter much in the way of understanding from them, on the business with Damien.

"To really enter into the experience of another person," Ramon said, "we have to let go of parameters, emotional, intellectual, spiritual, that we are accustomed to, and comfortable with. To look at a situation like Damien's, suspending judgment long enough to try to grasp what it is that has moved Damien, what it is that he is dealing with, why it is that he feels this is his best course – that takes some effort, Kendra. It's easy to judge, but not so easy to understand."

Kendra sat back in her rocking and cushioned patio chair, looking from Ramon to Damien and Isabel, now being greeted by Raquel and her husband. Damien had in the preceding weeks made it clear to the family that he would not try to force acceptance of Jean Marc. "I just don't feel I can judge," she said. "It's between Damien and Isabel, and when Isabel tells me she is all right with it, I ask myself, 'What objection are you going to raise? They have worked this out. Let them be and let it be.'"

"And that is the course the family is taking," Ramon said. "With a few bumps here and there. After all, it is a shock. And really, Isabel's own attitude almost as much as Damien's decision. She really has people scratching their heads."

"I marvel at Isabel," said Kendra. "What strength, what courage. What compassion."

"All of that is there," said Ramon, "but for most of the rest of us, there is another dimension to it entirely, there is the problem of trying to reconcile this with our Catholic convictions."

"Isabel assures me she is a woman of faith," Kendra said. "For her, the line of sight is clear. She says God loves gay people as much as He loves anyone else."

Ramon smiled. "She's right," he said.

"And I'm not entirely ignorant on this subject, you know. Not after marrying into this family. I understand that the Church holds that whether it is nature or nurture, gay people experience their sexuality as a given, it is not something anyone chooses."

Ramon smiled with approval. "Have you been reading the Catechism?" he asked. "Because that is what it says."

"No, but I've picked things up here and there," said Kendra. "The faith is just too big, in this family, for me not to."

Ramon lifted his glass to Javier, dressed in black boots, black jeans and a Hawaiian shirt. Javier re-filled it, part orange juice, part champagne. "Thanks, nephew," said Kendra, as Javier re-filled her flute as well. "This is better than a restaurant," said Kendra.

"Got that right," said Javier.

"So if people don't choose to be gay," said Kendra, turning back to Ramon, "they can't be 'blamed' for it. And in my view, to ask them to go their whole lives celibate is, well, in the mildest available term, unrealistic."

"It's certainly not an easy expectation," Ramon conceded. "Of course, it is nothing the Church does not ask of everyone else. Everyone unmarried, I mean."

174

"But straights have the option of marrying," said Kendra. "An option the Church denies gays."

"Well, on that score," said Ramon, "the Church's definition of marriage has been at odds with civil definitions since Henry VIII. It's got to do with understanding what a sacrament is, what a covenant is, and why marriage is more than just a contract."

"I'm aware that the Church's position is not rank prejudice," said Kendra. "But I am also aware of gay couples who have been together twenty, thirty years, a lot longer than any number of straight couples. Should they have remained celibate instead? Lived their lives alone? I mean celibacy is chosen among the clergy, among religious sisters and monks. No one HAS to become a priest, a nun, a brother. There's nothing wrong with choosing a celibate lifestyle, and in fact, I have an old-fashioned admiration for priests and nuns on just that score. But it should be a choice. No one should be told that sex is off-limits to them simply because of their preference. Our sexuality is too integral a part of who we are."

"Well amen to that," said Ramon. "That understanding, that our sexuality is a huge, and a precious part of who we are, is entirely in keeping with the teaching of the Church. What it really comes down to, is anthropology. This debate is about two widely different understandings of what it is to be human. The Church proposes that there is a rightness to the natural order, and that we can see that rightness in the way things are made. We can read meaning from the details of nature. I can't imagine that anyone would really try to argue that the complementarity of the sexes is not apparent, is not obvious. The Church tells us that we can trust that complementarity. The moral law of the Church both draws on and reflects arguments made from natural law."

"I'm a fan of the natural law, actually," said Kendra. "I'm a fan of the belief that reality is objective and knowable, not something we make up as we go along. And I agree with you that this is about anthropology, it is about competing theories of what it is to be human. Marxist-Leninism proposed an anthropology, man the worker, subservient to the state, to which the Church, quite rightly, in my view, took strong exception, condemned outright, in fact. If the Church had the right to object to atheist communism and its anthropology, don't gay people have the right to object to an anthropology which treats them as diseased?"

"Whew!" said Ramon. "I may need some more champagne before I can answer that!"

"All right, all right," Kendra said, sitting back and smiling. "I'll answer it for you. What I assume the Church would say about her anthropology is that it treats all of us as if we are diseased; human nature itself is fallen, and we all suffer because of that. Am I more or less right?'

"You HAVE been reading the Catechism!"

"Only on the beach," Kendra said. She sipped her mimosa, waved across the patio to Raquel, and indicated their table, which was thus far vacant. "I think it is obvious enough that the Church is going to carry the point on fallen human nature," Kendra went on. "Wasn't it Chesterton who said that Original Sin is the one Christian doctrine that is proved every morning on our doorsteps by the headlines in the paper?"

Ramon beamed. "He did say that."

"But I would still argue, from the suppositions of natural law," Kendra continued, "that homosexuality is a naturally occurring phenomenon, not a matter of subjective choice. It follows that gay sexuality is simply a normal variant on the spectrum."

176

"Here, try this," said Ramon. "This is an analogy which I found helpful, when I was studying for my ordination. Think of a gorgeous new car. Untouched. A beautiful new car in mint condition, everything in working order. It's obvious that the car has been designed, and designed for a purpose. The varied parts of the car show us, by their very design, what that larger purpose is. But just in case there are questions, there is a manual in the glove compartment that tells you how things work. Follow the manual and the car will run well. The moral law is like that; it's a user's manual."

"Give me a minute," Kendra said, a hand up, and looking with a thoughtful frown at the white lace tablecloth. Then she looked up, a bright questioning look in her hazel eyes. "It's a good analogy but for one thing," she said. "Shouldn't this car have a flat tire, a plugged fuel filter, carbon deposits on the valves and be leaking transmission fluid? Because isn't that how most of us experience ourselves?"

Ramon's eyes were wide, as was his smile. "Yes, I think that is how most of us experience ourselves," he said.

"Gets back to fallen human nature," said Kendra.

"Precisely," said Ramon. "In which case, I would argue, all the more need for the user's manual."

"Your point," said Kendra. "Now I'm the one who needs more champagne." She thought about it a moment and then said, "I suppose my response would have to be, 'Who designed the user's manual?'"

"That gets to subjectivity," Ramon warned, with an arch smile. "And you say you believe that reality is objective."

"Your point," Kendra conceded.

"Back to the car analogy," said Ramon. "What are various parts designed for? Wilfred Sheed once pointed out that the modern mind, encountering an object, asks not 'What is its proper use?' but rather, 'What can I do with it?' Everything is understood through the lens of personal and subjective preference. Yet design itself appears unmistakably in nature, and where there is design, there is intention, there is purpose."

"I grant that nature appears to be designed," said Kendra. "But I would argue as well that homosexuality appears to be so naturally occurring a phenomenon as to be part of the design. The only other possibility is to call it a design flaw, a flat tire, if you will. One of the defects in nature which the Church attributes to Original Sin. In any event, arguments about what the Designer intends won't cut much ice with people who do not believe in the Designer to begin with."

"Your point," said Ramon.

"So we're at a draw," said Kendra.

"We could take it to the next level," Ramon said. "The level of the questions of evangelization and of freedom of conscience, formation of conscience and so on, but only at the risk of boring anyone else who sits at our table."

Kendra smiled. "I need to reaffirm my general agreement with the suppositions of natural law," she said. "A morality based on the subjective lends itself quickly to just what we saw in Russian communism. Power ultimately dictates morality in such a case; might makes right, objective truth is trampled underfoot and justice is whatever the powerful say it is. That's what we get, when we abandon objective norms in our efforts to understand reality. Deep truth, not subjective reaction, must be the basis for our moral understandings."

Ramon was smiling.

"Get that look out of your eye, cunado," Kendra said with smile. "An acknowledgment of human weakness and wickedness is a long way from an acceptance of the Nicene Creed. I'm not about to convert."

"To my agnostic sister-in-law," said Ramon, lifting his flute. "And her fine elucidation of the doctrine of Original Sin."

Kendra, smiling, shrugged. She would not want to let Ramon down. They clinked their glasses. Meanwhile, Raquel and her husband Juan arrived and took seat at the table.

"As long as we are toasting," Kendra said, and turning to Raquel and Juan, lifted her glass. "It's Mother's Day, so I guess I can go ahead and let this out. David and I found out Friday. I'm six weeks pregnant."

"Rico!" Raquel cried, clapping her hands together. "Champagne at this table! A bottle, just for us!"

FIFTY-ONE

"Brother says come in," said Solange, smiling radiantly at Ramon, as she crossed into the shade. "He is with his sisters, and he says, 'all the siblings can be together now, bring my brother, bring Sandra and Isabel.'"

"We are going to wear David out with love," said Linda, after Ramon, Sandra and Isabel had gone in. "Literally kill him with kindness."

"He had a long nap this afternoon," said Kendra. "And this is Ramon's first visit in a week. The parish keeps him so busy, especially at the weekends."

"So funny that Ramon became the big do-gooder in the family, a deacon for the Church," Linda said. "I understand that he was the original wild child, when he was young."

Ramon had, in fact, had a rather mis-spent youth. While Damien was busy with the restaurant and the family, and David was driven in his pursuit of Hollywood success, Ramon had relaxed, smoked pot, tried cocaine, had a succession of beautiful girlfriends, drank with his buddies, drove fast cars, played the horses at Santa Anita, sailed off Catalina and in general, enjoyed life, for about fifteen years until, in his early thirties, he met a girl whose seriousness he could not pass by. That girl was Sandra, and after two years, they married.

"I think his experiences while young are part of what make him so effective as a deacon," said Kendra. "He's not judgmental because he himself has been there and done that, when it comes to sin. I love Ramon."

"Who doesn't?" Linda agreed.

FIFTY-TWO

Sandra's eyes were red, and her make-up smeared. "I'm just glad I held it together 'til we were out of the room," she said now, to Linda and Matt.

"Oh baby," said Linda, and rising, hugged her. "I know, I know. It is so, so hard."

"He was so strong," Sandra said, "just this winter. Oh, I thought maybe we had had a miracle. I really did. After Ramon blessed him with the Lourdes water, I thought, maybe, just maybe, David had been spared. He's so weak, Linda! He's so weak!" She collapsed sobbing in Linda's arms.

"It's okay, baby," Linda said, "it's okay. You are here, and he is so glad that you are here. That is all that matters. You've made him very happy, this afternoon, Sandra. So happy. Easy, easy, baby," she said, as Sandra sobbed. "Easy. Just be grateful for the chance to be with him. He is. He is so glad you came today. And you picked the best possible day, because he is so awake today, so alert."

"We almost didn't come," said Sandra, gathering herself and pulling back and up a little, from Linda's embrace. "We almost didn't come. I had the kids tonight," and she was speaking of her young adult group in the parish, "and Ramon had Bible Study. But when Isabel called and said she was going over, we found substitutes; we came."

"You came," Linda said, and beamed at her. "Of course you came. And David is so glad and so grateful. So take your cue from him, Sandra. Be glad. Be grateful."

"Oh my gosh!" said Justin, who was seated at the bar. "Look who's here!"

All eyes turned toward the glass doors through which yet again Solange stepped, this time with a tall and slender middle-aged woman with long blonde hair, dressed in a grey pantsuit and flowing yellow scarf. She would be the last guest that long afternoon.

Jessica leaned over for a better look. "Is that --?"

"Chrysta McAllen!" said Justin.

Linda turned with something like disbelief toward the back of the house. Sure enough, there, with Solange at her side, was Chrysta McAllen. Linda looked about the patio, seeing the overall reaction, realizing that not one of them, not even Matt, had the faintest idea. She turned at last to Kendra, seated at the bar in her white blouse and black skirt, talking with Isabel.

Kendra, hearing the hub-bub about Chrysta, turned and looked and said, "Oh my gosh! Is it six already?"

"Five past," said Tino.

"I'll be back," said Kendra, alighting from her high bar chair, and crossed the patio, a hand extended, to greet the newcomer.

"What the Hell," Linda breathed almost inaudibly.

FIFTY-THREE

A few months after the opening of the Century City restaurant, Kendra, thirty-six that year, became pregnant. She and David had been trying for a child, and were joyful at the news. She miscarried that summer, not ten weeks into the pregnancy. It happened at home, David was there. He had been working in his office when he heard Kendra cry out. He leapt up and ran to the light and airy breakfast room, where he found Kendra, clutching herself and staggering, trying to reach a chair or one of the cushioned window seats. Then he saw the blood.

He lifted Kendra in his arms and carried her to one of the window seats, but she was sobbing, "It's too late, it's too late, the baby's gone."

After getting his wife safely to the window seat, David turned and looked and saw the bloody place on the pale tile floor. He looked for a long moment at the little messy spot there on the floor, then turned back to Kendra, who was turned in on herself and crying.

"One moment, darling," he said.

Tears starting in his own eyes, David went to the kitchen sink, ran water in a juice glass, and came back to the breakfast room. He poured the water out on the bloody place. He raised his hand above the little mess and Kendra distinctly heard the words, "I baptize you in the name of the Father, and of the Son and of the Holy Spirit."

When he joined his wife on the window seat, taking her in his arms, David too was sobbing. He held her close and tight. It would seem to Kendra, in memory, that she had spent the rest of that day in David's arms.

Two years went by before Kendra again conceived. This second pregnancy was the one of which she spoke, at the Mother's Day brunch at Carmen's. Haunted by the memory of the first miscarriage, Kendra nonetheless accepted her doctor's assurances that there was no reason to fear with this second pregnancy; she was fine and the baby was fine, and for five full months, Kendra knew the joy of expectant motherhood.

The miscarriage occurred in early September, precipitated by a bloody show, while she was working on a script with Matt. Matt drove Kendra to the hospital. David was on location in Mexico. Carmen got through to him several hours later, but by then it was all over. Kendra had miscarried again, and this time, it was not just a "bloody little mess" on the floor. This time it was a very small, but perfectly formed little boy.

Kendra was in the hospital overnight, and returned home shocked and grieving. David flew home that same day, and spent three days with her. He was all solicitude, and Kendra in his arms felt safe, if disconsolate. When he returned to Mexico, Kendra felt herself alone as she had never felt before. This was not just some psychological reaction and she knew it. There was, in fact, a literal emptiness in her. There was inside her that empty place where their little boy had been.

At Linda's prompting, David flew home again about ten days after the miscarriage, staying two days. Kendra had not expected him; she knew the pressure to stay on schedule and under budget, while filming. Secretly grateful for Linda's intercession. Kendra would nonetheless not have troubled David to return to L.A. Neediness had never occupied a prominent place in her playbook. She assured David she was all right. He returned to Mexico and completed the location shots the following week. When he got back to Los Angeles, Kendra, busy with the kids, and working once more on the interrupted script with Matt, seemed to be herself again. In fact this was an act; Kendra was in deep grief. She talked with Linda, she talked with Matt, she talked with Polly, her mother, who flew down from the Bay Area a couple of times to be with her. But the one person who really could console her was David, and he was on the set with the new film twelve to fourteen hours a day; Kendra knew he had lost five days of filming because of his returns to L.A., she understood that he needed to get the picture completed on budget and on time.

Sleep became her new friend. She had always been a late-night type, often working on rewrites 'til well after midnight. Left to herself, Kendra would never have been in bed before two AM or out of it before nine. Her schedule was adjusted, of course, after she married, but in the weeks and then the months following the second miscarriage, Kendra found herself going to bed some nights not long after the children. She and David had evenings together. They had evenings together when something compelled it, a family party, some red-carpet event or other, a night at the symphony with Linda and Sam. But other nights David was at work late and Kendra in bed early. On good nights she slept, but on others she lay awake, wondering about the child she had lost, thinking about where she would be with the pregnancy had she not miscarried, sixth month, seventh month, thinking about who this little boy, her son with David, might have been. The second miscarriage had the effect of bringing vividly to mind her memory of the first, and so some nights she would let herself think about two children lost, about how life itself had twice been expelled from her womb. She knew there was no point in such thoughts, but she thought them anyway. Nor did she think her grief outsized or inappropriate. She might at this time have been the mother of two children with David. Those children were not here.

For the first time in their married life, she missed David. She missed him deeply. He did not see where she was, emotionally, and she supposed that that was hardly his fault. She had determined while he was still in Mexico to handle her grief with as little disruption of the family routine as possible. It was less for David than for the children that she resolved to appear capable and strong, no matter what she was actually feeling. Jessica, Justin and Jeffrey needed her as they always had, and she could not indulge the desire – as for instance sometimes occurred to her – to simply spend a day in bed. Much as she some mornings felt that there was no reason to get up, in fact, of course, there were three reasons to get up each morning, and later, looking back on this time, she would realize that it was the children who got her through it.

FIFTY-FOUR

It was a morning in March, bright and sunny, late in the morning, going on noon. It was six months since the miscarriage. Kendra was alone in the house. The kids were at school and David was that week in London, to attend the British premiere of one of his films. There had been some talk of Kendra accompanying him, but her heart had not been in it, and it was easy enough for her to beg off simply on consideration of the children's schedules. Kendra had over the winter completed work on the new script with Matt, and though she would, in fact, have welcomed extra work, simply for its value as distraction, none came that spring. Matt went to Spain for two months, after completing the script, and Kendra, missing now not only her husband but her writing partner and one of her best friends, became very quiet and rather withdrawn, there in the Brentwood house, whenever she was alone.

The silence of the house that spring, those many mornings and early afternoons that she was alone in it, struck Kendra. Normally, as a writer, she valued silence, even cherished it. But the silence of the Brentwood home that spring struck Kendra precisely for what it counterpoised: the gurgles, the cries, the laughter of a child. The baby would have been two months old, that March, had he been born.

She had found over that sad autumn and winter that there was a therapeutic advantage to simple domestic routine, and so she engaged herself more so than ever before in the maintenance of the household. The house-cleaning crew came Mondays and Thursdays and handled not only the rooms of the house, but the pool and patio; the gardeners came once a week, and David gave them their instructions. But there were certain aspects of housekeeping which Kendra had always reserved to herself, such as doing the laundry, such as picking flowers and bringing them into the house, such as planning meals when David was not there to take care of it, and these she retained and attended to, throughout those sad months. Washing clothes required no mental effort. It was simply something there to be attended to, a task which presented itself as necessary two or three times a week. Watering the indoor plants, of which there were many, was also an aspect of the domestic routine that Kendra could call her own, as was setting the table for dinner and clearing things away afterward. Kendra took refuge in these routines, she took solace in them.

It was while she was separating David's clothes, some for the wash, some for dry cleaning, that it happened, that she came across the note. She was checking pockets, as she always did, for keys and cash and credit cards, for anything else not meant for the soak-rinse-spin cycle. It was as she was going through the things to be sent out to the dry cleaners that she found it, in a grey sport jacket that Lana had given him ten or more Christmases before, a favorite among his many jackets. The note was in an inside pocket.

She did not, at first, even notice it. She simply laid it aside with the other things she had taken from his pockets. Getting the laundry into a basket, and separating the dry cleaning over a divan, she glanced at the little pile of things on the desk that she had pulled from David's pockets, and the note caught her attention.

It caught her attention because it was a hand-written note, rare, for e-mail was by this time commonplace. It caught her attention because of the well-formed inked letters of the message itself. It looked like a woman's handwriting. It caught her attention because she saw, in a glance, a signature to the note, the name Chrysta. She knew in an instant it was Chrysta McAllen. That fact sent a sudden and inexplicable shiver of fear through her. And with a sense at once of an impending and yet impossible discovery, she lifted the note.

189

"No, nothing has changed," Chrysta's note read, "except that everything has. Kendra is devastated. If you cannot see that, David, honestly, it is because she is indeed the actress you have always said she was. She is trying to spare you. But trust me on this. She and I have a lot of mutual friends, you know. She is devastated. She needs her husband. She has a right to him. I need a real, full-time and devoted lover, and whether or not I have a right to such a man, I intend to find him.

Bless you, dear, dear D. Thank you. For all of it – yes, yes, the professional, but truly, I will never forget the personal.

Take care of Kendra.

Always,

Chrysta."

There was no date, and the note was obviously the last page of a longer communication. Kendra read it a second time, then a third. She crossed toward the windows there in the master suite, for no reason other than that there were chairs and a love seat near the windows. She needed to sit down.

FIFTY-SIX

The summer of the birthday party for Carlos, David had offered Kendra a two-picture deal which she turned down. David had been surprised. Matt had been surprised. Nick, Kendra's agent, had been surprised. But Kendra had had her reasons, among them that certain "charge" in the atmosphere of which she'd spoken to Matt, when she found herself together with David. David was married and the father of three; what is more, Kendra found him very attractive. She said no to the deal.

David eventually cast different actresses in the two films. It was only Kendra he had imagined playing in both films, part of a cherished strategy David nurtured for several years, with Kendra: he believed she was destined for stardom, and he wanted to be the director who brought her into it. He cast separate actresses in the roles, one of them a recent cross-over from a hit television detective series: Chrysta McAllen. The film was a brainy comedy, and the role Chrysta took required an ease with irony and satirical delivery which Kendra would have brought off effortlessly. Chrysta, accustomed to drama and suspense, needed coaching. She needed repeated takes where Kendra would have gotten it on the first try. She needed to be shown how toss off more than a few of the lines, she needed to be taught the art of comedy then and there, on the set, with all the lights up and the cameras rolling. She needed, finally, expert editing: the most supportive camera angles, lighting that could help suggest what she was unable on her own to project, and she was helped as well by a certain number of dubs – she came back in after the shooting was completed and re-delivered several of her lines to achieve the best effect.

One result of all this hard work on Chrysta's part was that when the film was released she won general recognition as a fine comic performer. The film in which David had hoped to launch Kendra launched Chrysta instead.

Another result of all the effort the two of them put into the film is that Chrysta and David became lovers, while the film was in post-production. This was, of course, while David was married to Lana.

Lana never found out.

FIFTY-SEVEN

Kendra sat near the tall windows there in the master suite, Chrysta's note to David in her hand, staring in the direction of the balcony which gave off the bedroom, but not really seeing the balcony, nor its yellow-cushioned, wrought iron chairs, nor the brightly blooming climber rose along the railing. Nor was Kendra "seeing" anything in her mind. She saw only the note in her hand and its huge, its impossible ramifications, and, because these genuinely did seem impossible, Kendra could not really "see" them, could not imagine them.

David…with Chrysta? The possibilities crowded in on her mind, leaving her unable to visualize any of them; they were all too huge, too dark, their cumulative revelation too shattering.

She looked once more at the note in her hand, turned it over as if studying it, when in fact, the information it conveyed was just at that moment so impossible for her to absorb that it might as well have been written in medieval Icelandic rune.

David, with Chrysta? Chrysta in David's arms? David, Chrysta, together, where – a hotel suite, a foreign city, a bar above a beach, laughing, confiding, kissing…

She shut the images down for they threatened to overwhelm her. She felt almost dizzy with their force. She sat silent by the tall windows for several minutes, her breathing deliberately slowed and steady, an effort to calm her mind.

David was in London. It was Tuesday; he would not be home until Sunday. She did not want to ask David about the note, anyway.

Not until she had spoken with Chrysta. She was almost desperate to find some meaning other than the obvious one, for the note. She did not have personal contact information for Chrysta, but she could find her easily enough. Kendra's agent Nick was also Chrysta's agent.

FIFTY-EIGHT

"It started with EROS SHRUGGED," Chrysta said, when two days later she and Kendra met for a drink in Beverly Hills. "Not on the set, but after the filming, while we were in post-production."

"Lana never knew?" asked Kendra.

"No," Chrysta said, looking at the shining wood surface of their little table. The table was set in a curving sort-of alcove near the bar. It afforded a degree of privacy which Kendra had wanted for this conversation. "We were pretty careful, of course," Chrysta went on, lifting her glass of white wine, looking at it and putting it down. "But beyond that, we were also pretty infrequent. I guess we got together six or seven times those last two years of Lana's life."

She was an elegant green-eyed blonde, a couple years younger than Kendra. Since her film debut with EROS SHRUGGED Chrysta had become a major star. Patrons in the bar stole glances at her now and again, and the waiter had asked for her autograph, which she'd provided on a paper napkin.

Kendra had called Chrysta just hours after finding the note. Chrysta's shock had been palpable across the telephone wires; in the next moment she was sobbing, begging Kendra's forgiveness, assuring her the affair was over, volunteering information which confirmed all of Kendra's own worst fears. Kendra, cool and restrained, asked, "Will you meet me for a drink sometime this week? David is out of town until Sunday. I would like to get this sorted out in my mind before talking with him. If I am going to be fair, I need as far as possible to understand how this could have happened."

"Anything you want, Kendra," Chrysta sobbed. "Anything you want."

"How about Junior's on Beverly Glen?" Kendra said. "Thursday at six okay?"

"Thursday at six," Chrysta agreed.

"At the time we shot the film, I was not involved with anyone," Chrysta was saying now. "I'd divorced Mel the previous year and was not ready to try again, I mean, not even to date. I was gun-shy, after all the ups and downs with Mel. Here I was in this exciting new environment, film, not television, with this tough, this challenging business of comedic acting. I was excited and happy and I was – scared. Scared of blowing it." She looked directly at Kendra. "I have never had your talent. Not then, not now."

"EROS SHRUGGED was made two years before Lana died," Kendra said.

"Right. We were together, off and on, as I say, the last two years of the marriage. Lana was, well, their relationship was --" Chrysta hesitated, looking down again, and from right to left, as if hoping to find the appropriate word somewhere on the table.

"Difficult," Kendra suggested.

Chrysta nodded, sighed. "You know how it was. I know the affair troubled David, he was deeply conflicted, as of course, was I. But we had --" Again, Chrysta seemed to hope to find the word somewhere on the table. "We had one charged set of responses to one another," she said, and looked up, again meeting Kendra's gaze directly.

Kendra's breath caught at the word "charged." She looked at her glass, an almost-untouched chenin blanc, and said, "I can understand that."

"Of course it wasn't only physical," Chrysta said. "He had mentored me. He had reassured and calmed and coaxed me, he created that performance, he made me a star. I was grateful to him. I was reliant on him. I was a little in awe of him – after all, Kendra, he is a lot older than either one of us. There was a protective feeling in it, for me, which, I guess, after all the fireworks with Mel, was very seductive. I felt so safe with David, so appreciated, so loved."

"Yet you got together so infrequently," Kendra said.

Chrysta took a deep breath. "Well, he was married. Three very young children; Jeffrey was in diapers. And he loved Lana. Despite the affair, he loved Lana. She just sometimes, she left him feeling taken for granted, I guess. I don't want to say more than that, because I do not want to blame Lana in any of this. I am just trying to give you insight on how the affair developed.

"In any event," Chrysta went on, "I did not want or need a steady romance at that point. I mentioned fireworks with Mel. They can burn, fireworks. I had been burned, and as I say, I was very hesitant to take up right away with anyone. In a way, the affair was perfect for me, perfect at the time. Except for an affair, David was unavailable. I didn't have to worry about jealousy, possessiveness, nasty suspicions, raging scenes, emotional abuse. There would never be any of that with David, because David was taken, David belonged to Lana, to the children, to his family, to his career. David had too much else going on in his life to become a mad man about me. I could have him now and again and I did, forgive me, Kendra, but this is the truth, I did love having him. It was very comforting, consoling, to be found so desirable, and to feel so safe. David's love was stolen, I readily admit. But honestly, Kendra, it was a healing love, for me."

Kendra said nothing for a long moment. She lifted her glass, looked at it, set it back down. She looked at Chrysta. "Then Lana died," she said.

Chrysta nodded, looking down. Kendra saw a tear forming on her long lashes. It trembled there for a moment, then broke free and fell to the table. Another followed, and when Chrysta looked up, her face was a mask of anguished guilt.

"How I wished I could have undone the affair," she said. "Lana's death was a knife in my heart, Kendra. Oh! How I wished I could have undone it. It makes no sense, I know I was not responsible for Lana's addictions, but when the woman whose husband you have stolen, or okay, for the sake of argument, let's say borrowed, when the woman whose husband you have borrowed dies of a drug overdose, alone, in a Vegas hotel suite, well, you blame yourself. You ask yourself what would have been the situation between David and Lana if you had not been in the picture. Would he have been there for her, would her death have been avoided, if you had not entered the equation?

"I just assumed that David would want to end the affair," Chrysta said, and wiped her eyes with a tissue she had retrieved from her purse. "I told him how terribly guilty I felt. I hardly knew how even to try to console him, I would have felt like a hypocrite. I told him I could not attend the funeral --"

"But you were there," said Kendra. "At the church. I remember. And we spoke at the restaurant, afterward."

Chrysta nodded. "David asked me to come," she said. "He asked me to come to the house, afterward. That I did not do. It was at Carmen's. The nephews and nieces were all there, David's children were there. How could I face all of his family, after what we'd done? I'm not that good an actress."

Kendra was puzzling over David's desire to have his mistress at his wife's funeral.

Chrysta, as if reading Kendra's thoughts, said, "Do you think it is possible to love two people at once? I mean, you know, romantic, sexual love? I have never felt that it is, but I suppose it depends on one's definition of love, and on how one experiences oneself, in love. By my definition of the term, David could not possibly have loved both me and Lana. Love is all or nothing, as far as I'm concerned."

A small, careful smile crossed Kendra's face. She looked again at her chenin blanc, but did not lift the glass. "Sounds like we use the same dictionary," Kendra said.

Chrysta's eyes were a large part of her stardom. They were deeply expressive. In that moment they seemed to Kendra to express gratitude, hope and the deepest contrition, all at the same time.

"David told me he loved me," Chrysta continued, "but what, after all, could be done about it? He was married. And really, whether or not he loved me, he did love Lana. It was a tortured love, but it was love. Divorce was not an option, in his mind, because of the children. I doubt that he would have strayed if things had been different with Lana.

"After her death, I think David might have wanted to marry me, but I made sure that conversation never happened. I did not want to be the mother of three children. Period. Besides, David was grief-stricken. I could have had anything I wanted from him, those months after Lana died. Anything. All I wanted was to be a comfort to him – I mean as a friend. I swore to myself that the affair was over.

"But of course it wasn't. He was so hurt, just shattered. Kendra, in his abjection, in his vulnerability, after Lana died, I gained a whole new experience of David; a couple of times he cried himself to sleep in my arms, and I fell more deeply than ever in love with him."

"But you did not want to marry him?"

"Not David nor anyone else," said Chrysta. "This was still at the outset of my career, just two years since EROS SHRUGGED. I was free and strong, confident in new ways, able to imagine and accomplish things I never could have, while I was with Mel. I wanted my career and the future it was offering. And at that time, children were no part of my plan."

Kendra nodded.

"And the affair continued," Chrysta said, "until a few months before you and David were engaged. I saw what was happening between the two of you and honestly, I was happy, happy for you, because I saw as well that you COULD become the mother of three young children, and happy for David, because he deserved a loving wife, one who would not take him for granted, one who would love him and the children before and beyond everything else. When he told me he was planning to ask you to marry him, I was not surprised, I was ready to move on, and we ended our affair by mutual agreement, and on amicable terms. And that should have been that."

Chrysta sipped her wine, pushed her hair back with her other hand, looked across the bar as if looking for some way to avoid the rest of the conversation.

"You remember when he took over as director on BLUE HORIZONS," said Chrysta.

"Two years ago," said Kendra, this turn in the conversation confirming her own suspicions. BLUE HORIZONS was a picture in which Chrysta had had a leading role. The original director had quit early in the filming, and the studio had brought David in to salvage the project, which he had done: the film was completed on time and only slightly over budget and had done handsomely at the box office. It was the first time since EROS SHRUGGED that David and Chrysta had worked together, and Kendra had suspected that it was on the set of BLUE HORIZONS that they had rekindled their affair.

"Not on the set," Chrysta told her, as the conversation continued. "Just as it was with EROS SHRUGGED, it happened in post-production. One afternoon after going round and round about a couple of scenes with the editor and a couple of the producers, David called me and asked if I would meet him for a drink. He wanted to talk shop, he said, wanted to talk about the film, about the final cut of the film, I should say. He suggested the Polo Lounge. I should have suggested someplace else, because the Polo Lounge is where our affair started.

"I cannot explain this, Kendra. I cannot offer a satisfactory analysis. The spark, the charge, the attraction that we'd had in Lana's time, it was still there. We both felt it, working on the set of BLUE HORIZONS, but somehow, we got past it. I was unattached at the time, between lovers, but he was yours, and I assumed, on the set, while we were shooting, that though he felt the old spark, too, he was determined to ignore it. I respected that, and did my best to ignore it, too, and we finished the shooting and we were fine. Then came that call, that suggestion of the Polo Lounge, that drink and the one that followed, and the discussion of a joint project in which we both had a stake, the discussion of our mutual hopes for BLUE HORIZONS, and well…a week later, we were lovers again.

"There is no possible justification for either of us. It was sheer desire, animal instinct, radical selfishness. I felt awful, later, and told David we needed to avoid being alone together, avoid, in fact, even seeing each other, but events conspired to throw us together, after all, we were rolling out a new film and there were other things, too, a couple of charity events which you and David attended together – Matt's big fete at the family restaurant, for instance – we, David and I, saw each other, talked together, drank and laughed together, and we fell back into the old routine. It wasn't frequent, anymore than it had been with Lana. But it happened.

"And then you had the second miscarriage."

"Last September," said Kendra.

"I wrote David the letter you found right before Thanksgiving. The affair has been over, Kendra, for four months."

"From the phrasing of your note," Kendra said, "it appears to me that you ended the affair, perhaps even over David's objections."

Chrysta took a deep breath. She looked across the bar again.

Kendra smiled a sad smile. "Thank you for meeting with me. Thank you for your honesty." She reached up her purse, took out her wallet.

"Please," Chrysta said, a hand reached across the table and laid on Kendra's arm. She meant specifically the bill, but in fact was asking for something rather larger.

In the instant, Kendra was unable to give Chrysta that larger thing. "Thanks for the glass of wine," Kendra said, rising.

"Please, Kendra," Chrysta said. "Please believe me. The affair is over."

Kendra nodded, saying nothing. She turned and left.

Kendra's glass was almost untouched. Chrysta stared at it a moment and then hailed the waiter. Indicating her own nearly empty glass, "I'd like another," she said.

FIFTY-NINE

"Clifton Abbey Sauvignon blanc," said Linda to the waiter, young, Filipino and elegantly dressed in black slacks, white shirt and black vest. "How about you, darling?"

Kendra shrugged. It was the next day, Friday, early afternoon. Linda and Sam had been in Palm Desert all week. Kendra had called out to the desert a couple of days before and asked Linda for a lunch date as soon as she got back. Linda had unmistakably heard something "wrong" in Kendra's voice over the phone, but Kendra had revealed nothing, saying only that she had a problem and needed help. Linda said she and Sam were coming back over Friday morning, "So how about Friday lunch?" Kendra grasped the invitation as a drowning man would a life vest.

Other than Chrysta, Kendra had talked to no one all week. Matt was in Spain. Polly, Kendra's mother, was just a phone call away, or an hour's flight, in the Bay Area, but Kendra had not wanted to burden either Matt or Polly with this. Really, she had not wanted to burden anyone with it, but she had to talk to someone, she had to get her own feelings out in the open where she could see them and begin to understand them. Really, there was no candidate for this distinction but Linda.

She had found the note on Tuesday. It had been perhaps the longest seventy-two hours of Kendra's life. The silence of the house, with David in London and the children in school, for several months now a silence of sad emptiness, had taken on a new dimension, since the discovery of Chrysta's note. There seemed to be something almost sinister in it. Kendra had trouble sleeping and, had she not had the children to cook for, she very likely would not have eaten anything at all since Tuesday's discovery. She had no appetite.

And now here on Friday afternoon in a restaurant of Linda's choosing in Beverly Hills, Kendra could not make a decision about a glass of wine. It was overwhelming to Kendra, simply to be with Linda. For the first time since discovering the note, she felt safe, she felt sheltered, as if from a rain that had been falling for three days. She wished she could prolong her time with Linda indefinitely.

"Chardonnay or chenin blanc?" Linda asked.

Kendra had had a chenin blanc the previous evening, with Chrysta, and she had left it almost untouched. "I guess a chardonnay," she said.

"The best in the house," said Linda to the waiter, who nodded as if conspiring with Linda for Kendra's benefit and then was gone.

"So you've known how long?" Linda asked. "Three days?"

"Since Tuesday."

"This is Friday. One messed-up Friday."

"It was one messed-up Tuesday," said Kendra. "It's been one messed-up week."

"And Chrysta admits to everything."

"An on and off affair," Kendra said, "stretching over a decade. I guess it went into eclipse for two or three years after we were married. It was re-ignited while they were working together on BLUE HORIZONS."

"I loved that film," said Linda. "What a shame. I'll never feel the same about it again."

"Yeah, me either," said Kendra, with an ironic laugh. "Chrysta says it was largely animal attraction, a charged atmosphere, if you will. My deepest problem with it is that the affair is evidently over at her insistence. She felt for me, after the miscarriage. She couldn't continue with it. There's no indication that David could not have continued indefinitely. Of course, that is unfair of me, until I have heard his side of it. But Chrysta's account rings true to me."

"I don't know how I would handle this, if it happened to me," said Linda. "My gut is that I would walk out. Hit him with all the legal system allows, get every dime that I could claim, and be done with it, and actually, I would not be the one who walked out. That would be him. I'd keep the house, girlfriend. He could sleep in his car, for all I care."

Kendra heard Linda's response but could not connect with it. "I am at sea, Linda. I'm at sea. And rudderless. Too much in shock to know my own mind."

"Entirely to be expected," Linda said.

"So if it were you and Sam, you'd walk?"

Linda shrugged. "Oh, who knows? Just speculation. And remember, I'm the trophy wife. I'm the new model he traded the old one in for. It's different with a second and much-younger wife. She can hold her own in the discussions in a way a blowsy fifty or sixty year old can't."

"I'm not a blowsy fifty or sixty year old," Kendra said. She laughed and added, "I'm a blowsy thirty-nine year old."

"Oh baby!" said Linda. "Not like Chrysta is twenty-two. She's our age."

"Yeah, that's not an issue," Kendra agreed.

The waiter returned with their wine. Linda looked at Kendra. "Going to eat?"

Kendra shrugged.

"We'll both have the spring mix salad, chicken," Linda told the waiter, "with a raspberry vinaigrette for me and balsamic for my friend. And could you bring some bread?"

Linda turned back to Kendra, who was swirling the wine in her glass, staring at it. Linda just watched her silently. When Kendra looked up and met her gaze, Linda asked, "What are you going to do?"

"I am going to talk to David."

"And?"

"And I don't know," Kendra said. "It depends on what he says, I suppose. I mean, what are my options? I can stay. I can leave."

Linda sipped her wine, saying nothing.

"I mean, Linda, Chrysta is the reason the affair is over. Or well, the miscarriage is the reason; that, and Chrysta's compassion."

"Yeah," Linda said. "It's like Chrysta's more on your side in this than your husband."

"I never sold my condo in Santa Monica, you know," Kendra said.

Linda considered this statement. "So you are that close," she asked, "that close to leaving?"

Kendra shrugged.

"I just need to know where we are with this, so that I can help you," Linda said. "Are you giving serious consideration to leaving?"

Kendra shook her head, looking toward the restaurant's windows. "I don't know," she said and choked back a sob.

Linda was all solicitude. "Baby," she said. "Kendra. I am here for you. For you. What Kendra needs may she get from this girlfriend or may I be boiled in oil, burned at the stake and subjected to the Salem witch water test, not necessarily in that order. I am with you, whatever you decide. I am just ascertaining the fact: you would seriously consider leaving?"

"You think that isn't a realistic option?"

"Kendra!" said Linda. "I told you. I am one hundred-ten per cent on your side. Your decision garners my support, whatever it is. I just didn't realize, coming into it this afternoon, that divorce was on the table."

"You don't think I should leave," said Kendra.

Linda looked at her glass and took a deep breath. "Kendra. I am here for you."

Kendra smiled a small, quick, sad smile. It was funny, she thought, how we see ourselves in our friends. Quite clearly, she saw that the possibility that she might leave shocked Linda. In Linda's shock Kendra saw, not herself, but Linda's image of herself. And that image was important to Kendra. Clearly, Linda did not think Kendra capable of breaking up her marriage over an affair. Linda's impression of Kendra was that she was strong enough to get through this. That impression made an impression on Kendra. Linda would doubtless love her regardless, but her understanding of her friend Kendra would be forever changed, and perhaps diminished, were Kendra to leave.

And of course, Kendra knew the reason why. The three reasons why.

SIXTY

Kendra pulled the car into the gravel drive, and stopping the engine, sat there in front of the house for a long moment. The house was Georgian in style, with Southern accents, including a colonnaded verandah. Two large magnolia trees, one on either side of the front walk, deepened the suggestion of a confederate past. Azaleas, veritable hedges of them, many just now in full bloom, also contributed to the Deep South ambience, as did the touches and finishings here and there in wrought iron. Lana had apparently fallen in love with what Linda termed "the GONE WITH THE WIND back-lot look" of the place, and she and David had bought the house early in their marriage, before Jessica was born.

It was a beautiful spring afternoon. Bright sunshine and a light breeze, temperatures in the seventies. Kendra had had the window down while coming back from lunch, but put it up as she turned onto her street. Now, turning the key in the ignition but not starting the engine, she put the window down again. The trees rustled in the breezes; and not just the azaleas, but the roses, too, were riotous and so many colors -- red, yellow, orange, white, pink, purple. A yellow swallowtail butterfly rode the light wind across the front of the house; bumble bees were attending to the pomegranate blossoms, bright orange in the afternoon sun. One of the cats was stretched out on the walk toward the front door. Selcat, sleek and black, with golden eyes, punningly named for the Egyptian funerary goddess, Selket.

With the bright afternoon and the blooming garden Kendra in previous times would have taken a quiet joy, pulling up to the house. She'd have taken a serene pleasure in looking toward the house; she'd have taken a moment to let the garden impressions register in her mind. Simple moments such as this, and the deep appreciation they could evoke in her heart, were a part of Kendra's whole approach to living. But this afternoon she was hard-pressed to see beyond the anguish. The affair had ended because Chrysta could no longer continue it.

Kendra put the window up and got out of the car, leaving it in the drive for she had a strong sense that she and the kids would be going out for dinner, tonight; may as well leave the car out. The gravel crunching under her heels, she thought about the long-ago conversation she and David had had about a gravel driveway. He'd resisted the suggestion to pave it, because he did not want the children playing in it. That was the kind of father he was, and even in the sorrow of the moment, Kendra could hold clear in her mind that truth about him. She remembered him as well, carrying her to the sofa, at the very moment of the first miscarriage, she remembered him kneeling over the little bloody mess on the floor, with water. "I baptize you…" It was all he could do for the child they had just lost. So he did it. The gesture had struck Kendra at once as almost achingly pathetic and yet strong and true, really, something very like magnificent. There was no question of his being a good father.

The children, of course, were his. She and David had miscarriages, not children. The house was his; he had bought it with Lana, not with her. The garden was his; David supervised the crew that came in once a week and he made all decisions about plantings, prunings and so forth. The huge southern California family was his; they liked her, but David was their blood. The larger part of their joint income was his; Kendra had been happy to release much of her own earning potential in order to be with the children.

The marriage itself was evidently his. His to do with as he saw fit, and if that included having a decade-long affair with Chrysta

McAllen, well, that was what it was. She had married into this life, and she had come to realize the past several days that this life was not hers, nor hers and David's together, rather, this life she had married into was David's. In light of the affair, well no, in the darkness revealed by the affair, she realized that she was, evidently, sort of on loan here, a nice "extra" in the broader context of David's life. She could make herself as "at home" here as she liked, but in fact, she was hired help.

She crossed the gravel to the walk, stopping to play a little with the cat. Selcat rolled and stretched under Kendra's touch, her black coat glossy in the bright afternoon light. Kendra straightened up and continued into the house. It was just after three. The kids would be home soon.

SIXTY-ONE

Sitting by the pool some minutes later, Kendra heard a door open, and turning toward the back of the house, saw Jessica, then fourteen, and a freshman in high school, step out onto the patio. She was on her cell phone. She saw Kendra and waved, smiling, then turned and walked toward the curving flower beds, bright with orange kaffir lilies and California poppies, with geraniums, azaleas, iris and day lilies in many colors. The beds were shaded here and there by olive trees and there were several stone benches. Jessica took seat on a bench facing the pool and continued her conversation, her voice and her occasional laughter catching on the breeze and coming to Kendra in snippets.

Kendra rose and headed into the house, realizing that if Jessica were home, the boys would be, too. She came in through the glass doors that led into David's office. She stopped a moment at the entrance to the room, and looked about it, and was struck once again with the thought, "It is all David's."

She came into the broad hallway beyond the office and heard Justin and Jeffrey arguing, somewhere out toward the main rooms of the house. She followed their voices up the hallway and into what the kids had come to call "the computer room" because it was the room, a one-time playroom, where their shared computer was kept.

The kids shared the computer because Kendra did not think there was a reason for any of them to have their own. She and David had disagreed on this point, and Kendra had prevailed. The compromise was that at the start of high school, each child would receive a computer. Jessica thus was exempted now, from squabbles about the use of the computer, a fact much resented by

213

both Justin and Jeffrey, thirteen and ten, respectively, but on this point Kendra had dug in her heels and refused to budge.

"No ten year old needs his own computer," Kendra had argued, when she and David had discussed the matter. "Besides which, they need to learn to share. It would be easy to spoil them, David, with all we might give them. We need not to do that."

The argument currently in progress evidently involved Justin trying to bump Jeffrey from the computer, so that he could do his homework.

"He's not doing his homework!" Jeffrey protested to Kendra. "He wants to play video games!"

"No, that's what you're doing!" Justin shot back. "Kendra," he said, "I have to research the British Isles for a class report on Monday."

"On Monday!" Jeffrey cried. "It's Friday afternoon! You have plenty of time. And you are not going to do homework, anyway! I was here first. Mom, I was here first. Tell Justin to come back in an hour."

An hour each had been established among the family as the allotted time for a fair set of rotations in the use of the computer.

"None of this would be happening," Justin pointed out, "if I had my own computer!"

"You're right," said Kendra. "But you don't have your own computer. It's Friday afternoon," she continued, secretly very sympathetic with Jeffrey's charge that Justin was not likely to be doing homework due Monday on Friday afternoon. "There is plenty of time for you to do the research, Justin. I'll help if you like. It'll be fun."

Justin sighed loudly, seeing he had lost.

"Meanwhile," Kendra said, "as Jeffrey was on the computer first, let him have an hour. Then it's yours."

"Man, I'm the only kid at school without his own computer!" Justin said, and stomped out of the room.

"Thanks, Mom," said Jeffrey, and smiling, returned to his video games.

"One hour," Kendra said, leaving the room. "Then it's your brother's. Be thinking meanwhile," she said, calling the words after Justin, who was stamping up the stairs, "what you want for dinner. I'm not going to cook, so it's gonna be take-out."

Suddenly, Justin was over his pout. "Pizza!" he said, over the balustrade, while "Chinese!" came the vote from the computer room.

"We'll leave it to your sister to break the tie," said Kendra.

"I'm going to tell her pizza!" said Justin, and ran back downstairs and through the sunny rooms to the patio, to line Jessica up for his preference.

In the end, they had both pizza and Chinese, and some cut, raw vegetables, carrots, celery, avocado, tomato, which was as much as Kendra had the energy to get together on her own. The pizzas arrived first, around seven, and they put in a video they all loved, THE KARATE KID, and the Chinese arrived ten minutes into the film and "It's a feast!" delighted Jeffrey, as Kendra got everything laid out and, pausing the video, they began to serve themselves.

Kendra watched as the children filled their plates and poured their sodas. They were back in front of the tv in just minutes, and Justin re-started the video.

"Sit here by me, Mom!" Jeffrey said, patting the place on the leather sofa next to him.

Kendra smiled and put some of the raw vegetables on her plate.

"Is that all you are eating?" asked Jessica.

"I'll get more later," Kendra promised. "This is just an appetizer."

"I love this movie!" said Jeffrey.

Kendra let the film's dialogue and images wash over her, laughing when the kids did, and appearing to be as wrapped up in it as they were. Only much later would she look back and realize that this was the moment where she had her answer, where she realized that she had had her answer all along. The talk with David was still to come. But she could not consider leaving.

SIXTY-TWO

David sat alone in the family dining room, that is, the informal dining room off the kitchen, staring at the floodlit patio beyond the windows. The pool was translucent blue and the palms along the perimeter were also lit up. Their fronds lifted and rustled with the night breezes. It had been a warm day, mid-eighties at LAX when his plane arrived from London, but it cooled down rapidly after sunset, and it was chilly out now, March, after all, besides which, it was well after midnight. David would otherwise have gone out to the bar to sit, to sit and stare into the darkness and be silent.

He'd gotten in from the airport well ahead of dinner, as he had promised Kendra and the kids; he had assured them he would be here tonight, to barbecue. The children loved it when he barbecued, and he had asked Kendra to have tri-tip marinating this afternoon. He and Kendra had a drink on the patio around six, he got the fire going half an hour later and the steaks were on before seven. Jessica wanted to hear about London, Justin wanted to complain about not having a computer of his own and Jeffrey had just wanted to be with his dad – he helped with the grill-side prep and marinating. Kendra seemed herself, a little subdued, perhaps, but then, that had been the way of it, since the miscarriage. The loss of the second baby had had profound enough an effect on her that a quieter, more pensive Kendra was now the norm, that was Kendra "seeming to be herself." David told her about the week in London, asked how her week had gone, asked when Matt would be back from Spain, wanted to know if Sam and Linda were still in the desert. He had left himself no downtime, after this trip; had a meeting with someone at Fox at ten tomorrow, then lunch with the folks from Denver who hoped he'd select their city for a future film, then the tax guys at two, after that an interview with L.A. EXPRESS, and then the two of them had that charity event for

217

children with life-threatening illnesses – were Sam and Linda going, and if so, could Kendra possibly attend with them and let David bow out, "After all," David had grinned, "it's you the organizers want, not me." He added that, after London, the thought of one more night out just exhausted him; how much more he would rather come home to the children and make dinner.

Kendra said that they needed to talk about the charity event; she said it could wait 'til later. "These guys," she added, and indicated Justin and Jeffrey, who were sitting at the patio table with them, "need Dad time."

It was ten that night before Kendra told David. Jessica and Justin both were still up, but in their rooms, and within an hour of being in bed. Kendra knew David would be tired, would want to go to bed early, that is to say, before midnight; but she had also been determined that her concern not mar David's first evening back with the children. At ten, finding him with his laptop at a table in the family dining room, Kendra said, "David, the children are all upstairs and it's safe now, for us to talk about this."

David looked up from the laptop, an expression of mild surprise and certain interest on his face.

"Chrysta and I met for a drink on Thursday."

David sat there now at the windows of the family dining room, staring out over the floodlit patio, and recalled Kendra's calm, her cool, her eminent rationality.

"I am going to tell you something," Kendra had said, taking seat across the table from him. "If you had to select a mistress, you could hardly have done better than Chrysta McAllen. She is, in my opinion, a genuinely good person.

"She wept, David," Kendra had said. "Wept on the phone, wept in person. And you know, her story, the stormy first marriage, her fears, both professional and romantic, when you cast her in EROS SHRUGGED. I could relate to everything she said, I could understand how, from her side, this could have happened.

"I can also understand this from your side, in terms of how the affair developed. I saw what you went through with Lana. Well, no, of course, I did not see it, not by a long shot. But I caught a glimpse of it, that first night, that night at the restaurant, Carlos' party. I understand how it is that you may have taken comfort in Chrysta, both while you were married to Lana, and afterward."

She waited a moment, and appeared to be choking back tears which in fact is exactly what she was doing. "What I do not understand, David, is how the affair could have started again. I do not understand how you could have wanted Chrysta when you had me. And, and I do need to say this, I am at a loss to grasp how it is that the affair has been ended, and I do believe that it is ended, at Chrysta's insistence, almost as it would seem," and here, Kendra produced from a pocket of her blouse Chrysta's note, "almost, as I say, as it would seem, against your will. Chrysta is telling you here that the affair must end, and she is explaining why. I – ache, ache, David – thinking that had Chrysta not been the sort of woman she is, you would still be sleeping with her."

Kendra had then waited, watching as he absorbed the shock, took the note carefully in his hands and read it. For a long moment, he said nothing. Then he looked up and their eyes met and he said, "Kendra, it is over."

She nodded. "I believe that. It's late, and we don't need to settle anything tonight," she continued. "But I need to know, David. I need to know how it is that our love has not been enough."

Again he was silent for a long moment, looking down and clearly, looking within. That was four hours earlier and he was still looking within, looking out over the pool.

"What are you thinking?" David had asked, after a long moment. "I mean, what are you going to do?"

"The morning we took our vows, David," Kendra said, "that bright Saturday at the Mission five years ago, what I said to you that morning, what I vowed to you, I meant. For better, for worse. I need two things from you, David. I need to know what is missing in our love that you sought out Chrysta. I never realized that there was anything missing. I was happy. I thought you were, too. That's the first thing. The second thing is that I need to know that this is going to be the worst that 'for worse' gets."

She stood up then, straightening her skirt with a sweeping action of one hand. "It's late for a talk like this; you're tired and have a full day tomorrow. We'll talk. I am not going to the fundraiser tomorrow night."

Kendra went upstairs. David thought about following her, but decided against it. His brain was on stun, and he was, actually, glad not to have to explain himself tonight.

As if he could explain himself, he thought now, hours later, staring out the glass at the pool and patio, floodlit in the chilly night. As if he could explain himself. He ran a hand through his hair while running through the possibilities, in his mind.

Lana took me for granted. I felt neglected.

Chrysta was unsure of herself on the set, vulnerable. She needed me. I felt important and manly.

You, Kendra, had been my first choice for that film, and for the other, as well. You rejected the whole deal. I felt disappointed, and I will admit, part of it was that I wanted to be with you; I think you were aware of the electricity between us, as well. After all, I wasn't nineteen, I wasn't imagining it, wasn't making things up. The spark was there. Not that I was consciously looking for an affair with you, just that I was very attracted. I thought that if we could not be lovers we might, anyway, be creative partners together. I wanted to work with you.

It was Nick, your agent, who suggested I take a look at Chrysta. She was just coming off four years with that hot legal series. He said she wanted film, he said she was brainy, he said watch the tv show if you want proof. I watched the tv show. She was brainy all right. And witty. Not really funny, not like you are, not really a comic performer, but then the show was a legal drama. I saw potential, and I saw something else.

I saw – forgive the word, but after all, it's always intended as a compliment – I saw a lady, Kendra. I saw a lady in Chrysta. That consoled me, and it encouraged me to give her a shot, because as you know, I saw a lady in you, too. Classy, gracious, strong but unassuming. Frankly, I saw in Chrysta and in you, Kendra, a whole lot of things I did not see in Lana.

An excuse? No. It doesn't rise to the dignity of being an excuse. Lana was my wife. I loved her. She was the mother of my children. I needed her. They needed her. We all needed each other, but Lana needed all the rest of that, and she went out after it regularly, and we, the kids and I, were the losers. There are other things I might have done with these circumstances, rather than initiate an affair, but initiate an affair is what I did.

How to describe Chrysta, those first weeks on the set? She was so damned beautiful, Kendra! So beautiful. Those pale green eyes. That silky blonde hair, and the ways she wore it. Long and relaxed like a Swedish model or up and sophisticated, like Eleanor Parker as the Baroness in THE SOUND OF MUSIC.

How to describe Chrysta those first weeks on the set? Her ease and grace with the other actors, with the crew. She got to know everyone by name, and you'd find her talking – I mean real conversations about her life, theirs -- with the best boys and the wardrobe assistants. Only a lady behaves that way. Only a woman sure of herself, at home in her own skin, takes time to know the set crew. Not a whiff of the prima donna about her. Everyone loved her.

Which was a good thing for her because for all her personal poise and confidence, she needed help, doing her first comic picture; she had a lot to learn. She not only had the humility to learn it, and learn it well, she had the love and support of the entire cast and crew, and that, plus her willingness to work long and hard at it, is what launched her.

I remember one morning seeing her with a couple of the make-up guys, just talking, nothing special about the moment at all, really, except what it produced in my mind. They were talking about the weather, for crying out loud; it had been raining for three days and everyone was sick of it. Anyway one of the make-up guys saw me and he looked alert all of a sudden, as if he were expecting me to give some kind of order. Chrysta and the other guy turned, following his lead. Chrysta was wearing a red wool sweater, v-neck, a little loose, kind of hid her curves. Her hair was down. When she turned, I saw the line of her torso under the sweater. That's all. I saw her slim curves beneath the sweater, and I had my first – conscious reaction – to her. She saw me and smiled. And I had my second conscious reaction to her. Not as an actress, you know. As a beautiful blonde in a red sweater.

Factor in the rest of it, the long hours making her performance and I do mean MAKING her performance; her recent escape from her first marriage; my feeling neglected by Lana; her being such a lady by contrast to Lana; her neediness, professionally, which created a gratitude on her part, emotionally, which I turned to my advantage, sexually.

I turned the situation to my advantage. I did it. I initiated. Chrysta simply responded. Did I "need" Chrysta? Hell no. Did I want her? Hell yes. And what happened between us was electric.

What were my feelings for her? They were there. I've always said that I might have married any of a thousand women and made it work. I have never been the dreamy romantic poet type; you know that. My feelings for Chrysta were there. They did not need to be expressed the way they were expressed. The affair was hardly inevitable.

It was also, as I gather Chrysta has told you, sporadic, off and on; hardly some all-consuming torrid romance. Light, breezy, fun; romantic precisely because it was not conceived by either of us as some grand passion. An occasional escape into sensual joy. That is what the affair was, from my side, anyway. You'd have to ask Chrysta what it meant to her. I would not presume to speak for her.

I have sometimes wondered what would have happened, had Lana found out. Thank God she didn't. I am not sure how she would have reacted, but I know her reaction would not have resembled yours.

When Lana died, Chrysta tried to disengage. I know it sounds awful – but I am not interested in lying, at this point, Kendra. I've done enough of that. I wanted Chrysta more than ever, after Lana died. We were together within a month of her death. I suppose that is shocking and I know it is inexcusable, but there you are.

And as Chrysta told you, we continued to see each other for the next two years. I suppose that is understandable enough. I would have married her, had she wanted marriage. I knew all along she didn't. We parted amicably, three or four months before you and I were engaged. I told her you and I were serious; I told her I was going to ask you to marry me. She was happy for us. As I say, a lady.

So…you. Us. The rekindled affair, two and one-half years after you and I were married. Kendra. Kendra. Kendra. God help me, Kendra.

I don't know what to say. I mean, I do. But I do not want to say it to you.

Why did I re-light the flame with Chrysta? What was missing, you ask, in our love, in our marriage, in our happiness? Shall I lie to you?

Shall I say that Chrysta's dissatisfaction with the producers' plans for BLUE HORIZONS threw us back into the old roles of protective director and new star? I suppose you could say that Chrysta fell back into a certain neediness and reliance with me, regarding the final cut of the film, regarding the next stage of her career. I suppose you could say that we simply reverted to form, her neediness and insecurity, my experience, my power, and we took it, literally, all the way.

You could even make some kind of argument, I suppose, about how Chrysta appealed to me in a way you couldn't, because Kendra, I have never seen you needy. I have never seen you dependent. I was the one who was rescued by you, after Lana's death. You were the strong one in the situation, I was the one who relied on your strength. But you know as well as I do that I was only too willing to be taken care of, to surrender to your judgments and recommendations, to do the whole thing, our whole courtship, your way, rather than asserting myself, because I knew you were thinking of the children. And that was everything to me.

Yeah sure. I could say, Chrysta helped me feel strong and protective again, which I liked, and which I don't especially experience with you. But actually, what I experience with you, Kendra – an equal partnership – I prefer. It is an entirely new way of being with a woman, for me, this love between equals. It's bracing and unpredictable. I am NOT in charge, not with you. WE are in charge. And I like that.

So what was missing, you quite rightly ask, from our love, that I re-kindled the affair with Chrysta?

It was while we were in post-production with BLUE HORIZONS. I had problems with the final cut being proposed by the producers and so did Chrysta. I suggested we meet. I suggested we meet at the Polo Lounge. True enough, it was convenient; she lives in Beverly Hills. But as I have said, at this point, why would I lie to you? I recommended the Polo Lounge because that is where our affair had started and…and I was thinking how much we had enjoyed each other.

Chrysta arrived wearing a beaded black dress, classy cut, low neckline, hem at the knees, a matching jacket. The ensemble overall hid her curves. She walked into that fabled cocktail lounge, in modest but glittering black, her hair up and her eyes so expressive and green and her need for me worn on her sleeve, and well…I was reminded of the rainy day that she had turned to me in the red sweater, and smiled. I was reminded of my first conscious reaction to her as a woman, not as an actress, as a woman. I thought how much sexier a woman can be, sometimes, fully dressed, than naked. And then I thought of her naked. The affair did not actually re-commence for another week, but in fact, I think we both knew then and there that we were headed back to bed together.

Would you believe that, Kendra? I'll bet that you would have trouble believing it, because our own romantic life has been so deeply satisfying. I can't fake what we have, Kendra. Nor can I tell you what you mean to me. Just at the moment I see how everything we have together, the whole life we have built, is headed for a cliff. I am struck through with the thought of losing you; too late, a damned fool, too late, I am realizing all that is at stake here, my serenity in our life together, the happiness of the children, how much I cherish what we have. Too late, Kendra, too late, I am realizing the stupidity of the affair, the thoughtless selfishness and all that I put at risk to indulge it.

So why did I re-engage it? What was missing from our love, Kendra?

What am I to say? Blonde hair and a red sweater?

And we are going to talk tomorrow, Kendra? I don't look forward to it. I don't know what I can possibly say to you.

God help me.

SIXTY-THREE

"Pigs," Matt had once said to Kendra, years earlier, on the subject of men and sex. "We are all pigs, when it comes to sex, and actually, I think I am probably maligning a perfectly decent little barnyard animal, in using the term. Real pigs, I think, behave nothing like the ordinary human male, when it comes to sex. Pigs may be random and self-serving – I don't know the mating habits of the porcine species. But if so, at least they are honest about it. Males of the human species, no. Because we know damned well that honesty will get us nowhere with most females of the human species. We want sex, they want romance. They want it wrapped up with tissue and bows, and we go out and buy the tissue and bows, happily at first, resentfully later, after we have made the conquest and feel it's a done deal. Remember that Christine McVie song, TELL ME LIES? Christine McVie is a woman who figured men out. We tell lies, when it comes to getting what we want. The anguish women would save themselves, and the headaches they'd save us!" Matt added with an ironic laugh, "if they could just get that equation right. Men lie to get what they want."

The conversation had been prompted by Matt's summary dismissal earlier that week, of a girlfriend he'd been with almost two years. Kendra had been surprised, and asked him what happened. "I thought you loved Angie," Kendra said.

"I loved being with her," Matt corrected. "Angie was fun. And she got the whole writing thing, she got that my work comes first." Matt had dropped other girlfriends because they'd objected to his unavailability owing to his hours and many hours, with his scripts, his meetings with directors, producers, his agent. Matt's career always trumped any other consideration, and more than one of his girlfriends had tried to challenge that fact, had tried to become his first priority. One of them had even joked with him, "I wish I were one of your film scripts. I'd get to see you every day."

This had not been the case with Angie. She "got" Matt the writer, and was happy with the time and energy Matt devoted to her.

"So what happened?" Kendra asked.

Matt looked at her. "She just recently began to object to the time I spend with you."

Kendra was surprised. "Me?" she said. "She was jealous of me?"

Matt shrugged. "Don't underestimate yourself," he said. "You're talented and intelligent and fun to be with and – oh yeah! You're not just movie star gorgeous, you ARE a movie star! And you appear to be available," for this was before Kendra married. "Yeah," he went on. "Angie objected to you. So, I gave her the heave-ho."

"Wow," Kendra said. "I'd thought the two of you might be headed for the altar."

Matt laughed. "Yeah, well, that was another thing," he said. "Angie was starting to get serious. That was part of her objection to you. She didn't see how she could be married to a man who spent so much time with another woman." He waited a moment, then said, "I assured her, I didn't see how that could be, either. And I told her in any event, she needn't worry about it."

"Wow," Kendra said again. "You don't seem very broken up about it."

Matt laughed, the short, ironic laugh again. "I'm not," he said. "I'm relieved, actually."

"You're not going to miss her?"

"Of course I am," said Matt. "'Til I find someone else. But meanwhile, along with the mild regret, there is a much more than mild relief: I had no intention of marrying Angie."

"At the risk of sounding repetitious," Kendra said, "wow."

And that is when Matt explained to her that when it came to sex, men were pigs.

Lying awake in bed that Sunday night, following her conversation with David, Kendra remembered this conversation with Matt. David had not articulated the reasons he'd resumed the affair with Chrysta. But Chrysta had: "radical selfishness," she'd called it. Inexcusable, without any satisfactory rationale. Comparing Chrysta's words with Matt's, Kendra was satisfied that she had her answer. Her heart ached. She felt anger. But in her rational mind Kendra clearly saw that her marriage was not threatened. She saw as well that, henceforth, she would wield a moral authority in her marriage that she had not possessed before. Any sort of power at all can be a dangerous thing and Kendra knew it. Yet she felt secure that she could use this new unsought and unwanted power, carefully, judiciously to hold David close, to hold him contrite and true.

That was enough.

SIXTY-FOUR

Kendra woke as dawn was breaking. She had left David in the family dining room and come upstairs to bed, but she had not slept. She lay awake, waiting for David to come up. He did not come and he did not come. Eventually Kendra dozed fitfully, stealing glances at the radio alarm clock when she woke, two-forty, three-fifteen, four-thirty-five. Finally, as it was getting on toward six in the morning, and light was beginning to show beyond the plantation blinds, Kendra rose, sufficiently rested though she could not have had more than three or four hours of sleep, and pulling on a silky black robe, went downstairs.

She went first to the family dining room, where she'd last night left David, but he was not there. She crossed into the formal dining room, not, of course, expecting to find him there. She went into the front living room; he was not there. She crossed to the library; again, no David. She looked in the west living room, so named because it faced the patio and pool, faced the afternoon and setting sun. David was not there.

Kendra began to worry. She decided to short-circuit her fears and crossed to the garage, where, seeing their three cars, she was able to ascertain that David was in the house, or well, at least somewhere here at home, on the property. She thought then of his office, and crossed down the broad carpeted hallway and, seeing the door open, stepped through it.

David lay on his back on the room's single sofa. At the instant she saw him, Kendra's breath caught, it flashed through her mind that David was dead. She dismissed the idea as soon as it occurred, but it had the effect of sending a deep and terrible pang of fear, of regret, of incalculable loss through her, and she trembled with the feeling, she felt her heart race with it.

She crossed over to him. She knelt down beside him, and took his hand in hers.

David started awake, looked blinking about himself as if trying to figure out where he was, saw Kendra, and showed still more surprise.

"Kendra!"

Then, clearly, it all came back to him. A look of pain, really, of anguish, swept over his face. He covered his face with his free hand.

"Kendra," he said again.

"I had begun to worry," she said, his hand in both of hers. "You didn't come to bed, and then I could not find you, downstairs."

David looked up at her from under his sheltering hand. Tears started in his eyes. Then suddenly he was off the sofa and kneeling on the carpet with her, his arms around her and hugging her tight, close, as if for dear life itself.

"Kendra," he said. "Kendra. Please," and his voice was a sob. "Please, please, please don't leave us. Please Kendra, forgive me. Forgive me." And now he was sobbing, the words finding their way out in gasps and spasms. "Oh God, Kendra! I'll make this up to you. Please, please give me the chance. For the children's sake, please, Kendra, please. Don't leave us."

He collapsed into her, sobbing, so violently that Kendra had to steady them both with her hand on a nearby coffee table. His tears soaked through her robe to her shoulder, and Kendra had the sense that if she did not keep holding him he would sink to the carpet entirely.

A few moments later, each of them settled in the other's arms, and still on the carpet, Kendra stroking his hair and David's grief for the moment subsided, "You have to promise me something," Kendra said.

"Anything," David said in a husky whisper.

"You have to promise me that you will search as diligently as I, to discover what was missing between us, what left you unsatisfied, what made Chrysta possible. There's only one way to accomplish this," Kendra continued. "We will look together for a good therapist, and find one, and this week."

SIXTY-FIVE

Kendra woke the next morning feeling rested for the first time in she could not say how long. She had had a real night's sleep for the first time in a week, and for the first time since perhaps the miscarriage, she woke feeling bright and refreshed, eager to start the day.

David had risen early; meetings with investors in Orange County. Kendra got breakfast for the children, but did not eat herself, just coffee, just juice, then drove the kids to school. On her return she heard the birds singing in the trees, she saw the swallowtail butterfly again. She sat in the car a moment, there in front of the house, and looked at the azaleas, looked at the roses. This time, these things made her smile.

She crossed up the walk to the veranda. Cleocatra yawned and stretched on a cushioned chair. King Tut-tut-tut, a Maltese-alley cat mix, followed along at Kendra's heels. She got out her house keys, the cats accompanying her toward the door. She crossed into the house, and she realized two things. One, the period of sorrow about the miscarriage was over; she had come through it to the other side. Two, she realized that she was already in a new place with regard to her marriage. She realized that as a direct result of what she had just come through with David, she had a newly-formed purpose. A plan which had evidently been arranging itself in secret all the past week now stood revealed, in the morning's bright light.

She crossed into the kitchen. She took a bottle of orange juice from the refrigerator and went into the breakfast room, bright with morning light. She sat down at a table, looking into the front garden, King Tut rubbing against her legs. She reached her cell phone from her purse. She went to her contacts and hit the speed-dial, sipping the orange juice and waiting for the receptionist to pick up on the other end.

"Good morning," she said, a moment later. "This is Kendra Collins. I need to speak with Mr. Braxton."

SIXTY-SIX

"How are you?" Alan said, hugging her when, two days later, they met at the Bistro for lunch. "Wow," he said, taking a step back and looking her up and down. "You look great."

Kendra smiled. She was dressed in black and yellow, colors which became her. "I've lost weight," she said.

"As if you needed to," said Alan, as they crossed in to the host station. "I've been worried about you, you know."

The thought flitted through Kendra's mind: "I'm glad someone has been." But she let the thought pass. It was at variance with her new outlook, her new hope. What she said was, "I so much appreciated the flowers, a couple months ago; the note."

Alan had written Kendra, and sent her a bouquet, on the baby's due date. "I meant to get a written thank-you note off to you but --"

"Oh Kendra, please. You CALLED me, remember? Braxton," Alan said to the host staff. "Party of two, twelve-thirty. You called me," he said, returning to Kendra. "We talked half an hour."

Kendra shrugged. "Thank-you notes are important," she said.

The hostess invited them to follow her to their table.

"I'll bet you don't know what today is," said Alan, after they were seated.

Kendra smiled, questioning with a hands-up gesture. "Thursday," she said. "March twenty-ninth."

Alan smiled, nodded. "Our twelfth anniversary," he said.

Kendra looked at him with amused bafflement. "Of what?"

"Today is the day," Alan said, picking up the menu, "twelve years ago, that you first stepped onto the set of GIRL THURSDAY."

Kendra's jaw dropped, and her eyes went wide. "Good Heavens! How do you remember such things?" Though, in fact, everyone was impressed with Alan's memory. "Like a computer," Matt had more than once said of it. David, too, had remarked on the way Alan never forgot a friend's birthday. And Alan alone, among all her friends and family, had remembered the baby's due date.

Alan smiled. "I note the day every year. That was such a great day for me, as a writer, as a director, the day Kendra Collins walked onto the set for the first time. Don't worry, I'm not even a cyber-stalker. I'm just a big fan of Kendra Collins, actress. I remember the day because it was such a happy one for me. I think it especially auspicious, that we are meeting on that anniversary."

"Wow," said Kendra, sitting back and smiling at him. "Why didn't I marry Alan?" she asked herself. "What might it have been, if I had?"

Alan himself had been widowed tragically and young. He had not remarried.

They exchanged information on David and the children and a number of mutual friends and then Alan said, "All right, so tell me again what you told me Tuesday morning on the phone. I want to SEE it as well as hear it."

236

Kendra smiled. "I want to work, Alan. I want to act."

SIXTY-SEVEN

"Just so – so uncanny," Alan was saying, as their drinks arrived. "I mean, how these things work out. I always dreamed of you as Teresa. I wrote the part with you in mind, not that I ever dreamt you would play it. But it reminded me so much of your first role, in GIRL THURSDAY. I just saw you, that's all, and as I wrote Teresa, I thought Kendra, and Teresa took shape and took wing, and she is, really, the surprise character in the script. If scenes are going to be stolen, it's Teresa who is going to steal them. Naturally, I never thought of asking you. Sam and Tommy and Jennifer wanted Macy," Alan said, of the film's producers, "and for sure, Macy could have brought the part to life. But I thought of you."

"Lucky for me," Kendra said, "Macy's in Buenos Aires."

Alan grinned. "Why not? They love her there."

"They made her a star," said Kendra. "L.A. was way behind time, recognizing her."

They were speaking of Macy O'Brien, a popular singer and a mutual friend. Macy had appeared in supporting roles in a couple of Alan's films.

"Anyway," said Alan. "I was so stuck on you as Teresa that when Macy couldn't do it, I sent you the script." He took a deep breath, exhaling with a sigh. "There was more to it, though, than just how right I thought you were for the role."

Kendra said nothing, just held his gaze. Or rather, more accurately, she let herself be held in his gaze. Intense. Blue. The gaze of a man who had once truly loved her and who still cared.

"I was, as I said, worried about you. Your friends knew how the loss of the baby had affected you, Kendra. We all wanted to help, no one was sure how. Here I had this part, Teresa, in my new film that I really had written for you. Macy was unavailable. I thought, 'What the Hell, send Kendra the script. When she says no, you've lost nothing. If she says yes, you've cast Teresa with the actress you wrote her for.' And really, I thought getting out of the house, having the healthy distraction of the set, would be good for you."

Kendra smiled. She felt like crying, but she smiled. Alan's solicitude touched her deeply. But there was more. A baby or a part in a film? What a tragic choice, what a ridiculous choice, for truly, who would choose a role in a film over a child? But of course, that was not really the choice, not really the way it was. She had never been given any choice. The baby was gone, the film was here.

"I was only sorry that we would not be shooting 'til June," Alan went on. "Because I thought that your need was immediate."

"It was," Kendra agreed. "But the irony in it is that as long as I remained there, in that sad, dark place, I would not have contacted you about the film. I had to," and she stopped and searched for the right word, "I had to recover on my own, before I knew what my next step would be."

Alan crossed his arms on the table and leaned in a little. "Kendra is better then?"

Kendra smiled. She lifted her glass, a favorite chenin blanc. "I feel the need to propose a toast," she said, "but I am not sure to whom or what. Here's to Macy being in Argentina, I guess!"

Alan grinned, and lifting his bourbon, touched his glass to hers.

SIXTY-EIGHT

"Just seventeen lines," Alan was saying, over lunch at the Bistro, of the part of Teresa which Kendra, having called her agent from the restaurant, was now formally committed to play. "Seventeen lines, four scenes. Not twelve minutes' total on screen, and I can guarantee you a ten-day shooting schedule. Guarantee it. You'll have your cherished summer with the kids.

"The really fun part of the role for you, though," Alan continued, "is that Teresa is a singer. She has songs in three of her four scenes. MAS QUE NADA, which we'll probably feature because it's suave and sexy, like Teresa herself. MAS QUE NADA I am planning to transfer in its entirety to the screen."

"I like that song," said Kendra.

"So do I," said Alan. "That's why it's in the script."

"And then there's the other two, which will be partials, that is, we'll run a minute or so of you singing them, but not the whole song. They're great songs, too, though, WHERE OR WHEN which is actually the first scene, and then, about two-thirds of the way through the film, AND THE ANGELS SING. They fit perfectly with the film's retro ambience. And they are unabashedly dreamy, romantic songs; they poise an ironic counter point to the way Ben and Sheila go about pursuing their romance."

Alan was describing the film's main characters; the movie, a gentle romantic comedy, with an ironic L.A. film noir motif, was titled THE LOVE BROKER.

"WHERE OR WHEN I know," Kendra said. "But I am not familiar with AND THE ANGELS SING."

"Oh my goodness," said Alan. "You are in for a treat. Benny Goodman tune. Johnny Mercer did the lyrics. One of the biggest hits of 1939. Big trumpet solo in the second half of the song. Kate Smith had a hit with it, so did Della Reese decades later. Bouncy, bright tune, but when you get to the trumpet, it soars, it makes you believe that there really are angels and that they really are singing."

SIXTY-NINE

"Mom's making a movie!" Jeffrey told his friends, when later that spring, filming of THE LOVE BROKER drew near. "She used to be in the movies, then she quit, because of us. Now she is going to make another one! I can't wait to see it."

Justin and Jessica were excited at Kendra's return to the screen as well, Jessica telling friends that she had seen the storyboards and that the part her step-mother was playing was very glamorous.

"A singer in a nightclub," Jessica said, to girlfriends. "You should see the costumes!"

"Has Alan really guaranteed you a ten-day shoot?" Damien asked, sitting at an umbrella table at Carmen's, on Mother's Day that spring.

"Iron-clad," said Kendra. "Teresa is easy to shoot," she said of her part, "because all of her scenes are at the club. No exteriors. It's all there on the set."

"It's exciting," said Isabel, sitting between Damien and David. "I loved you in GIRL THURSDAY and this sounds a lot like the same sort of role."

"Very similar," Kendra said. "Except Teresa is not a rock singer. The film is set present-day but deliberately evokes the L.A. film noir genre, right down to a mystery sub-plot. So the songs are from the thirties and forties."

"I liked you in GIRL THURSDAY," said Jean Marc, "but HEART OF BRASS is my favorite Kendra Collins film. All those jazz

243

tunes. All those sexy costumes. And so damned funny."

Kendra smiled. "That was a fun film," she said.

"My favorite is RAINSHADOW," said Damien. "So romantic. And you were actually the star, in that one."

"My favorite is every film Kendra Collins has ever appeared in," said Carlos, down for the weekend from his graduate studies at Berkeley. "I am still your biggest fan, you know."

"And I'm still yours," said Kendra, "diamond stud or no."

"You may be Kendra's biggest fan," said Jean Marc, seated next Carlos, "but I think Alan Braxton is her most loyal fan."

Kendra smiled. "Or anyway, the most strategic," she said.

"So all Hollywood wants to know," said Jean Marc, "and it seems like all Hollywood is asking me, because we're friends. Is this a one-shot deal, or does it signal a return to the screen generally? Is Kendra Collins going to become a star, after all?"

Again Kendra smiled. "Keep watching," she said.

David looked from his wife to the others, saying nothing. Rico and Angelo were at the next table, re-filling mimosas. David signaled his nephews, and raised his flute.

SEVENTY

"Mom," said Jeffrey, swimming up to the side of the pool where Kendra sat with her legs in the water. "I can't decide whether I am bringing Tim or Aidan to Disneyland."

"Well, you've still got a couple weeks to make up your mind," Kendra said.

"I want to go on Star Tours and Indiana Jones both days!"

Kendra smiled. "I'm sure we can arrange that."

"I wish we were going tomorrow!"

"We can't go tomorrow," Kendra said, "because Mommy has to go to work tomorrow. But it's just two weeks. It will go fast."

Each summer Kendra and David took the children to Disneyland for two or three days, staying at the Disneyland Hotel despite Brentwood's proximity to Anaheim. The nights at the hotel made it an overall vacation, and in any event saved them time on the freeway. Each of the children was allowed to invite a friend, as well. The family had only once gone to Disneyworld in Florida, staying five days. The place's size had overwhelmed both Kendra and David, and in any event, with Disneyland so close, there was no reason to go all the way to Orlando.

It was the second Sunday in June. The children were out of school for the summer. David was home for most of the summer; the children would be with their father throughout the days that Kendra was on the set. This June had proved an auspicious time, for her to resume her acting career.

"How old is Macy?" David asked Kendra, later that day, as he was setting up to barbecue. He meant Macy O'Brien, the singer Alan had first asked to take the role of Teresa.

Kendra, opening a beer for him at the bar, shrugged. "Early thirties somewhere. Younger than I am," she added, satisfied to nail any possible ramification of meaning in the question. Did David want to suggest that Kendra was too old for the part? Kendra did not know and did not care. The age of the character she was playing was not defined; it didn't come into the film's plot or theme. All the same, Macy O'Brien was five or six years younger than Kendra.

"She should spend more time in the States," David said, of Macy. "The only reason she's not bigger here is that she spends so much time in Latin America."

Kendra shrugged. "They love her down there," she said, and she thought that perhaps there had been no implied meaning in David's question, after all. It was entirely possible that David was simply saying that Macy should maximize her opportunities just as he had once been so keen on Kendra maximizing hers. Kendra was sorry, if she'd misjudged him. But such questioning, even in their simple conversations, was a frequent thing now, for Kendra. Trust, once lost, is only with time and determination rebuilt. With their therapist, she and David were working through it, once a week, every week.

The following morning, while David slept, Kendra rose early. She showered and dressed quietly, went downstairs and crossed to the garage. She started her car, a charcoal-grey Audi, and drove to the Paramount lot.

David woke a couple hours later. He saw the other side of the bed empty, and he thought of Kendra on the set with Alan Braxton. On the set with Alan rather than here at home with him and the children. He thought of Kendra back at work as an actress for the first time in the five years of their marriage. She had never said that she took the part because he had the affair.

She didn't have to.

SEVENTY-ONE

"Oh!" said Alan, with a delighted smile, as he encountered Kendra coming out of her trailer on the Paramount lot. "How that baby does shine!" He was referring to the blue-sequined sheath Kendra was wearing for the filming of the next scene, her last.

It was eight AM on the third Friday in June; Kendra had been on the set each day for ten days, as promised. They had one final shoot, for the character of Teresa, a simple set-up and no dialogue; the scene's dialogue sequence had been shot several days before. All they were doing this morning was shooting Kendra's singing of AND THE ANGELS SING.

"It's not MAS QUE NADA," Alan told the set crew, as they were preparing the first take. "This needn't be flawless start to finish, it just needs to be good. We are very likely going to leave half the song on the cutting room floor, but the half we keep, we want nice. Real nice. As nice as Kendra looks."

Kendra smiled. She waited while the technicians went through the drill. Jan, the hairstylist, suddenly wanted to fix something; it had to do with bringing out the flame-red highlights of Kendra's hair. Alan agreed it needed to be attended to. "Teresa's hot," he said. "We want the audience agreed on that fact."

The moment to roll film came. Silence descended on the set. Kendra was in place. She was relaxed and happy, very much at ease with this last shot. She had been at ease the entire ten days. From the moment she stepped onto the set 'til now, she had felt at home, almost, indeed, as if she had come home. Come home to music, to singing, to the bright lights and club stages of her twenties.

And she was with Alan. Alan and his crew, many of whom she had known since GIRL THURSDAY a dozen years before. She had stepped back into the roles, actress and singer, she had taken on with them in her late twenties, and she had delivered easily and confidently from the first day. This morning, or at any rate, by this afternoon, she would finish with them, and she knew she would finish strong. Even if half the song ended up cut, she would deliver, and the half that remained would do her, Alan and the crew credit.

The moment came. The set was darkened but for the lights which found Kendra. The band started to play. Kendra started to sing.

"You smile," she sang, "and the angels sing..."

Only a few notes into the song, Kendra could feel the melody coursing through her. She could feel herself becoming one with the music, one with the words. It was as it had once been, many years before, when she had played in the clubs. Kendra's delivery of the lyrics was cool and poised, almost off-handedly relaxed, despite the song's joyful passion. It was a nice counter-point, Kendra's smiling and breezy nonchalance, and the song's dreamy romanticism. Kate Smith may have belted it in 1939; there on the Paramount lot with Alan and his crew filming, Kendra delivered the song with an understatement that only suggested the flame within: she left it to the trumpet to take the song to the next level.

Which, when once she had finished singing, and stepped back, the trumpet did. Just as Alan had said it would, the trumpet solo soared through the set, reached to the rafters and made everyone there, including Kendra, for a moment at least, believe in angels. The solo came back to earth. The song was ready to be wrapped. When suddenly, with a glance between the musicians and herself, and a smile, and a nod, Kendra stepped back into the spotlight, the music flared rather than died, launched back into the song and it was Kendra, this time, who took it to the next level, took it to the

249

heights, took it to the angels. She dropped the cool, breezy delivery and went for the fire, went for the passion, went for the song's soaring hope, its bright and airy promise. She herself seemed transformed in the moment, radiant and joyful, almost an angel herself, flame-red and spangled blue. Kendra for a moment almost lost track of where she was, for where she had taken herself in the song was a place of such rich and deep happiness.

Then it was over. With a glance, a smile, a nod, Kendra and the musicians brought it all home, Kendra cool and clipped once more, the melody returning, though airily, to earth. Kendra smiled ironically, delivered the last of the lyrics with a wink and they finished. And Kendra stepped back, suddenly aware of what she and the band had just done.

And the doubts set in. Good grief. She had not sung like that in a dozen years. She had been clipped and cool with MAS QUE NADA, when they filmed it last week. She had been smooth and sultry, with WHERE OR WHEN. She was suddenly gripped with alarm and fear: what had she been thinking, singing with such joy, such abandon, singing, really, her heart out? This was a sophisticated film, a brainy comedy, precisely the sort of film, the sort of comedy, she liked to play. Hadn't Alan wanted something suave and ironic from her? Hadn't he simply imagined she would rise to that expectation, rather than…rather than sing her heart out? What had she been thinking? What had the musicians been thinking?

The lights came back up. Kendra suddenly saw the set and the crew again, in their regular places, not transported, as she had been, by the power and the beauty of the song. She looked apprehensively, apologetically, at Alan.

And then at once she relaxed. After all, this was Alan. What had she to fear? She was ready to offer him a laughing, a self-deprecatory apology. "I'll get it right on take two," she was about

250

to say, when suddenly the absolute stillness and silence of the set was broken by…

Applause. Loud, long, enthusiastic, accompanied by hoots and whoo-hoos. Applause.

Kendra stepped back. And stepped back again and hit the set wall. She stopped there, breathing all at once deeply and heavily, looking with astonishment at the three dozen men and women round about her, putting their hands together in her honor, Alan, smiling radiantly, at their center.

"I think," Alan said, when it had died down, "we might need to re-think the importance of this song in the final cut."

SEVENTY-TWO

Alan did re-think the song's placement in the film; not one note of it ended up on the cutting room floor, and indeed, AND THE ANGELS SING – rather than MAS QUE NADA – became the principle musical number in the picture, reprised instrumentally near the climax and used in the final credits. Kendra, actress and singer, had knocked it out of the park. Alan knew a showcase moment when he saw it.

It would be the following spring before the film was released. Kendra, meanwhile, sat down to lunch in West Hollywood with her agent.

"I hear you are set to soar," Nick said, "with THE LOVE BROKER."

Kendra smiled, "Let's hope so," she said. But she had no time to consider an achievement already past. "I want to do television, Nick," she said.

"Television?" said Nick.

"Quality television," she said. "I want guest spots this season on top twenty shows or I want a mini-series or an HBO movie or well – you get the idea. I don't need to star, you know that. I just need to be seen. Widely seen. In addition to shows and tv movies, think telethons, award shows, tv charity events. I have been out of the action for five years, and when the film is released next March, I want the public re-acquainted with me."

"You know, Kendra, I don't think you need tv. The very fact that you are back on the set has sparked interest. I've had a couple film inquiries," Nick said.

"Do you have scripts?"

"I can get them."

"Get them and send them over," said Kendra, "but I want tv this fall, this winter. I need exposure. Besides, I have my next film lined up already. It's only a supporting role, but it's a good one. I should know, since I wrote it."

Nick looked surprised. "Were you planning to inform your agent of this project?"

"Matt and I are going to produce," Kendra said.

Nick's jaw dropped. "Kendra!" Nick had been urging Matt, also his client, to produce for years.

"We'll talk," Kendra said, "you, me and Matt. But meanwhile, I mean business, Nick. I want to act. I need just one thing from you: I need you to tell all Hollywood that Kendra Collins is back."

SEVENTY-THREE

"Oh Kendra," Chrysta said, after spending a quarter of an hour with David, and then re-emerging on the patio. "Oh, I cannot thank you enough for arranging this."

"You have our gratitude," Kendra said. "He wanted to see you."

Which was true. In February, after his first hospitalization, David, at home and in his office, which had just been turned into his sick room, had spoken to Fr. Cesar about Chrysta.

"I hurt her," David said to the young priest. "I used her. I have never adequately apologized to her."

"Do you know where she is?" Cesar asked.

"No. She married a Brit, a few years back. I think she is in London a lot. I think Kendra would know how to reach her, but I am not sure I should mention it to Kendra. I don't want to hurt Kendra. But I want Chrysta to know how sorry I am. I could simply send her a letter."

"If you do not want to hurt Kendra," Cesar said, "it seems to me you need to tell her of this desire. How would it look if you were to write Chrysta without Kendra knowing, and then Kendra found out?"

"You're right," David agreed. And he later that day asked Kendra if she would mind his writing Chrysta, and if she knew how to reach her. "I have never adequately apologized to her," he said.

"I'll find her," Kendra said.

Chrysta was in London filming a cheeky espionage series all winter. She would be back in L.A. in April.

Kendra herself arranged Chrysta's visit.

"I am so grateful, Kendra," Chrysta said. "I am shocked to see him like this – I know it showed on my face. I really do fail, at times, as an actress. I know it showed. Oh Kendra what a heartbreak for you, for the children."

"They are all here this week," Kendra said. "They've been making regular visits all spring. On that subject, how are your boys?"

Kendra remembered with irony their conversation so many years ago, at the bar with the untouched glass of chenin blanc: Chrysta had not married David precisely because she did not want three children. But now she was herself the mother of three, twin boys first and then a couple of years later, a third boy, a child with Down Syndrome. His name was Carl. He was now nine. Chrysta and her husband had considered but ultimately resisted the doctor's recommendation that they abort. Chrysta had since gone on to tell the world of her gratitude in making that decision. She had become a national spokesperson for Down Syndrome children.

"Carl is such a gift," she was saying now, to Kendra. "All these children know how to do, Kendra, is love. They are walking and waking innocence. Not that he can't be a handful, at times. Of course, we are very fortunate; we can provide for Carl easily. But when he slides in quietly beside me, when I am watching television, or when he follows his father about in the garden, oh!, Kendra. We can't imagine our lives anymore without him. Carl is such a gift to me and Robert."

"And the twins?" asked Kendra.

"Oh!" Chrysta laughed. "They are eleven now. And never a dull moment. My gosh, Kendra, what an adventure motherhood is proving to be!"

"I remember," said Kendra, and smiled. "And brace yourself, the wildest part is still to come!"

SEVENTY-FOUR

Kendra had experienced some adventures of her own, in parenting. Above all, she had dealt with the sudden and perplexing difficulty of being step-mother to a rebellious teen aged girl, in what Kendra would come to call "the year from Hell" with Jessica.

Kendra really did not know where it came from. Almost overnight, it seemed, Jessica went from being the smiling if strong-willed high school freshman who loved her family and enjoyed school to a sullen and uncooperative sophomore who seemed to resent her parents' – but especially Kendra's – very presence. She spent hours on her cell phone and made a point of avoiding the family; locked away in her room, or out back, wandering the paths or sitting on the benches amid the flower beds. Though there were periods when the old Jessica still seemed to be there, they were infrequent, unpredictable and no one could guess how long they would last. Nor could anyone know just what might set off one her moods. A request that she pick up her room or clear the table could result in a sullen and protracted non-response, a non-response that said, in effect, "Make me." A suggestion that she take the time away from her cell phone to join the family for dinner could become the starting point for an argument.

She had a lot of friends, was a class officer at school, and was on the debate team. Her grades remained high. She spent a lot of time with her friends, a lot of time in after-school activities – it looked good from the outside. It was at home that she was a little monster. She talked a lot with Justin, but was dismissive of Jeffrey, seemed annoyed by him more than anything else. Once when some unnecessary put-down of her little brother caught Kendra's attention, Kendra asked Jessica to be more respectful of Jeffrey's feelings. Jessica's response was a put-down to Kendra.

Kendra arched an eyebrow and asked Jessica if she liked having a cell phone. Jessica said dad won't let you take it away. Kendra said she did not need David's permission and one more word like that and she would take it away. Jessica sullenly backed down.

Kendra was at sea with it, she really had no idea how or why her once loving and attentive step-daughter had suddenly become, as she would put it to Linda, "a raging little something that rhymes with rich."

David, too, of course, was part of the household drama. When once he came upon Kendra and Jessica squared off in the kitchen, and heard his daughter's caustic reply to a warning from Kendra, David said, "Jessica, do not talk to your mother that way."

"She's not my mother," Jessica shot back.

David looked at her. "I am your father. And I will not be spoken to in that tone of voice. You will apologize to me, and now."

Jessica said she was sorry.

"And you will apologize to Kendra."

With a melodramatic sigh, Jessica apologized to Kendra, sarcastically.

"That does it," said David. "You're grounded the rest of this month. Hand over your cell phone. Now. And your computer stays in my office, and you use it only when I am there."

"How am I gonna get my homework done?"

"That's your problem, not mine," said David. "You should have thought of that before you disrespected Kendra."

Though Kendra was truly mystified at her step-daughter's hostility, she did get a glimpse at a possible contributing factor to the dynamic. It was when Kendra had tried to explain to Jessica her reasons for wanting her to attend a family event in San Gabriel. Jessica replied, "Cut the crap, Kendra. Save it for the set. There's nothing to be gained by acting here at home. They don't give Oscars, you know, for Best Step-Mother."

SEVENTY-FIVE

"She's right, Kendra," Linda said. "You're not her mother. Lana is. Remember that. It absolves you of huge responsibilities."

"I do sometimes think of that, of course," said Kendra. "But the rebellion is not aimed at Lana, it is aimed at me."

They were having lunch in Westwood. The lunch had not been planned because of Jessica; but she happened to come up and they wound up talking half an hour about her and her rebellion.

"I just want Jessica back. I think she resents me resuming my career."

Kendra's schedule with the children was not what it used to be, of course. After she completed filming on THE LOVE BROKER with Alan, Kendra began to take guest roles on television shows. Nick had taken Kendra at her word, and found her work as a one-time guest on two top-ranked television series. A more time-consuming commitment developed with the offer, in November, of Kendra taking a six-episode role on a major prime time soap. This role went a long way toward re-establishing Kendra as an actress in the public mind. Nick had also landed her a comic cameo in an HBO movie; Kendra's presence, two minutes on screen, was widely publicized and she received before-the-title-billing, something that clearly said, "star." Kendra was a presenter that year at the Golden Globes, and in the spring she appeared several times as a guest host for a series about 1950s Hollywood on THE HISTORY CHANNEL.

All of this meant time away from the home, away from the family. But Kendra had not been concerned about it. Number one, most of her television work required only two or three days' commitment, and it was never more than a couple times a month. In other words, five or six days a month Kendra was away from home, away from the children, for her television work. Two, there was a new understanding between her and David. When she could not be at home, David would be. They had agreed to this in their therapy sessions, and David kept his end of the bargain. The kids were rarely alone, and in any event, number three, they were old enough now to be on their own for the occasional afternoon or evening.

"Could be that she's angry about your career," Linda said, evidently considering the possibility for the first time. "You were like the fairy Godmother to them. You swooped into their lives lovingly and gently and made them your central priority. The rest of your life fell into place around them."

"That was how it should have been," said Kendra.

"No argument. And now, you are taking time for yourself, which, all things past and present considered, is also as it should be. Yeah," Linda said. "Yeah. Could be. Jessica could be jealous of your career. Or it could have nothing to do with that. Teen-agers don't need reasons."

Kendra gestured rueful agreement with a slight upward movement of her eyebrows.

Linda sipped her wine. "Tell me, with you back on the set, has the CAR Show offered to help?"

"Busy with grandchildren," said Kendra, of David's sisters. "The thing is, this isn't really about my not being at home some afternoons. It's about testing limits, establishing independence, and to some real degree, I think, it is about insecurity. And that worries me, and it worries me in part precisely because Lana is her mother. You know how Lana dealt with her insecurities."

"Oh boy," said Linda. "Are you worried about drugs?"

Kendra shrugged. "Well, possibly. Blood is thicker than water, right?"

"Her friends," said Linda. "The wrong kind of kid?"

"No," Kendra said. "That's part of the mystery of it. Her friends are cheerleaders and club presidents and honor roll students. She's on the honor roll herself and is a class officer."

"Well, that's an encouraging set of circumstances," Linda said. She sipped her chardonnay, considering it. "In a way you sort of did yourself in, in being such a great step-mother. MY stepkids never had any expectations of me. I was never the fairy step-mother, in their eyes. More like the wicked witch of the west coast."

"It was different," Kendra said. "Sam and Maureen divorced."

"It was different," Linda agreed.

"And Maureen set the children against you."

Linda shrugged, sighed. "It was what it was," she said. To this day, more than a quarter century later, Sam's three children gave Linda only lip-service respect.

"I'm wondering if I can help," Linda said. "I mean, Jessica has always liked me. We've always had a nice rapport. I wonder if I could help by being there for her a little – you know, maybe an occasional lunch date, a shopping trip, that kind of thing. If there were even a chance of her opening up with me, it seems worth aiming for."

"I would be very grateful to you," Kendra said.

SEVENTY-SIX

Linda was as good as her word.

She took Jessica shopping for her prom dress, a day which included lunch at Spago.

"This is fun!" Linda said, at lunch. "We ought to do it more often."

Jessica was delighted.

After that Linda and Jessica became lunching galpals, getting together once or twice a month, fancy places, funky places, all over the West Side. Linda and Sam together took Jessica and two of her friends to the Huntington-Hartford for a touring production of LES MISERABLES and a few weeks later to the Hollywood Bowl for an evening of Brazilian jazz. In taking Jessica to these places, of course, where Linda was really taking her was to a place where she could begin to spread her wings, outside of that parental supervision which she had lately found so oppressive. Jessica talked happily with Linda of her activities at school, of her hopes and her plans for college and beyond, and in time, she even talked to her a bit about her frustrations at home. Linda listened sympathetically, and kept all confidences, meanwhile only hoping she was helping Kendra in all of it.

The summer after her sophomore year, Sam and Linda took Jessica to Chicago. They stayed two weeks. Jessica spent time in the city not just with Linda and Sam and the Stefani family, but also with Anneke, the beloved au pair from her childhood. Anneke had married a Chicago attorney and now lived in the city with their two young sons. They had a sailboat and took Jessica out on the lake.

Jessica came back from the trip beaming. She loved the city's fountains and plazas, she loved all the water, the river and the lake. She loved the parks and the busy boulevards, the flower stands and the quick-lunch kiosks. She loved the skyscrapers that did not crowd the sky.

"Chicago is a western city in terms of the sky," she said, "but eastern in terms of the sidewalk, the crowds, the pace." She laughed and added, "And the pigeons!"

"You haven't seen it in the winter yet," David cautioned.

But she did, that December, going to stay with Anneke for a week before Christmas, having finished her finals ahead of time with special permission granted precisely for the trip. She came back enchanted not just with the snow, but with the snowplows, with the city's whole snow-clearing operation.

"Chicago knows how to handle winter," she said. "It's not like cities farther south that get paralyzed by snowstorms. Chicago shows winter who's boss. And they actually GET a winter. The seasons actually change there. I love Chicago!"

The following spring Sam and Linda again took Jessica with them for a ten-day visit. Jessica babysat Anneke's boys a couple of evenings – "Talk about the wheel coming full circle!" she said.

Jessica came home from this third visit observing, "Everyone in New York lives in L.A. for a few years and everyone in L.A. lives in New York at some point. But there's another REAL city in this country, and that's the one I want to live in. I want to live in Chicago."

And she did, applying as a freshman to both the University of Chicago and Northwestern, choosing the latter for undergraduate work and then going to the former for law school. It was in a first-year law class that she met Brett. They had married the previous September, they were both now third-year students, very close to graduation. Neither Jessica nor Brett was in law for the money. They were in it for the chance for justice, for the hope of making a difference for the poor, the marginalized, those who faced discrimination . Brett was interested in immigration issues; Jessica simply wanted to work for and with the poor.

Kendra was pleased, relieved, satisfied, and deeply grateful to Linda, for the way she had taken Jessica under wing. But she wondered in the end about how her decision to return to acting, let alone the decision to start producing, had in fact come at an unforeseen cost. Jessica saw her return to film as a betrayal. Though their relationship improved greatly, the closeness she and Jessica once shared had never returned.

SEVENTY-SEVEN

There had been trouble as well with Justin. Not as spectacular as the problems with Jessica; Justin did not upend the normal household routine with his rebellion. But he did go through a rebellion. It was in a way more frightening than Jessica's, precisely because of its being so much quieter, so much more under cover.

It too began to take shape his sophomore year in high school, when his grades suddenly nose-dived. Reasons for this change were not immediately apparent. Justin's friends, as was the case with Jessica, were good kids. Good kids from loving families, but bright and frequently bored with school; idle and maybe rather spoiled – these kids had had their own computers when they were nine.

It was a lucky accident that told David and Kendra what was up with Justin. Riding in an SUV with three friends on the Pacific Coast Highway one Saturday afternoon, Justin escaped serious injury when the young driver lost control of the car on a curve. The vehicle slammed into the guard rail, then skidded across two lanes of traffic to hit the center divider, where it came to a wobbly rest, other vehicles screeching and swerving to avoid it.

"No," David said, over the phone to Carmen, that evening, "no, by the grace of God, Justin was not hurt. Nor were the other boys. But the driver was legally intoxicated, and when the police swept the car they found traces of pot – and cocaine."

"My goodness!" Carmen cried.

"The kid driving evidently said the drugs were his parents', if you like."

"Heaven knows, David," said Carmen. "That could be true. Are they Hollywood people?"

Kendra and David grounded Justin for three months, imposed a new and earlier curfew when the grounding was lifted, forbade him to ride with teen friends (which in any event was law in California) and they got Justin into therapy. Whatever demons Justin had been dealing with his sophomore year, he too had straightened up by late junior year. He'd wrecked his chances of getting into a great university but went to Santa Monica Community College and then transferred to UCLA. From there he went to Emory for law and had been in Atlanta since, having met Monique there through his legal work with – troubled teens.

SEVENTY-EIGHT

There was then Jeffrey. After what she had been through with Jessica and Justin, Kendra was virtually holding her breath as Jeffrey started high school. She had always had a special bond with Jeffrey and the thought of him, too, rebelling, was a sad one, a hard one for her. But after what she had been through with his siblings, she was braced for it.

Except that in their youngest child, and the one who called Kendra "Mom," David and Kendra never experienced a rebellion of any sort. Jeffrey was an easy, relaxed, happy teen. He had a sweet temper and a trusting nature. He expressed gratitude for even everyday things and occurrences, such as a lift to school when he was running late, or help with his math homework, which he detested.

He was, perhaps, lacking in direction and drive – his grades were good, not outstanding, and unlike his siblings, he did not hang out with student leaders. His friends were like Jeffrey, relaxed, pleasant to be with, unambitious. He finished high school and knocked around at the community college for several semesters, surfing and snorkeling whenever he could get the time. He talked about four-year colleges, but made no applications his second year at the junior college, and none his third. Finally, when a pretty brunette classmate named Janette told him she was transferring to Cal Poly, Jeffrey discovered a motivating factor strong enough to move him along on his educational path. Janette was not his girlfriend – "Just a friend," he would shrug, when Kendra would occasionally ask about their relationship.

At twenty-four, he was still a year from finishing with unexceptional grades a degree in computer graphics and design at the campus in San Luis Obispo. He was assistant manager at a surf shop and had a nice girlfriend whose name, it turned out, was Janette after all. He had no particular ambitions beyond a genial enjoyment of life. He prized his friends and especially his family. He called his parents a couple times a week: "Hey Mom," he'd say on Kendra's voice-mail when she was unavailable. "Just calling to chat. Give me a call when you've got a few minutes. Beautiful afternoon here. You should see the ice plant above the beach. It makes me smile."

So Kendra had weathered the adventures of raising her step-children.

In all the ups and downs with her stepchildren, though, Kendra never encountered anything like what she was to find herself facing, with yet another member of the younger generation of the family. She never could have guessed what would almost come to be, between herself and Tino.

SEVENTY-NINE

Kendra's second miscarriage had occurred the September that Tino started as a freshman at UCLA. He was thus on the West Side that autumn, that winter which had been so hard, so sad and lonely for Kendra. Tino called Kendra several times that autumn, just to see how his "favorite aunt" was doing, a fact which much consoled her. When the Cal-UCLA game was played, on a bright, warm Saturday late in October, Tino got tickets for Kendra and David. David was unable to attend; Matt came in his place.

"Two UCLA boys here," Matt joked, with Kendra, "and one Berkeley girl. We're going to be at cross-purposes with each other right through to the after-game happy hour."

They went to drinks and dinner in Westwood, afterward, celebrating UCLA's win, even Kendra, who had felt deeply happy, during the game, for the welcome distraction, the excited and happy crowd, the bright, fresh air, the memories of youth, but above all, for the fact of having Matt on one side and Tino on the other. At one point Tino, speaking into her ear so that she could hear above the loudspeaker and the crowd, put his arm around her shoulders. It was only for a moment, but going to sleep that night, Kendra could still feel her nephew's embrace.

They had had so much fun at the Cal game that when the Big Game came, the one against USC, the Saturday before Thanksgiving, Matt got tickets through the alumni association on the forty yard line. This time David was able to attend. Kendra sat between Matt and David, Tino on his uncle's other side. But she and Tino talked and laughed and high-fived each other throughout the game, and at dinner that evening above the beach in Santa Monica, Kendra was aware of her nephew's occasionally stolen glances. She had to chuckle inwardly at the thought of Tino's appreciation; it was flattering, of course, but she couldn't take it seriously. After all, he was a boy, eighteen, and her nephew. And not even the first de la Fuente nephew to develop a crush on her, if indeed that was what his glances suggested. She had been there for him, the previous spring, in his hurt over his parents' situation, over his father's decision to move in with Jean Marc. If he felt gratitude to her for that, if he felt compassion for her, over the miscarriage, if he felt anything else at all and if all of it were mixed together in a way that left him a little shy, a little hesitant and unsure, well, really, that was all right. Tino might be a little at sea with his mix of feelings, but Kendra wasn't. He was half her age. He was her nephew. That was that. Besides, it was only weeks since she had miscarried, and she was so very sad. Tino's attention and appreciation gently consoled her. There was nothing to worry about.

EIGHTY

There was nothing to worry about with Tino. Until there was.

Isabel, determined to hold things together for the family, had issued a general invitation for Thanksgiving, at her house in Arcadia. Her own children, Tino and his sisters, and the grandchildren would be there, along with, of course, Damien and Jean Marc. Kendra was not in the habit of preparing Thanksgiving dinner – as a matter of fact, she had never in her life done any such thing. On the kitchen, generally, her attitude, as she once joked with Matt, was that of Mae West: "Nobody ever asked me to cook." In previous years, Kendra and David had gone to San Gabriel for Thanksgiving, rotating among family celebrations. Kendra suggested they this year attend with Isabel and Damien.

"It is no longer Isabel and Damien," David said. "It is Isabel, hosting us, and others, including Damien and Jean Marc."

Kendra shrugged. "Precisely why it is important that we be there."

David sighed. "Carlos is going to be down from Berkeley," he said. "And he'll be at Ana's, and I haven't seen him since the summer --"

"No, neither have I," said Kendra. "We can go to Ana's for the afternoon and then over to Isabel's. I've talked with Raquel," Kendra went on. "She and Juan are going to Isabel's, along with all the kids. And Ramon said that he and Sandra will be there for a drink. What's more, Matt will be there. He can't take the time to drive to Salinas, this year. We are under deadline, with this script, and it's my fault, because of all the time we lost, after the miscarriage."

David shrugged and, surprising Kendra, acquiesced. They went to Isabel's for Thanksgiving.

"Jean Marc's all right," David said, when, at well past midnight, they were driving west from Isabel's on the freeway. "He's actually rather entertaining, isn't he?"

"He has been a friend of mine for years," said Kendra. She glanced to the Range Rover's back seat, and saw that the boys were asleep and Jessica busy with texts on her lit cell phone. She felt it was all right to have this conversation with David. In any event, they were speaking quietly.

"I really would have no problem with Damien and Jean Marc if it were not for the fact that, one, Damien is my brother; two, Isabel is my sister-in-law; three, there are four children and – oh yeah! - five grandchildren involved; four, we are, ostensibly, anyway, a Catholic family; five, I am still suspicious of Jean Marc's motives. Damien has money and Jean Marc doesn't. Other than that, really, I would have no problem. All the same, Jean Marc is witty and engaging, and, I must admit, he seems to really care for Damien."

"Of course he does," agreed Kendra. "They love each other. Is it really so hard to grasp?"

"Not hard at all," David answered. "But real love cannot be selfish, and in abandoning his family, Damien is being selfish. And I am not sure that selfishness – or at least, self-interest -- does not figure into Jean Marc's considerations."

Kendra shook her head. She smiled regardless. This conversation on the late-night west-bound freeways reminded her of the one she and David had had years before, after Carlos' party, about Lana.

Then, David had looked for reasons to excuse his wife's behavior. Curious that now he would be so determined to judge his brother. Kendra could not have known, of course, that Chrysta had only the week before sent David the letter, ending their decade-long affair. She could not have known the ulterior motives David might have had for his judgment of his brother.

Kendra in any event was not really thinking about Damien and Jean Marc. She was thinking of Tino. She had noticed him looking at her from across a couple of rooms, for Isabel's home was open and spacious and from any given downstairs room, one could see into two or three others. Their eyes had met and Tino had glanced immediately away, as if he'd been caught. At another point she had crossed into Isabel's large stone kitchen and seen Tino in conversation with a couple of the cousins. His demeanor became more animated, more joyful, as she crossed into the kitchen, and at some point he looked in her direction and feigned, Kendra was sure of it, surprise at seeing her. "Tia!" he'd said, and rising, took her in his arms, a hug that lasted just a few seconds longer than usual.

She was thinking as well of how Tino had attended to her, this autumn, her autumn of emptiness, her autumn of missing David. The occasional phone calls, "Hola Tia! Como estas?" The two or three visits to the house in Brentwood, family dinners, but her nephew's focus subtly laser-like on her.

She felt herself bouyed by her nephew's attention, she felt herself somehow protected by it. She all the same became alert that Thanksgiving, as she had not been before, that this feeling of safety and quiet happiness in Tino's affections was with her all the time. That fact was, when she considered it, a potentially alarming one.

EIGHTY-ONE

It was mid-January that same winter, the sad, hard winter following the second miscarriage. It was the start of the winter quarter at UCLA. Tino was enrolled in a photography class that would, by the end of the quarter, that is, by late March, require him to present a completed project as his final. The project was to consist of a mixed-media presentation, including photos grouped around a theme, black and white and color. The subject of the photos, the theme of the presentation, was left entirely to the student's discretion. Tino knew what he wanted as his theme: movie star glamour; in particular, the glamour of his favorite aunt.

On January seventeenth Tino called to wish David a happy birthday. David was in New York that week. Tino talked to Kendra instead. He mentioned his project almost as if in passing; when Kendra asked him specific questions about it, he told her he had toyed with the idea of making her his subject. Kendra gathered that he had "toyed" with it not at all, that he wanted it, and was a little shy about asking for it, deference being a natural instinct with him. She felt her senses becoming aware, as Tino described the project to her, over the phone. The project itself sounded very much like something she would be glad to help him with, but it was the fact of his enthusiasm for her as his subject that Kendra was really responding to – and she knew it. She told him she would be glad to pose for him.

Kendra hung up and felt a different set of emotions for several hours, as if her world, which had turned grey following the second miscarriage, had suddenly been lit in Technicolor.

The following week, of course, it was her birthday. Tino called. Kendra answered. They talked. David was back from New York, but had meetings with investors that morning, at the Malibu house. Kendra was alone in Brentwood, and yes, she had time to talk. Hanging up almost an hour later, Kendra experienced the same heightened sensations as she'd had following the previous conversation with her nephew, a set of feelings which included a quiet excitement and some kind of nebulous, but bright, happy promise.

Later that day, attending to the kids' laundry, Kendra experienced an unbidden image of her nephew as he had been, here in Brentwood during the Christmas holidays, at the pool in a pair of black board shorts . This remembered image was followed by an imagined one: Tino out of the board shorts. The image flashed through her mind so quickly that it was gone before she entirely realized she had experienced it. But her shock at it brought the image, Tino naked, back into sharp focus. She replayed it both willingly and unwillingly, several times that afternoon.

She was glad for the distraction shortly provided by the fact that it was her birthday, glad that Sam and Linda were coming to dinner; that David would be home soon to start preparing it. Celebrating her birthday in a quiet way at the house had been planned a couple of weeks before; Kendra when asked had told David she preferred a simple night with the family to anything big, to any real party, or to a night out. Despite her relief at having her birthday dinner to focus on, Kendra found herself thinking that it was a shame that they had not thought to include Tino. She resisted the temptation to call him and issue a last-minute invitation.

She understood all of it in all of its complexity. She had miscarried a second time; she had longed for David, he had not been there. She had been comforted by her nephew's attentions and concerns. She had been flattered, a woman close to forty being found attractive by an eighteen year old, and a veritable Adonis, at that.

276

She got all that. It did not seem to make any difference that she so well understood the underlying emotional dynamic at work. That day, her thirty-ninth birthday, with a recurring and sensual image of Tino going through her mind, Kendra was glad for every distraction, and especially for David's amorous attentions in bed late that night. "Feliz cumpleanos, bebe," he whispered huskily, beginning the caresses.

Kendra lay awake later that night, looking at her thoughts, at her desires. Her husband sleeping contentedly beside her, Kendra thought of Tino, acknowledging to herself that she wanted her nephew. The fact at once appalled her and intrigued her; literally it intrigued her. She found herself spinning fanciful intrigues of the seduction. Amazed at herself, she nonetheless allowed full range to an unknown voice in her mind, "He isn't really your nephew, you know. There is no blood relation at all. He is deeply smitten, possibly a virgin, he would be playful and joyous and wildly excited. He would have a puppy's devotion. You already have a deep friendship, a deep trust with him; no doubt an affair could be fit easily and naturally into that context. He'd outgrow his fascination in a few months, and you would quite possibly recover your equilibrium, your very joy in living. And as if pre-designed, he's over here on the West Side now, just on the other side of the 405. Really, what would be the harm in having him?"

She heard this voice out fully. She was more than appalled at it. She was unnerved by it. Unnerved by it because she was so deeply attracted by it, by its whispering reassurances and lovely lies. She knew the reassurances were lies. But she heard this voice out because she had to. If she did not accept the truth of her feelings for Tino, she might be tripped up by them. And Tino himself would be the victim.

She looked to David, asleep amid the covers, his head flat on the mattress – she could never understand how he slept without a pillow – and settled more deeply into her own pillows, thinking about, seeing in her mind's eye, Tino. But not now Tino the potential lover. Rather what she saw was the little boy at Carlos' party, shaking his father's hand and promising to be good. The teen talking about student government and taking photos over the balustrade at the opening of the Century City restaurant. The broken-hearted son, talking about the love of his parents, at the Japanese restaurant, after Damien and Jean Marc had made their alliance known.

Tino. Her nephew. Her precious, loving, vulnerable nephew.

From now on, she needed to avoid being alone with him. That was the first thing. There were second, third and fourth things, as well, sensible precautions including custody of the eyes and a careful attention to what she said to him and how she said it, but this was first and foremost: she must avoid being alone with him. And there was already a problem, an obstacle to this resolution. For surely, he was planning to be alone with her for the photo sessions. She could, of course, rescind her promise to pose for Tino. But on what grounds? She'd already told him she was not working this winter. She had plenty of time, and he knew it. Really, she reflected, lying there in the dark next to her sleeping husband, she this sad winter had too much time; that was half the problem. The other part of it, of course, was that she very much wanted the time with Tino. If she could not actually become his lover, she might at least let him "make love" to her with his camera. Kendra had found that some dangers were best dealt with by an indirect approach, neither avoided entirely nor met head-on. The way not to be eaten by the wolf was to feed it.

She had it in a flash. She got her answer in an instant, and it was an answer that made her smile.

"Yes, sobrino," she told Tino in a phone call the next day. "I'm committed to the project. As I mentioned last week, I'm between scripts right now, so I have time. Just a matter of finding dates that work. Look at your calendar and get back to me. We'll set it up."

EIGHTY-TWO

Kendra took control of the situation, not because she wanted to but because she had to. Tino was eighteen. He was a good boy, a fine young man, but he was hurting from the situation between his parents and he was no doubt feeling some anxiety about his feelings for his glamorous aunt. Tino could not be expected to lead, in this situation; that was Kendra's clear and only responsibility.

And she in fact did want the time and the attention from him, and she knew it, and she made no excuses for or about it. She wanted to be photographed by her dreamily intoxicated young nephew. She was fully cognizant of her motivations. Denying herself the satisfaction would result in frustration and a mild bitterness. She had decided that the time and attention she wanted from Tino, and the neediness which underwrote that desire, could be corralled, could be domesticated, could be made safe for both her nephew and herself.

They would shoot at the house, indoors and out.

They would shoot outdoors at UCLA.

They would shoot at a studio, in West L.A.

They would do it all in one long day.

And they would be chaperoned.

"Damien," she said into the phone, one bright late winter morning, from the house in Brentwood. "It's Kendra."

The day of the shoot, the whole time, Damien and Jean Marc would be with them. It made perfect sense. Damien was a photographer himself. Reconciliation between Tino and his father was a family-wide goal. Helping Jean Marc to feel like family was a goal Kendra shared with Damien and Isabel. For Kendra, it was a win-win.

It was early March, a Thursday, from ten AM 'til seven in the evening, with a bright and laughing lunch in Westwood in the middle of it, not the several shoots drawn out over weeks that he had hoped for, but Tino got his shots, Damien got precious time with his son, Kendra made it unambiguously clear to Damien and Jean Marc that they had her love, and Kendra got the attention she so craved from Tino. And she got it in a manner which kept her relationship with him in its proper and safe context.

Was Tino disappointed? Kendra imagined he was, but at the same time, she saw what happened that day, between her nephew and his father, she saw the embrace between the two of them, at the end of the day. In the context of that relationship, a far more important relationship to Tino than his relationship with her, Kendra saw clearly that Tino, too, had had a very good day.

Only a couple of weeks later, Kendra found the note from Chrysta. The complex set of emotions triggered by the note included Kendra's own recently renewed understanding of human frailty in general: she had just had a close-up look at what she might be capable of, in terms of violating trust and relationship. While she had every right to know the truth about David and Chrysta, and while she was hurt beyond words at the thought of the betrayal, Kendra instinctively tempered her reaction. Any of us, she thought, could be capable of anything.

And in fact, the desire to seek comfort in her nephew's arms is part of what drove Kendra instead to Alan. For Alan also admired her, Alan also had once wanted her, Alan also knew her, cherished her.

281

But her association with Alan was entirely professional and appropriate. David had, essentially, gone missing from her life, the past few months, and then had come the shock of his betrayal. It was David she wanted and needed, but feeling almost abandoned by him, she had naturally looked elsewhere for consolation, for affirmation. Though no one could take her husband's place, Kendra saw of course that Alan was a far better emotional stand-in for David than was her nephew. Kendra signed with Alan to do the film. And when sometime later that spring she heard that Tino was spending almost all his spare time with a leggy blonde Tri-Delt named Cindy, Kendra breathed a sigh of smiling relief.

EIGHTY-THREE

Later that same year that Kendra returned to the set, Jean Marc, too, found a new career path: with Damien's help he opened a French market-bakery on Melrose. Damien, principle owner of the Century City Casa de la Fuente, was becoming rich. He shared profits from the Century City restaurant with his siblings, but after each of them had recouped their initial investment, he was not legally required to do so. He continued to do so because Damien loved his family. David, the one sibling not involved in the operations or the profits of either restaurant, all the same had a question about how much money Damien was spending on his lover's new enterprise, and asked Ramon to look into it. Ramon, who did accounts for both restaurants, assured David that Damien was spending only his own money.

"He's got quite a lot of it these days," Ramon said.

"I guess so," said David, "what with an executive home in Los Feliz and now Jean Marc's restaurant, or whatever it is, in Boys' Town."

Boys Town was how David referred to West Hollywood when he was feeling out of sorts with Damien and Jean Marc. As for Los Feliz, Damien had sold the Westwood condo and bought a Spanish-style house on a palmy hillside. He'd chosen Los Feliz for its proximity both to the West Side and to the San Gabriel area; Damien was twenty or thirty minutes closer to Isabel and his children in Los Feliz, than in Westwood.

"In any event," Ramon answered, "it's Damien's money. He has certainly earned it, with all those sixty hour weeks over the years. He can do with it as he pleases, and a nice home in Los Feliz and a

French market and bakery in West Hollywood are probably sound investments."

"He might think about Isabel and the children," said David.

"They're hardly broke, bro," replied Ramon.

That was all that came of it.

EIGHTY-FOUR

Meanwhile, Kendra became a star.

It was immediately following the photo shoot with Tino that Kendra discovered the affair between David and Chrysta, that she placed the call to Alan Braxton, that she returned to the set, that she told Nick to find her work on top-ranked television shows, that she and Matt decided to produce. Never in her life had Kendra asserted so much control over her own direction, her own destiny.

THE LOVE BROKER garnered generally favorable reviews and did good business, but even critics who panned the film raved about Kendra Collins' return to the screen. She had indeed stolen her scenes, just as Alan had predicted. Critics lamented that hers was not a larger role. Her rendition of AND THE ANGELS SING became the film's most talked-about moment, and would, over time, come to be regarded as the iconic moment of her film career, "the essential Kendra." The ultimate compliment on her performance was probably the one that came from Buenos Aires.

"Kudos to Kendra for an utterly captivating Teresa! Brax wrote her with you in mind, and no one, girlfriend, could have brought her to life as you have. I cannot regret being unavailable for the part, seeing what you have made of it. It's a star turn, Kendra. This one's got legs, including here in Argentina, and you are the reason. Bravo! Hope to catch up with you next month, when I am in L.A. Love to David and the children. Macy."

Kendra made the cover of several magazines that spring. Not yet PEOPLE -- that would come the following year. There were talk show appearances, there were print interviews, there was online chat, all following a similar narrative, one shaped and supported by

Kendra, by Nick, by Alan and his press office, "After five years away to learn the role of wife and mother, Kendra Collins returns to the screen and looks, walks, talks and sings like a superstar."

Kendra and Matt wrote and produced together her next film, an adaptation of Edith Wharton's THE CUSTOM OF THE COUNTRY. They updated the hard-edged, satirical storyline about early twentieth-century social-climbing New Yorkers, setting it in contemporary Hollywood. Kendra played a supporting role and though it came to nothing, there was talk of an Oscar nomination for her performance. The film itself won awards all over the place and Kendra and Matt took the Golden Globe for their screenplay. This triumph led to the cover of PEOPLE, but the more important and remembered interview that year was with ROLLING STONE.

"You've won a Golden Globe for your writing," the young interviewer, bearded and ambitious and at least on the surface, genial, said. "But it is as an actor that you have caught the public fancy. Can you comment on that?"

"I am sure I can," Kendra smiled, "but let me comment first that it is all right to call me an actress."

The interviewer's bright eyes widened just a bit.

"There is really nothing wrong with the word and never has been," Kendra added. "It's been in use for a long time."

"But words change over time," the interviewer said.

"They do, it's true, by a sort of natural linguistic evolution," Kendra agreed. "The word 'terrific,' as an example, was once much closer in meaning to the word 'terrible' than it is today. It has evolved naturally to mean something very much the opposite of terrible. But words can also be changed by deliberate wrenching of the language to serve a political and/or economic agenda. As a writer, I am suspicious of such agendas. There is an agenda behind the drive to call women performers 'actors.'"

"But the word writer is a good example," the reporter countered. "We don't say writeress, or authoress."

"As a matter of fact, authoress is not without pedigree," Kendra replied. "But you are right, we do not say writeress. Nor do we say singeress or danceress. We do, on the other hand, say actress. We always have. It's awkward and artificial, calling me an actor. Why is there a movement, and by whom is it being guided, to eliminate the word 'actress' from the English language?"

Silence.

"Let's look at it this way," Kendra went on. "Consider the Academy Awards. Will they one day be giving Oscars for Best Actor in a Leading Role, Male, and Best Actor in a Leading Role, Female?"

The interviewer considered it. Then, "Why not?" he shrugged.

"We will never see it," Kendra said, "and I'll tell you why. Because that precise distinction, male and female, is what this particular agenda is seeking to blur. Whether its proponents like it or not, they are stuck with the word 'actress' when it comes to the Oscars. Think about the agenda behind this drive to eliminate a perfectly useful word from the English language. Who wants us to stop saying 'actress,' and why?"

The interviewer laughed. Nervously. Then, "Are you into conspiracy theories?"

"Let's stay on point," Kendra said, smiling. "Words exist to make reality transparent, not to obscure it. They are at the service of reality, helping us to understand the world in which we find ourselves. They are not, by their nature, at the service of artificial agendas, though of course, they can be put to use by such agendas. Put to misuse, I might say. We call that propaganda."

"You speak of words revealing reality. Yet the concept of reality is itself a nebulous one, isn't it?" asked the interviewer, recovering a bit of his footing. He was a Yale grad in the social sciences; he had his journalism degree from Columbia. He did not need to be bowled over by an actress. Actor. Female performer. Film star of the feminine gender. "I mean, isn't reality more or less what we say it is?"

"Is it?" asked Kendra. "Tell me, what would happen if all the air were sucked out of this room this instant? What then would be our reality? What would happen if I were to step off the observation deck of the Eiffel Tower? What would happen if I were to attempt to dive to the bottom of the Marianas Trench without diving equipment and oxygen? Is reality really so nebulous, so open to human manipulation?"

"There are hard physical facts, like mountains and oxygen – though quantum physics seems to undercut even these certainties," said the interviewer, rising now to what he clearly saw as a challenge. "There are hard physical facts. And then there's the rest of reality, which is constructed, in large part, by the way we speak of it."

Kendra smiled. "You're younger than I," she said. "Tell me, do they still teach Orwell and Huxley in school? Have you read 1984 or BRAVE NEW WORLD?"

This was also the interview in which Kendra said that she did not have enough faith to be an atheist, a line which would prove over the years to be among her most quotable.

The young reporter, so taken by surprise during the course of the interview, found his moxie again, writing it up from his tape recorder and notes:

"An interview with Kendra Collins is not your typical celebrity-chat assignment," he began. "Never mind how she looks in sequins, never mind her jazz-temptress voice, or all those comparisons to the great clear-eyed and raven-haired beauties of the silver screen, Gardner, Russell, Taylor. Spend a couple of hours in real conversation with her, and Kendra Collins will show her true colors, the colors of a lover of the world of the mind. That her opinions can run from cutting edge to archaic is beside the point. The point here is sheer intelligence. How many actors come to an interview prepared to debate Nietzsche? In answer to a single question Collins may with one breath touch on the thought of Aristotle, the theology of Aquinas, the musings of Voltaire and then wrap it all up with a quote from Marlene Dietrich or Zsa Zsa Gabor."

The interview was quoted all over the world. It was headlined "The Professor's Daughter."

Kendra would appear in several other films over the next few years, but in fact, her greatest achievement came, with Matt, in her writing. Twenty years of experience now showed forth its fruits. Three times in five years as she was moving into her mid- and later forties, Kendra was nominated, with Matt, for a screenwriting Oscar. Each time, the nomination was for an adapted screenplay – Matt's long-ago desire to bring his favorite novels to the screen had finally been realized. The third nomination, for their adaptation of Aldous Huxley's classic portrayal of 1928 British high society, POINT COUNTER POINT, proved the charm.

Kendra stood on the stage at the Kodak Theater, in beaded maroon silk, a handsomely formal Matt at her side, complete with a maroon cumberbund which all the delighted and sniping

289

fashionistas picked up on in their columns the next day. Matt and Kendra kept it brief and funny, handing the coveted statuette back and forth between themselves almost as if it were a bomb, and it was thoroughly agreed by all commentators that evening, the next day and for as long as that Oscar telecast was written about, that the writing-producing team of Kendra Collins and Matthew Chase Trevino had arrived.

From his seat in the audience David watched as Kendra and Matt traded witticisms and the Oscar. Then he watched as the film's director accepted his Oscar – it was the first Academy Award win also, for Alan Braxton.

It had been suggested by some of the film's major backers, including Sam Stefani, that Kendra or Matt take a turn at directing, with POINT COUNTER POINT. Kendra and Matt both balked at the suggestion. "Our most ambitious screenplay," Matt said, "and you think we want an amateur director?" It was a classy project, a lot of A-listers even among the many supporting roles, six weeks mid-summer on location in London, lavish sets and Roaring Twenties costumes, a film a lot of people wanted to be associated with, and in fact, David had let himself hope that he might be tapped to direct. But there was never a question in either Kendra's mind, or Matt's, about the film's director. It was Alan to whom they offered the coveted job, "We owe him," Kendra said to David, one afternoon at the Malibu house, waiting for family to arrive for a barbecue. "He gave us our first real successes. And too, he single-handedly re-launched my acting career."

The day after the Academy Award telecast the papers were full of photos of a radiant Kendra Collins between her two closest male friends, Matt Trevino and Alan Braxton, all three of them with their Oscars. And when a few weeks later her actual, engraved award arrived and Kendra placed her Oscar in the niche where David had always dreamed of placing one of his own, David's pride in his wife's achievement, his joy for her, was not unmingled with a certain quiet rue. For her innocence in their love had been forever shattered, by the affair. She had made the decision that, should he ever let her down again, she would have a place to go, more than that, she would have someone to be, she would have a life to step into, independent entirely of him.

She had, indeed, become the star he had always said she was.

And he was the reason why.

EIGHTY-FIVE

Seven years after they had made their relationship public, Damien and Jean Marc broke up. To the surprise of everyone but Isabel, it was Damien who left. Left to return to Isabel, to the family home, to the original restaurant and the San Gabriel Valley. Jean Marc himself did not know the reasons why. He was shocked and heartbroken at Damien's decision, and Isabel, who had always been friendly with Jean Marc, found herself in the curious capacity of counselling and attempting to console her husband's rejected lover.

No one but Isabel ever heard of it, but Damien found himself sitting awake at four one morning in a pricey suite at a downtown hotel, a young Jamaican musician asleep in the king size bed. The musician's name was Nigel Rhodes. Damien had known him about four years. Damien had instituted live music in the bar at the Century City restaurant on weekend nights and Nigel's band had performed there several times. Nigel had caught Damien's attention for his bright, deeply dimpled smile while performing; he seemed to embrace the entire room with that smile. He was a captivating entertainer. He was young; still in his twenties, he wore his hair in dread locks or beaded braids in corn-row style, he worked out and played beach volleyball to stay in shape, he was a good-looking young man.

After performing at the restaurant three or four times, Nigel dropped in once for lunch. He was alone, and Damien spent some time talking with him. He came back a week later, again alone, and then showed up one evening with some friends at the bar, and over time, Nigel and Damien developed a friendship. They never saw each other beyond the restaurant, but their talks there were not insubstantial; Damien heard a lot about Nigel's boyhood in Kingston, his family, his artistic ambitions, his surprising antipathy toward the music of Bob Marley. And Nigel knew not just about Jean Marc but also about Isabel and the family in San Gabriel; he knew the names of all of Damien's children and grandchildren.

Two or three times a year, Jean Marc would go to Quebec where his family lived; Damien only occasionally accompanied him. The trips were typically a combination of business and pleasure; several of Jean Marc's principle vendors were based in Quebec. Jean Marc had become quite serious about business now that his French market-bakery had been expanded to include a café. The café was very successful; Jean Marc loved playing host and worked ten or twelve hours a day, six days a week. Damien felt that some of the spontaneity had gone out of their relationship, and he missed that. The night in question here Jean Marc was in Quebec.

There were other factors at work, of course, leading to the night with Nigel in the downtown hotel. The first of these factors being that Damien and Nigel had spent several nights in hotels together the last time Jean Marc had gone to Quebec. That had been some months before. Damien had been seized with remorse, afterward, and swore that he would never again cheat on Jean Marc. As it happened, however, the very evening that Jean Marc next flew to Montreal, Nigel stopped in at the bar. It seemed to Damien almost as if arranged by fate; he knew the instant he saw Nigel how the evening would end. He chatted Nigel up off and on throughout the evening, and had little trouble persuading him to stay 'til closing. They spent the night at the Century City Marriott.

Previous commitments kept them apart for two nights. But a night after that was spent at the Embassy Suites followed by a couple of nights at the Bonaventure. The night in question here, their fifth together in nine days, they were at the Sheraton. Damien changed hotels so as to avoid recognition by desk staff, and he wanted brand-name anonymity; no Chateau Marmont for him. Nor for that matter the Beverly Wilshire or the Beverly Hills Hotel.

Damien and Jean Marc had friends on the staff at all these establishments.

Nigel was happy with the big hotels and the spacious suites, with the limitless room service, the good booze. He and Damien talked about everything: family and friends, music and the restaurant, sports, movies, the California state water situation, national politics, both American and Jamaican. Nigel's smile made the evenings themselves smile. He was light, playful, free and easy in expressing his affection. Nigel was everything Jean Marc had been before he'd begun to succeed, before he'd begun to make real money, before he'd started following the stock market, before, basically, Jean Marc had settled so surely and, to Damien, so surprisingly, into a hard-working but comfortable middle age.

Nigel knew all about Jean Marc. He understood there was no future with Damien. That was fine; he was not looking for a future with anyone. He had lovers – of both sexes -- as he pleased, and his future was with his band. He was happy with the prospect of ongoing gigs at the restaurant, happy having Damien as a friend, and enchanting to Damien, he was evidently happy as well with the prospect of a rotating series of evenings of pleasure and passion, sporadically dependent on Jean Marc's travels.

This was the background to that four a.m. awakening Damien experienced, there at the downtown Sheraton. It was a true awakening, as if to reality itself. He was a man in his mid-sixties, a father and a grandfather, with a wife who still loved him in Arcadia and a loyal young lover in Quebec, and here he was with a Jamaican musician barely past his twenty-ninth birthday.

It was too much. Too much. He had sworn to himself that he would not violate Jean Marc's trust a second time. Disgusted with himself, Damien sat there in the dark and quiet hotel room, and wondered at his weakness, his self-indulgence, his radical abandonment of responsibility. This kid was young enough to be his son. What would Damien think of a man – or a woman – his age who would go to bed with Tino? Why should Damien think any differently of himself? Then Damien put it to himself another way: Nigel had spoken often of his parents in Jamaica. They were ten years younger than Damien. What would they think of a man such as himself, seducing their son?

What would Nigel himself think of him, Damien wondered, years from now? For Nigel was innocent. That is, he was, as was his entire generation, simply untrained, amoral by sheer osmosis, his convictions formed by Madison Avenue and cultural relativism, not at all his fault that he thought of sex as a purely recreational activity. But surely time and maturity would bring about a change in his attitudes, and when that change came, what would Nigel himself think of him, remembering these stolen nights in the big hotels?

Nigel was also trusting. It was precisely because Nigel did trust him that Damien was so astonished at himself, so appalled. He knew something of the young man's hurts, his insecurities, his hopes and his needs. And what he knew pointed to what he did not know, to deeper realities, unexplored depths – why, for instance, had the boy wanted to be with a man old enough to be his father? To eliminate the obvious, his interest was not pecuniary: when Damien gave Nigel a gift of cash on his most recent birthday, Nigel said it was too much and tried to give it back. Damien would not let him. Nigel used it to take his band, and Damien and Jean Marc, to dinner at Spago.

All of which left Damien with the question, what psychological needs had impelled Nigel toward this set of developments? Of course there were the shallow and obvious needs: the boy liked being looked at, he made his living on the stage, after all. If there were such a thing as a healthy and happy streak of narcissism, Nigel seemed to possess it. There was the fact of the enjoyment they took in each other's conversation. But there was clearly more, there was clearly an unexamined emotional dynamic at play. The boy wanted to be loved by a man his father's age. What unmet needs were operative in that desire? Where might those needs leave Nigel in ten years' time? In twenty? Damien did not know, and in taking the kid to bed, it was apparent that he did not care. Say what he might about his fondness for the boy, Damien evidently saw Nigel as a plaything. A toy. A living, breathing, walking, talking, thinking, feeling toy.

"We're not just animals," Jean Marc had once said to Damien, with regard to a mutual friend who was known for his promiscuous alliances. "We're built for relationship."

Well, what relationship did Damien have with this kid sleeping amid his beaded braids in the king size bed? He'd developed a friendship with him. It should have been a good thing, for Nigel, having that friendship. Damien might have been something of a mentor, his affection and guidance should have been a blessing for the boy. But no. He'd had to bring it and him to this. What did he owe this boy? Far more to the point, what did he owe Jean Marc? What did he owe Isabel?

Moving quietly because he did not want to wake Nigel, did not want to have a conversation with him, did not want to be tempted to delay or avoid the course of action he had in that moment decided upon, Damien found his wallet, took five one hundred dollar bills from it (for Damien had always carried cash) and laid the bills on the table on Nigel's side of the bed. He then took a piece of the hotel stationery and crossing quietly into the bathroom and closing the door, switched on the light and wrote the boy a note. "I have been unjust to you, Nigel" Damien wrote. "I ask your forgiveness. Be assured of my prayers and best wishes always. Take care of yourself." He signed it. He did not for a minute expect Nigel to understand, but Damien needed to leave this note.

As he was laying the note alongside the cash, Damien inadvertently pushed a room service menu against a small reading lamp. The lamp tipped over, hitting the clock radio and then bumping against the wall. Damien belatedly tried to catch the lamp and only succeeded in making yet more noise. Nigel stirred. Damien looked apprehensively toward the boy and saw in the darkness that he was stretching – he was awake.

"Poppy?" Nigel said sleepily, with a questioning intonation.

Poppy was one of Nigel's several nicknames for Damien.

The youth rolled over toward the side of the bed, the beads in his braids clicking. "What's up?" Nigel asked. "What time is it?" He yawned, stretched again, reached for the light, which Damien meanwhile had straightened. Nigel got the light on and, blinking, looked at Damien with a questioning frown.

"What's going on? Why are you up? Is something wrong?"

"Yes," Damien found himself saying, for he had not planned on saying anything, of course; he had wanted to avoid this conversation entirely. "Yes, something is wrong."

Nigel's eyes widened. He pushed himself up on one elbow. "In San Gabriel? With the family? Isabel?"

"They are all fine, but something is wrong, yes, Nigel."

Nigel blinked, still accustoming his eyes to the brightness. Looking at the clock radio he noticed the cash and the note on the bed table.

"What's this?" he said, and sat up amid the pillows and covers. Seeing that the note was addressed to him, he picked it up and gestured lightly with it in Damien's direction. "Are you leaving?" he said. He read the note.

He looked from the note to Damien and then to the cash, his eyes growing wide even as his brow furrowed into a frown that suggested a wondering incomprehension, and too, a certain emotional pain, this last fact not lost on Damien. That Nigel was such a good kid only intensified Damien's guilt and shame. It would have been much easier to walk out on a hustler.

"Damien," Nigel said. "I don't understand."

"I know you don't," said Damien. "Please, Nigel, just accept my apologies and this little gift --"

"Apologies for what?" said Nigel. "And a gift? The money? What for? I don't want money from you, Poppy!" And Nigel actually laughed. This seemed almost a joke of some strange kind. "Tell me. What's wrong?"

Damien turned away. "I have to go," he said.

"Go where?"

Damien did not answer, but turned toward the suite's living room.

"No!" said Nigel. He threw the covers back. He snapped up his robe, which he had left over the back of a chair. With one stride he was even with Damien. He took Damien by the shoulders and looked directly into his eyes. "No, Damien!" he said, smiling a questioning smile. "Why? You said something's wrong – what? What's happened? I'll help, if I can. You know that."

This of course would be the moment to reassure Nigel, to try to let him down gently. Damien didn't dare. Already he felt his resolve weakening. He shrugged himself roughly out of the boy's hands and started again for the outer room.

"Damien! What is this about?" Nigel said, his braids swinging with the force of his movement. "Have I done something? Are you upset with me? Tell me!"

Damien had to answer that question. It was unfair not to do so. "You have not done anything. I have obligations to others, Nigel. And I had an obligation to you. I was meant to be your friend. I'm not."

"What do you mean?" Nigel asked, truly incredulous. "You're a great friend!"

"I can't expect you to understand."

"I don't understand. Please, Poppy," and Nigel had him by the arms. "Sit down. Talk to me. I'll get you a drink."

Damien again shook himself free.

"What have I done?" Nigel said.

Damien ignored him, heading toward the outer room.

With eyes that suddenly flashed, Nigel crossed to the bed table. He reached up the cash and closed quickly the distance between the two of them, blocking Damien's exit. He threw the bills at Damien. "I don't want your money!" he said. The gesture was angry, but his voice was pleading. "I don't want your money!" he repeated.

Damien looked at the bills where they landed on the carpet. He pulled out his wallet. He emptied it of its remaining cash, fanning it out in his hand. He then flicked it forth toward Nigel, a fluttering shower of ones, fives, tens, twentys, fiftys and hundreds. Nigel stood open-mouthed, speechless, watching the bills as they floated to the carpet. He looked up questioning, gestured with his hands as if in supplication.

"What have I done?" he asked.

"Nothing."

"Then what are you doing?"

Damien locked his gaze with Nigel's. "I'm loving you."

He turned and strode quickly to the outside door, hurrying down the corridor to the elevator. He took with him the image of the boy, standing still as a statue in his shock, bills in every denomination scattered about his feet like so many fallen green leaves.

EIGHTY-SIX

Downstairs, Damien checked out at reception, making sure that all the room charges were run on his card. He paid as well the voucher for Nigel's parking. He was gratified by the efficiency of the lone desk clerk; he was afraid that Nigel might at any moment appear, dressed and pleading. He wished he'd had the strength to break with the boy more gently; perhaps even, to have explained himself.

It was winter and by the standards of Los Angeles, a cold night, perhaps fifty degrees, with a brisk wind. There had been several recent rainstorms which had cleared the air and left the city sparkling during the day, but it was chilly, at four in the morning, and as he crossed toward his car, Damien drew the collar of his overcoat up against the cold air.

Driving away Damien was leaving more than an astonished young Jamaican musician behind. Hunger – for the glamour, adventure and excitement of life in the fast lanes of the West Side – had driven him to found the Century City Casa de la Fuente. Despite his indulgence of it, that hunger had not been satiated. It had only demanded more. Hooking up with a twenty-nine year-old! Damien knew what he had to do.

Shortly after the night at the Sheraton Damien retired from the management of the Century City restaurant. It was a seamless transition; Tino was already in place there. But the great surprise to all who heard of it was that Damien left Jean Marc as well. He drove from the Sheraton to the home he and Jean Marc shared in Los Feliz. Jean Marc was in Quebec another few days; the house was dark and silent. Damien packed a couple of bags and drove to

Arcadia. He left no note; there would be plenty of time for him and Jean Marc to talk.

Damien had keys to the family home. He had been in Arcadia, as Isabel had said he would be, many, many times over the years. He let himself in quietly just before dawn. He slipped a note under the door to the master bedroom so as not to surprise Isabel, then went down to the big, airy kitchen, and made coffee. Pouring himself a cup, he sat at the breakfast bar, looking out the windows. The house sat on a low slope and commanded spectacular views. A pink and gold sunrise was spreading above the San Gabriels. The recent storms had left the peaks covered in snow. They were beautiful in the spreading dawn light and in striking contrast to the long line of palms, also visible from the kitchen windows, which marked the neighborhood's principal thoroughfare. One of Isabel's three Lhasa Apsos wandered in from somewhere in the house and sat at Damien's feet, looking up at him with bright eyes. Damien bent down to scratch the dog's head. The dog leapt up onto the next chair, a paw extended toward Damien. Damien smiled, and sipped his coffee. He was home.

No more West Side glamour, no more art-and-entertainment-crowd parties in West Hollywood or Santa Monica or Venice, no more nights on duty at Century City, greeting "the famed, the named, the sleek and the chic," as Linda joked of the restaurant's clients. No more ogling young Jamaican musicians. No more failures in loyalty and love to those he had originally promised both. The first and longest-standing of those promises had been to Isabel. She was his wife, the mother of his children. He could only go forward now, by going back.

If he'd chafed at his treatment of Nigel, how much more would he despise himself, for what must soon transpire with Jean Marc? Yet it did need to transpire. Jean Marc was solid and true, but Damien knew he had to make a clean break. He knew himself too well. There would be other Nigels, if he stayed on the West Side. The only place he could find the support and strength he needed now was at Isabel's side.

An hour later he heard Isabel upstairs. She liked rising early, as did Damien. He heard his wife's light footsteps on the carpeted stairs; she had evidently seen the note, and decided to come down immediately. Not that he had meant to alarm her with the note; he'd simply told her he was downstairs. But she must have intuited the bald fact of it; she must have guessed why he had come in at dawn.

He turned from the window as she entered the kitchen. Her dark hair was loose and wavy above her full-length, sky blue negligee, a sexy nightgown, very Isabel, even though she'd spent her nights alone, these past seven years. Isabel had gotten into the habit of looking like a movie star in bed early in their marriage; it had been part of her campaign to hold her husband, to strengthen her marriage. Damien smiled inwardly, a rueful smile, to think of those days and that effort on her part; also to see how the habit had stayed with her all these years, for this morning, at sixty-two, light and flowing in that negligee, she was as beautiful as she had ever been.

She came into the big stone kitchen, lit by the early morning light, and her gaze met Damien's. What Damien saw in her eyes brought tears into his. He held her gaze as she took seat at the bar alongside him. For a long moment, they simply gazed into one another's eyes.

Then Isabel said, "Does Jean Marc know?"

Damien looked down, shook his head. "He's in Quebec," he said.

Isabel nodded. "This is going to be hard for him."

Damien looked up and met her gaze again. "It seems that all I do is hurt and disappoint others."

Isabel laid a hand on his harm. "Your life is bigger than that," she said. "It always has been." She looked to a nearby counter and smiled. "Oh good," she said. "You've made coffee."

EIGHTY-SEVEN

"Not take him back?" Isabel replied, astonished at the question, which she found herself several times asked, over the next few weeks. "Not take him back? Why wouldn't I? We love each other."

Kendra heard of this reply of Isabel's and she smiled, deeply proud of her sister-in-law. "We love each other," Isabel had said, including Damien in the dignity of their love, making sure others understood this was not some regally magnanimous gesture on her part. Kendra revered Isabel for that response.

At the same time, Kendra's heart hurt for Jean Marc. They had been friends for years before she and Matt had introduced him to Damien. Kendra could imagine the shock to Jean Marc of Damien's desertion, she could imagine the grief he felt, at no longer being a part of the de la Fuente family. She went out of her way to make sure he knew that she still considered him family, and she made a point of patronizing the café and the market on Melrose. She urged him to accept invitations from Isabel, who was no more inclined to desert him than had she been inclined, years before, to abandon Damien.

"You have a true friend in Isabel," Kendra assured Jean Marc. "We all do. Once she loves, she loves. There are no conditions."

"Poor Jean Marc," Matt said to David at a cocktail party at Sam's and Linda's, honoring a retiring studio head, a few weeks after Damien moved back in with Isabel. "I guess he's really pretty broken up."

"He'll get over it," said David. "He's got plenty of admirers, now that he is doing so well thanks to Damien."

"He's put on a few pounds the last couple years," Matt observed. "He may need to hit the treadmill to rebound adequately."

David snorted. "Jean Marc's turn for a mid-life crisis. How old is he now?"

Matt shrugged. "Early forties somewhere, maybe forty-two, forty-three?"

"In any event I wouldn't worry too much about Jean Marc," said David. "He got a restaurant out of it."

"More than that," agreed Matt. "He got a twelve-room house in Los Feliz with poolside views of downtown. Not bad for a charming ski bum."

"Crying all the way to the bank," agreed David.

Ladylike hands with glossy nails suddenly came to rest, one on Matt's shoulder, and one on David's. Both men turned as a cascade of blonde hair came between them.

"You know," said Linda, with wide grey-green eyes and a tight smile playing about her pink lips, "when it comes to snarky gossip, you two really separate the men from the girls."

She withdrew as lightly as she had arrived, leaving Matt and David open-mouthed, staring at each other. Then Matt laughed out loud.

"Busted!" he said.

EIGHTY-EIGHT

Damien and Isabel had six good years reunited. They celebrated their fiftieth wedding anniversary with the renewal of their vows at Mission San Gabriel, followed by a huge party at the restaurant, the original restaurant, the first Casa de la Fuente. By that time, they had ten grandchildren and two great-grandchildren. The party might not have happened: Damien did not feel he had earned it.

Isabel took Damien's face in her hands and smiled, kissed him. "You may not have earned it," she said, "but I have." She sent word to the family and to many friends, and the party was held.

Just weeks after their anniversary, Damien suffered a stroke which left him weak on his left side, and in need of speech therapy. Isabel set up the study as a sick room and with the help of Carmen, Ana and Raquel, Damien was nursed by Thanksgiving to the point of being able to walk unassisted and make his words understood. He had one last holiday season with his family.

During the first week of the new year, Damien suffered the second stroke, the one that killed him. He lay unconscious in the hospital for four days as the family gathered, the MDs offering no hope. He died late on a Thursday afternoon with Isabel at his side.

The funeral was held at Mission San Gabriel and the reception at the original Casa de la Fuente, ever the site of the family's rites of passage. Kendra found herself at a table with several of the nephews; they were all so grown up now, in their late thirties and early forties, mostly married and with young children. Yet, they remained the nephews.

"We were undecided on a name 'til last week," said Julian, in answer to Kendra's question about his baby, due in a couple of months. "His name is Damien."

"Yeah!" said Rico, and lifted his glass, which was empty. He noticed it after he got it in the air and said, "Where's a waiter? I need a re-fill."

Isabel had given the entire staff the day off, so that they might attend the funeral as guests. The family had hired in a catering service.

"Not the same as when it's our people," Rico said now, and lowered his glass.

"I'll get you another," said Santino. "I'm empty myself and they've got serving tables in every room --"

"To Hell with the serving tables," said Angelo. "Raid the bar. This place is ours."

"Not the same," Rico repeated, looking at his empty glass. "This would never have happened on Tio Damien's watch."

Angelo took his cousin's glass. "CC?" he asked.

"Crown Royal," said Rico. "Rocks."

"You gonna marry Miss Istanbul or what?" Javier asked Carlos.

Carlos, who was seated next to Kendra, smiled. "She's from Izmir, actually."

Carlos, now a tenure-track professor at, of all places, the University of Chicago, had become quite serious, over the past year, with a beautiful young native of Turkey named Farah.

"Izmir schmizmir," said Javier. "You gonna marry her or not?"

"I don't know," Carlos smiled.

"Jessica likes her," said Javier. "Jessica likes her a lot. Says she's real down-to-earth, a lot of fun, our kinda girl."

Jessica and Brett saw Carlos often, in the Windy City.

"I like her, too," said Carlos and Kendra laughed. "Problem is this whole religion thing," he went on. He turned to Kendra. "I have never been so serious about being Catholic 'til I fell in love with a Muslim."

Kendra smiled. "I'd love to meet her. Bring her out sometime."

"What are your kids gonna be?" said Rico. "Cathlims? Muslics?"

Carlos laughed. "That's the problem!"

"Bring 'em up nuthin'," said Rico. "Let 'em choose for themselves."

Carlos shook his head. "It's actually a question. It's the one issue Farah and I have."

"Don't bring them up nothing," said Julian. "Children have a right to know God."

"I was just joking," said Rico. "Geeze Louweeze. Bring 'em up Jewish."

"There you go, dude," said Angelo, returning Rico's glass, and, not taking any chances with the hired help, carting a fifth of Crown Royal, plus a bottle of Finlandia and a bucket of ice from the bar.

Santino was right behind him, with two bottles of wine, a merlot in his right hand and a chenin blanc, special for Kendra, in his left.

"That'll hold us for a bit," said Rico.

"Til happy hour, anyway," agreed Angelo.

"Hey!" said Javier, and rising suddenly from his seat embraced Tino, who was making the rounds of the tables. "Baby cousin!"

Kendra watched as the other nephews rose to hug Tino. Their hugs were long and hard. The sons of Carmen, Ana and Raquel, none of the other nephews had yet lost his father. Tino looked to Kendra, over Julian's shoulder, as the latter hugged him. Kendra's smile was small, slow, sad.

"Where's Maribel?" Julian asked Tino.

"Who cares?" said Javier. "Tino, Maribel can't sit at this table. The only woman allowed at this table is Tia Kendra!"

Kendra laughed:

"Get a chair for Tino!" Rico said.

"There ain't none!" said Santino.

"Sit on Javier's lap, Tino," said Rico.

Everyone laughed. Javier said, "Auntie Kendra," and patted his lap. Kendra laughed – and kept her seat.

"Sit here, cousin," Carlos said, rising.

But before Tino could accept the offer, Jeffrey was at the table, with a chair for his cousin.

"Talk about baby cousins!" said Rico. "Where did you come from? And how did you know we needed a chair?"

"The whole restaurant knows you need a chair!" said Jeffrey. "Tino," he said, and gestured toward the chair.

Tino took the seat.

"Now where's Jeffrey gonna sit?" said Julian.

"Rico's lap," said Javier.

"It's been a long time," Carlos said to Kendra, resuming his seat and content to let his cousins settle the issue of where Jeffrey would sit. "A long time, since the night you first came here, the night of my high school graduation party."

Kendra smiled. "That's the night I met all of you," she said. "You're the reason I'm in this family."

Carlos shook his head. "I think Uncle David is the reason you are in this family."

David was seated several tables away, with Sam and Linda, among others. Sam asked David if he were going to be at a charity event at Santa Anita the following day.

"No, actually I have a doctor's appointment tomorrow," said David. "I'll be staying close to home."

"Nothing serious," Linda said, more a statement, a declaration, than a question.

"Let's hope not!" David smiled.

EIGHTY-NINE

"If we put Gayle in the office that afternoon," said Matt, from the big leather recliner near the bookcases, "we run into a problem with the Jennifer-Scott plot point three scenes later. They don't know that Brady has cut Gayle out yet."

Kendra sighed. "You're right," she said. "So where is Gayle that afternoon?"

Matt shrugged, looking at the pages Kendra had just moments earlier printed out. "She likes fast cars and the beach," he said, with a smile, a smile that said, "I'm stumped." "Maybe have her cruising PCH?"

"Hey," Kendra said. "That could work."

"Could it?"

"Hang on," Kendra said, her fingers above the keyboard, for though Matt still did all rough draft work in ink on a lined yellow pad, Kendra composed at the computer. "Let me think. If Gayle's cruising the Pacific Coast Highway – for whatever reason, nice day, restless spirits, or maybe lunch with a cousin in Orange County, who knows, who cares, then she's not in the office when Jill and Brady send Scott the suspect e-mails..."

Matt smiled. Kendra was a natural at the construction of plot; she understood it as an extension of character, as did Matt himself.

"The problem with Gayle is that she really is good," Kendra went on.

312

"She is," Matt said. "Not a devious thought in her head, ever. So much easier to make plots work with characters who really are plotters."

Kendra laughed. "What did Flannery O'Connor say? She knew of nothing more difficult in the writing of fiction than making good characters believable?"

It was a few days after the funeral. A wet and windy Monday, a strong storm out of the Gulf of Alaska that had pounded the north state over the weekend and now was soaking L.A. They were at Matt's townhouse, at work on an original script, not an adaptation, hence their need to get the plot right themselves.

"What's the news with David?" Matt now asked, while Kendra sat thinking at the keyboard. "The MDs, I mean?"

Kendra turned away from the computer and looked at him, gesturing hands up. "Some tests this week, x-rays, an advanced blood draw. They are saying maybe an intestinal obstruction."

"Huh," said Matt. "He in any real pain?"

Kendra shrugged. "No, not really. Low-level, sporadic. The thing is, he hasn't much appetite."

"Yeah, I don't think he ate a thing at the reception."

Kendra sighed, turned back to the computer, her mind on Gayle and the drive along the coast. She had an occasional flash of fear about David's stomach problem, whatever it might be, but really, she could not imagine it was anything serious. In any event, they'd know more after these tests this week.

"The reception was something," said Matt.

Kendra looked again toward him, understanding that he wanted to talk. "It was," she agreed. "I was with the nephews for a couple of hours."

"I saw that," said Matt, and smiled. "I think that was the table everyone wished they were at. Looked like you guys were having fun."

"Well," Kendra laughed. "Rico and Javier, after all. All of them, really. They keep it light, even when they're sad. I talked a lot with Carlos. It was the right place to be. With the young, I mean. The right place to be at the funeral of my brother-in-law."

Matt nodded. "I'm gonna miss him," he said.

"I know. Me too."

"He always said he admired me," Matt said, and laughed a short, joyless laugh. "Damien always said he thought I had taken a smart path through life, because I had never made a commitment and then broken it. He so deeply felt, and so deeply regretted his failures. Failures in commitment, I mean. Leaving Isabel, then leaving Jean Marc. His kids having to deal with all that."

He shook his head. "He didn't exactly want to trade places with me, but he had this idea that I'd shown prudence and restraint where he had been foolish and headlong. Can you imagine? Foolish – the man who was the family's professional anchor; the restaurants are what they are because of him. And after all, and despite all of it, fifty years with Isabel. Fifty-four, really, if you count the four before they were married. Whatever may be said about him, it has to be said that Damien had the guts to dive into life, to really live according to his heart and his passion. He wasn't afraid to love."

Kendra nodded, saying nothing.

314

Matt sighed. "Maybe that's why we were such good friends," he said, looking toward the windows, where the storm lashed the palms. "Because he went one way in life, the way of passion and its messes, and I went another." He paused, then said, "I went the way of cool and rational calculation. He tried to love everybody and failed. I set out to love no one, and succeeded."

"What?" Kendra said.

Matt shook his head. "No one," he repeated. "I set out to love no one. And I succeeded. Funny thing, reaching fifty, and maybe especially reaching it as we have, with such a roaring success. You realize there is less time ahead than behind, and you look at the time that is gone, and you," he paused again. Then, "And you look for what has come into the world, as a result of the time that you have spent, as a result of where and how you have invested your energies, and for some of us, anyway, that can be a chilling view. To have succeeded in loving no one. That is one scary accomplishment."

"Matt," Kendra began, clearly ready to take issue with him.

"Remember Angie?" Matt asked. "Who was jealous of you?"

Kendra nodded.

"Remember Beth, who I was so sure was scheming to get pregnant?"

Kendra nodded again.

Matt laughed again, that short, joyless laugh. He shook his head. "Pregnant! With me! With Matthew Chase Trevino! Pregnant! Poor girl. Poor girls, all of them." He looked at Kendra. "Do you know I never once, not once, took the risk? I was always 'safe' and 'protected.' I could never have countenanced an abortion –

there was that much of the former altar boy still operative within me – so I made sure, every single time, no matter her assurances, or her protests, that the girl, whichever girl it happened to be, that the girl and I would not be making a baby. I made sure of it. After all it's not rocket science."

He sighed and ran his hand through his darks curls, leaning back in the chair, his gaze now toward the ceiling. "I may as well have been born a eunuch," he said.

"Matt!" Kendra protested. "That's ridiculous."

He cast his gaze her way. "Is it? Is it ridiculous to take a long, deep breath at this point, and wonder about how I have lived, and why?"

Kendra made an equivocal gesture. Put like that, no, it was not ridiculous.

"I've no natural children, either," Kendra now said.

Matt grinned and scoffed at the same time. "Not for lack of trying," he said. "And you are one extraordinary mother. And you know it." He smiled at her. "I'm proud of my friend Kendra," he said. "She wasn't afraid to love, either."

"Matt," Kendra said, shifting to face him directly. "The idea that you have not loved in life is preposterous. Look at your nephews and nieces."

Matt had twelve, by his three brothers in Salinas. He shrugged. "Easy to love a nephew or a niece," he said. "When they were little, as soon as they started to fuss, I handed them back to their parents. Now that they are grown up, it's just easy adult friendship. None of the baggage from parenting. Easy to love a nephew or a niece. There's no real self-sacrifice involved, no real self-surrender."

Kendra shook her head. "I disagree but for now, let's call it a draw on that point. Consider this. There are various calls to love, in life, various ways to love. Look at the Church, you should understand that. How do priests love in the world? How do sisters love?"

Matt practically guffawed. "Good grief, Kendra," he said. "You can't seriously mean to compare me to a good priest. And most of them are good, you know, to Hell with media portrayals. You can't consider comparing the way I have lived to the way a dedicated priest lives."

"I'm talking about different ways to love in the world," said Kendra.

"The opposite of a priest," Matt said, steady on his point, "is not a married man. Priests and married men actually have a lot in common. The opposite of a priest is a playboy. The priest shares his love with everyone and makes love to no one. The playboy makes love to everyone and shares his love with no one. It's even a question whether he has any love to share, as love is a living and dynamic quality of character. You cannot have it if you do not practice it."

"Great art requires passion, sacrifice and love," Kendra said. "You dedicated yourself thirty years ago to a risky and unknown path. That took guts and anything that takes guts takes love. There are different ways to love in the world."

"Matthew Chase Trevino, Academy Award-winning screenwriter," Matt said, "loved his talent for the way it could serve his ambition."

"The ambition to create great cinematic art," argued Kendra.

Matt shook his head, smiling. "The greater my scripts," he said, "the more they glorified me. Do you know how I felt, the night we won the Oscar?"

Kendra gave him a quizzical look. "I assume you were as exuberant as you appeared," she said.

Matt indicated with a slight inclination of his head that he had, indeed, been exuberant that happy night. "POINT COUNTER POINT took six Oscars," he said, "but missed for Best Picture. I was overjoyed with our win, with Alan's, with the others. And yet, ambition knows no rest. I vowed in my heart that triumphant night that you and I would take Best Picture, next time we were nominated."

Kendra could not help but point it out: "We just might, this year."

She was talking about their latest film, released the previous fall, a nearly three-hour adaptation of Thackeray's VANITY FAIR. The picture had so far done two hundred-fifty million at the worldwide box office. It was up for eight Golden Globes, there was talk of a sweep. And with Oscar nominations due out later that very week, there was excitement, there was anticipation.

Matt shrugged. "I made the golden boy my idol," he said, meaning the Oscar. "And not because I loved film, although I do love it. Because I loved me. I loved, and love, Matthew Chase Trevino. I worship his image and am in servitude to it."

"Bullshit," said Kendra, with feeling. "Can you count how many teens from East L.A. and South Central have been given opportunity and hope – hope, Matt – because of LA Futures?"

"Window dressing," said Matt.

"Wrong," said Kendra. "Wrong. You have helped an untold number of disadvantaged youth --"

"Window dressing," Matt repeated. "All Los Angeles knows what a great guy Matt Trevino is, raising all that money for deserving youth. When you give, give in secret and your heavenly Father who sees in secret will repay you. That's more or less a quote from one of the gospels, I don't know which, but it was Jesus himself who was speaking. Trust me, Kendra, I know how good it feels to be recognized citywide as such a wonderful and generous guy. Kendra," he said suddenly, sitting up and looking at her. "I drive a seven series BMW. You know what that car cost."

"It's modest, by Hollywood's standards."

"To Hell with Hollywood's standards. How did I see my way clear to spend one hundred thousand dollars on a car? How many inner-city youth have sunk into despair, drugs, crime, violence, because that hundred grand, and the hope it might have provided, was not made available to programs that might have helped them?"

"Matt," said Kendra. "We've had this discussion before. You cannot save the world."

"No," Matt agreed. "But I can help a small part of it, here in Los Angeles. And that small part suffers because I prefer my comfort and my ambition."

Kendra shook her head. She never knew quite how to lead him back out, when he went to this place.

"The care homes," she said finally.

Once a week, every Tuesday morning, Matt packed his guitar and drove to San Gabriel, where he met up with Carmen, Ana, Raquel and a handful of other parishioners at the Mission, and visited local

319

convalescent hospitals, three in all, on a rotating basis. The sisters had been involved in this ministry for years; Matt had started accompanying them only a few months before. They did a prayer service, brought communion to the Catholic residents and sang a few songs, hence the need for Matt's guitar.

"Raquel roped me into accompanying them," Matt said now, "one morning when I was over there visiting Damien and had nothing else to do."

"But you went back the next week," said Kendra.

Matt nodded. "Isabel usually joins us for lunch afterward," he said. "Ramon and Sandra have come a couple of times. It's my own selfish desire to be with my adopted family."

"You told me you went back," said Kendra, "because of the smiles on the faces of the residents."

Matt was silent.

"Do you remember the time you told me how you felt about care homes?" Kendra asked. "So many years ago?"

Matt nodded. "I still feel the same way. My folks will never go into one."

"But you're there for folks you don't even know."

Matt shrugged. "Do you imagine I would be there on my own?" he asked. "I'm there for a nice long lunch with Isabel and the sisters."

Kendra threw up her hands. "Catholic guilt," she said, with a helpless laugh.

"Guilt, Catholic or otherwise," Matt said, "is not a bad thing to feel when it is the right thing to feel. I am guilty of failing to love."

Kendra sighed, her arguments exhausted.

"I am guilty," Matt said. "Guilty of missing life's only point: learning how to love. My God, Damien may have missed a lot of his shots, but at least he was in the game, he wasn't afraid to take aim. I've lived my life safely and smugly on the sidelines, not willing to risk injury."

Matt looked again toward the windows, and the sheeting rain. "I was with Isabel," he said, "at the house in Arcadia, sometime last summer. After they'd gotten Damien home from rehab and had the den set up as his sickroom, recovery room, home rehab station, whatever. The sisters were there every day, helping Isabel, and I was there two or three times a week, mostly getting in their way, but talking with Damien, trying to encourage him, letting him know," and Matt's voice broke, "letting him know that --"

"That you loved him," Kendra asserted.

Matt smiled ruefully. "All right," he conceded. "Yeah, that I loved him. Well, one sunny afternoon Isabel and I were there together and Damien pointed to the crucifix on the wall. Carmen had put it there, where he could see it. She said it comforted him, to see it. One afternoon while Isabel and I were with him, Damien pointed to the crucifix and said that was the price of sin. He said it as clearly as he said anything last summer. Both Isabel and I heard it. Then he said he deserved his suffering; he said it was payment for his sins."

Matt laughed the joyless laugh again. "Talk about Catholic guilt! Anyway, Isabel said something that struck me, and that has stayed with me since. She said that when she looks at a crucifix what she sees is not the price of sin but the price of love."

Matt stopped. He took a deep breath, his eyes wet, and continued. "And that is a price I have never been willing to pay."

Kendra said nothing. She sat silently staring at Matt, who was sitting forward, staring at the carpet. She wanted to take him in her arms.

Before she had made up her mind to do so, however, Matt looked up, his cheeks tear-stained but his eyes now clear. He took another deep breath. "Well," he said. "This isn't getting us any closer to that second Oscar. I guess we better get back to Gayle and the Pacific Coast Highway."

"I guess not," said Kendra.

Matt looked at her.

"Get your raincoat and grab an umbrella," Kendra said, "it's wet and wild out there." She got up and crossed to where she had laid her coat. Matt followed her with his eyes.

"Get up," Kendra said. "Get your coat and an umbrella. We're done working for the day." She got her raincoat on. "It's not, unfortunately, a day for a drive along PCH. But we are going to the beach. To Santa Monica. To a restaurant where we can sit back and relax over a glass of wine and watch the storm rolling in. Maybe two glasses of wine. We can take our time, mulling the menu. No hurry."

She crossed to him, her hands reaching for his. Matt took her hands and let her pull him up.

"I don't know where we'll go or what we'll do, after lunch, which will be long and leisurely," Kendra continued. "But I know this. I am spending the rest of this wet and windy afternoon just kicking around. Kicking around with a man whose capacity for love long ago earned my love. Kicking around," she repeated, and kissed his cheek, "with my best friend."

NINETY

Six weeks after Damien's funeral, David received the definitive lab reports. And so it was that he and Kendra came to be sitting at the patio bar on a sunny February afternoon, she with a glass of white wine, he with his Glenlivet neat, discussing his cancer.

"It's all begun to wrap up rather suddenly," he observed. "Our life, the family life of the siblings, I mean. Funny, how life works. How it goes. Damien gone. Me going." He shook his head. "We never saw any of this coming. I am sure Ramon and my sisters will last another twenty years, but it will never be the same. The lion is loose among us, as Matt said a few weeks ago. It's the beginning of the end, in terms of the life we all have known."

He sipped his drink. "This is going to be hard on the family, coming so soon after Damien."

Kendra had urged him to fight with non-Western approaches. David's response had been a solitary tear.

NINETY-ONE

"Mama Chow's," Linda said, answering over her iPhone Sam's question of where dinner was coming from. "And no, you do not have to pick it up. Tino and Jeffrey went a few minutes ago. How far away are you?...Good. Then we'll see you soon. I'm glad you're coming, sweetheart. This is the day to see David."

"I haven't had Mama Chow's since I moved to Chicago," Jessica was saying to Monique.

"I've never had it," said Monique.

"It's a beautiful restaurant," Justin said to his wife. "The interior is all done up like some kind of pagoda."

"Temple," said Jessica. "Pagodas are Japanese." Then she stopped and thought about it. "Aren't they?"

Justin laughed and Monique shrugged.

"You'll be pleased, Monique," Linda said, coming among them. "I love their Mongolian beef, their lemon chicken and their hundred blossoms lamb, just out of this world. And they do chow mein right. It's not just a bunch of noodles, at Mama Chow's. We've ordered the whole menu, so don't worry, there will be something for everyone."

"We could have done hamburgers for all I care," said Monique. "What matters is that the whole family is here."

"There's the door," said Linda. "But it can't be the boys with the food, they just left."

"Besides, why would they ring?" asked Jessica.

Solange, in any event, had crossed to the foyer to answer the bell.

"Can't be Sam, either," said Linda. "He was at Wilshire and Veteran just now --"

She stopped talking as she heard the voice from the foyer. Then Linda grinned a great and happy grin. "Braxton!" she cried, and headed for the foyer.

NINETY-TWO

The food arrived in boxes and boxes but meanwhile Solange said David was awake again. He heard a party. "'Tell them to bring it in here,' David says," said Solange. "But only just to peek in and say hello," she advised. "He is more tired than he realizes."

They put dinner on hold for a few minutes and as a group followed Solange to the sick room. David was sitting up amid the pillows, looking alert. He looked around the room and smiled. "What a party!" he said, his voice weak but happy. "Is someone dying?"

This joke brought laughter and tears both.

"Brax," David said next. "You came back!"

"Of course," said Alan, and was suddenly very grateful that he had returned. He crossed to David's side. "Of course, amigo," he said. "Linda told me it was her turn to do dinner. I knew that meant take-out from Mama Chow's, so here I am."

David's smile was radiant. He said, "Put THE LOVE BROKER on, just that scene."

Alan turned to the family for help. Tino crossed to a dvd file cabinet and found the film. He turned on the flat screen tv and loaded the dvd, locating the scenes feature. He looked to Kendra. "Which scene is it?" he asked.

Kendra found the scene and hit "play."

They all watched for several minutes, as Kendra sang AND THE ANGELS SING. They smiled and turned one to another, commenting on the cool, breezy initial delivery. Then everyone got quiet, as the trumpet took over. Then everyone got even quieter, as Kendra took over. Then Kendra and the band came back to earth with a smile and a wink, and the scene ended. The room erupted in cheers and applause. Kendra and Alan exchanged a glance. They had both gone back to that happy day on the set. Alan smiled. So did Kendra.

David looked about the crowded room. "See the response?" he said, speaking to Alan, who had remained at his side. "Even today, after it has become so famous, after everyone knows that scene. That's the scene that made you a star, baby," he said to Kendra. He looked at Alan. "And you are the director," David said, his voice weak but full of joy. "You are the man who made Kendra a star. You gave her to the world."

Alan grinned. "Her greatest role," he said, "is the one that she shares with you."

Solange and Linda exchanged a meaningful glance. In less than three minutes, the room was cleared; Mama Chow's was waiting. Kendra and David were alone.

"I loved you in that scene," he said. "The whole world did. And does."

"It was fun playing it," Kendra acknowledged. "And it is a great song. But," she added, taking his hand in hers, "it's not our song."

David gave her a questioning look.

"Think," Kendra smiled.

David smiled. "Quiet nights," he whispered to her.

"Of quiet stars," she whispered in response.

328

Kendra had left, had returned to the dinner party in the other rooms. Solange sat reading in a large recliner. David looked at her and thanked God for this angel with orange curls, coffee-and-cream colored skin and a French-Caribbean accent who had been sent, and that was now the way David saw it, Solange had been sent, only a few months before his diagnosis. He had imagined that he was hiring a housekeeper. She had done far more than keep house, the past two and one-half years. This beautiful woman from the French Caribbean had been, for twenty years, a registered nurse in Martinique, her specialty oncology. She started for David and Kendra less than six months before his diagnosis. David could not see that as a coincidence.

No coincidence, either, that it was Father Cesar who came to the hospital that day a couple of months ago to pray with him, to give him the last rites. It might have been a sad and scary encounter; Father Cesar turned it to joy. Father Cesar had all of them laughing at one point; he brought light and peace into that hospital room; he brought trust in the love and tender mercies of God. David had seen him three times since, here at the house. When he considered the way he'd neglected his faith most of his life, how could David be anything but grateful, for Cesar's confident smile, his radiant joy? He had done nothing to deserve the gift of Father Cesar. But God sent Cesar anyway, just as God had sent Solange.

He loved Father Cesar, he loved Solange. He loved all of them. Oh! How wonderful it had been to see Chrysta, to be able to tell her, "I am sorry." She had wept. She had held his hand. She was happy now, with a good man and with three sons, three boys! She was happy, she had built a good life for herself; oh, of course, she had her worries and troubles, but she had a good life, she was happy. David could see that. He was glad.

He had a good life, too, after all – had it even still, despite this sickness and what it had done to him. Look at today, look at the day he had had.

His siblings. They had all come through life together; faced the same challenges, setbacks, trials, shared the same hopes and joys. They had talked this afternoon mostly about the younger generation. Three new babies on the way: not just Jessica and Brett, not just Justin and Monique, but also Carlos and Farah, in Chicago. They had been out at the spring break and told the family the happy news then.

"Due in October," said Ana, Carlos' mother, this afternoon. "But we don't know yet, boy or girl."

"You have one of each coming," Isabel smiled, speaking to David.

And David had smiled. Two grandchildren soon to arrive. The whole family was hoping he would live to see them, but David was at peace either way. He would see his grandchildren. And though they would not in this life know him, he would know them.

Linda and Sam; Matt and Alan. His closest friends. His co-creators in this wonderful work they had been trusted to do: making movies. Telling stories. Exploring the fears, the hopes, the questions, the joys everyone has through the medium of film. What a privilege! To have had such work – what a privilege, what a trust, what a joy. For most of his professional life he'd placed great store by the hope that his films would outlive him; that his contribution would be a lasting one. He could still see value in that, but from the perspective of this hospital bed in his converted office, eternity opening out before him, the term 'lasting' acquired a weightier significance. All the same, it had been a wonderful way to spend his working life, and he felt only gratitude for having been able to do it.

Tino. His brother's boy. Tino. A nephew who might as well have been a son. "I'd wanted to put him in pictures, you know, Damien," David mused addressing his brother as if he were present. "But Tino was so sharp and precise in his reply. 'Do we really need one more self-absorbed and marginally talented pretty boy cluttering up the screen and making headlines in the tabloids? No thanks, Tio. I want to work with Dad.' Good job, Damien. The restaurants thrive today because Tino loves them, loves the family the way you did. He's also an exceptionally skilled amateur nurse. Funny, bro, how the circle comes around. I remember changing Tino's diapers. Now he changes mine. Thank you, Damien. Thank you, for giving us Tino."

Jessica, Justin, Jeffrey. "We did all right in the end, I think," David said now, as if in prayer, to Lana. For he had always believed that Lana was close to them. "They've turned out well, don't you think? Justin a lawyer working with troubled youth in Atlanta. Jessica about to finish law school and determined to make a difference for the poor in Chicago. And then Jeffrey. Your favorite. Don't try to deny it, baby. I saw it even if Jess and Justin didn't, and it's okay. He's Kendra's favorite, too, you know. It's all right. Not like she spoiled him, or actually treated him any differently than Jess and Justin. Just that sweetness of temperament, I guess, that instinct for gentleness. He won a special place in your heart, Lana, and in Kendra's. Yeah, Lana. Yeah. I think we can be proud of our kids. And Brett, Lana. Don't you love him? Aren't you proud of Jessica, for loving him? So strong and empathic, so attentive to Kendra. I'm sorry for Kendra and Jessica. Brett sees it and tries to bridge the gap; he's a great kid, don't you think so, Lana? And Monique!" Thinking of his daughter-in-law, David's heart was so full that his mind went blank. "I just smile, Lana, when I think of Monique. Remember how you loved New Orleans? That love inspired us to buy this

331

house. Well, your daughter-in-law is from New Orleans. Funny, isn't it, Lana? How things come around again, how they work out?"

Kendra.

Kendra. "Oh God, Damien, Lana. What did I ever do to deserve Kendra?"

He remembered what he had said to her that long-ago night, driving west on the freeways, the night of Carlos' party: "Well, whoever you marry, I hope that the guy is worthy of you."

He smiled a bittersweet smile. "No," he said, "the man whom Kendra married did not, in fact, deserve her."

Kendra had seen it and decided to dis-empower it, decided not to let his unworthiness wreck their marriage, wreck the family. She had stayed. She had loved him in spite of it. No. Not worthy. He had not deserved the life she had agreed to continue to make with him.

Oh Kendra! Even now, even this happy evening so many years after the fact, he could hear her plaintive question, that Sunday night in the family dining room. "What was missing? What did you need, David, that you did not find with me? Because I was happy."

Oh! What he would have given then to have taken it all back, to have been able to undo the affair, to have saved Kendra that grief. She had dealt with it in a manner that seemed now precisely suited to her, so sensible, so straightforward, so rational and calm. She took care of herself while hurting no one else. She built herself into a star. Who could blame her? In some twisted way, the world itself might have been grateful for the affair, for without it, Kendra would never have returned to acting, would never have started to produce with Matt, would never have become the star the world so now loved. Peculiar, to think of it. To think of the good that had come from his evil.

And now today, this evening, here they all were. His children, his siblings, his best friends. Kendra. What a day it had been. What an evening.

He did not have to leave them. Not yet. Not after a day like this. His was a rich life, to have produced such a day. He would have liked to be able to prolong this day, this evening, indefinitely.

No, he did not have to leave them. Oh yes, of course, certainly he did have to leave them – and sooner rather than later. But not now. Not imminently. Would it not be good for all of them, to enjoy a few more days like this one? He could manage it. He could manage it for Kendra. He could manage it for all of them.

After all, what was so hard about staying alive? It was simply a matter of taking the next breath.

NINETY-FOUR

"He's been asleep since I relieved Solange," said Tino. "Solange said she heard the death rattle a couple times before midnight, but he's breathing normally now."

It was almost three-thirty in the morning. Kendra had awakened half an hour earlier and been restless; after twenty minutes or so she'd risen, put on a yellow silk robe and crossed downstairs to David's office, to David's bed. Tino was sitting up with the previous day's LOS ANGELES TIMES, not reading the paper, however, as Kendra had come in. Rather, he was simply sitting at his uncle's bedside, watching David sleep. Solange supervised a team of round-the-clock attendants, but when Tino spent the night, he spent it in the sickroom, and the attendant got a night off.

Kendra had taken seat on the other side of the bed from her nephew.

"Couldn't sleep," she explained, as she had come in.

"Me either," said Tino. He typically would spend his nights with David in a comfy leather armchair with ottoman; it was easy to doze off and on through the night. "I have been wide awake since I spelled Solange." He sighed and added, "You would think we'd be exhausted, after the day we've just had. The whole family was here. And the most important friends."

"Yeah, and all day," Kendra agreed. "He's wiped out, in any event," she added, of her sleeping husband.

"I'm glad to see him asleep," Tino said. "Not just for the fact that he is resting, but for what I assume is a sort of respite, a temporary escape from the reality he faces when awake."

"I've wondered," Kendra said, sitting forward and looking at David, "what his dreams are like. I mean, is he well in them? Is he himself again, strong and fit, and in command? I'd like to think so. I'd like to think that he is able to escape, in his dreams."

"What I would have given," Tino said, "for a few more years of his company. I just assumed he'd be around 'til I was fifty."

Kendra nodded. "I made assumptions, too," she said. "David and I both did. It's like what we were talking about at the pool this afternoon. None of us saw this coming until it hit us. Hobbes called life short, nasty and brutish. I can't enthusiastically endorse such an assessment, but I can see his point. There was so much more that we had looked forward to, so much more that we had thought and talked about doing. We assumed we would have the time."

"I think grieving is as much about the future," Tino said, "as it is about the past. It's not just the memories that bring our tears. It's the hopes, it's the dreams that now will never be. We grieve as much for the future as for the past."

David woke. He looked right at Kendra. He smiled. She smiled. "David," she said. "Kendra," he said, and his smile was deep, it seemed to be the visible manifestation of some radiance within. It transformed his face, from a mask of sickness and suffering to a countenance shining with quiet joy. She could almost see eternity in his smile. He held Kendra's gaze for a long moment, with that smile. He closed his eyes again.

Kendra turned to Tino. "Did you see his smile?" she asked.

335

Tino's smile answered her.

"I suppose there is this to be said about death from cancer," she said in a whisper, for she was very careful about talking about his death in front of the bedridden David. "You have this time, this precious time, to get things – well, sorted out. I think he's sorted a lot out, the past few weeks."

Tino nodded and Kendra saw the tears in his eyes. Oh! How she wished they might form in hers. It had been weeks. This was evidently the price of strength, or what was anyway perceived as strength by others.

Tino looked again toward his uncle. A moment, and then a slight frown and then he looked at Kendra, alarm in his dark eyes. He looked again at David.

Kendra looked at David.

Tino put his hand an inch from David's lips, which were slightly parted. Kendra reached for his arm, feeling for his pulse.

NINETY-FIVE

Linda sat bolt upright in bed. She placed a hand to her mouth in astonishment.

"David!" she cried, yet cried in a whisper.

It was only a moment, only a flash, an instantaneous recognition, lit up radiant and unmistakable. Then it, then he, then the light was gone.

There was a lamp beside her bed. She fumbled for it in the darkness; she got it on. She reached her iPhone from the bedside table.

Sam, awakened by her movement and the light, turned toward her, confused. "Linda?"

She was busy getting her phone open and placing the call.

"What?" Sam asked. "Who?" He blinked and tried to fully wake up. "Linda, who are you calling? Do you know what time it is?"

"Three thirty-five A.M.," she answered, putting the phone to her ear.

She knew exactly what time it was.

NINETY-SIX

Tino withdrew his hand from David's lips and looked at Kendra, who was still feeling for his pulse. Their eyes met; Tino's welling with tears. The tears spilled over.

"Tio!" he cried, turning back to David. "Tio!" He took David's hand in his and began to kiss it.

Kendra kept hold of David's wrist. She felt a sudden superstitious fear about letting go of it, letting go of him.

"I didn't think this," Tino said, through his quiet sobs. "Not tonight. Not tonight. Not after such a perfect day." He held his uncle's hand in his and wept.

His iPhone, left on a nearby end table, suddenly vibrated, for he had turned the ringer off. Both Tino and Kendra reacted with surprise.

"Who on earth?" said Kendra, and in her surprise, let go of David's wrist.

Tino reached the phone and looked at its lit-up face. "Linda," he said.

NINETY-SEVEN

Sam pushed the excess pillows – so very Linda all these years, all these unnecessary pillows – aside and sat more fully up amid the sheets. Linda was out of bed, pacing the floor. She had tried one number and then another. "Kendra," she had said, when he had repeated his question, "Who are you calling at this hour?"

Frowning, Sam watched his wife, statuesque in her white negligee, lustrous blonde hair falling to just below her shoulders, as she paced, agitated but focused. It flashed through his mind, as it often enough did, how much he loved her. He had hurt her, early on in their marriage. Too late, too late he had regretted it. He might have lost her, but she had stayed with him, after all. He thanked God every day for that fact.

"Tino!" Linda said. "Are you with David?"

Sam gathered that Tino answered in the affirmative.

"Where is your aunt? I called her just a moment ago, but there was no answer." A moment, while Tino responded, inaudible of course, to Sam, and then Linda said, "Put her on."

A moment more and then Linda said, "Kendra. I know what's happened…Never mind how, I know. I am on my way, darling. Give me a few minutes. I need a quick shower. Meanwhile, don't worry about a thing. This is one phone call, Kendra. Just one call. Solange knows what to do. But tell her to wait for me.

"I need," and here Sam watched as his wife hesitated, watched with curiosity as she seemed on the brink of tears and then caught herself, "I need to talk to you, but it can wait, it can wait. What

matters now is you, baby…No, no, I'm fine. Trust me, I am fine.
What matters now is you…Like I said, girlfriend, never mind how.
I knew…I just knew, that's all. We'll talk. I am on my way. I love
you, Kendra."

Sam moved toward Linda's side of the bed as she returned the
iPhone to the table. "Linda, what has happened? Has David
died?"

"Yes. Just now. Two minutes ago. Three thirty-five A.M., in
fact."

"I – sweetheart – I don't understand. How did you know?"

Linda looked right at her husband. "I saw him," she said. "Two
minutes ago. He was standing at the foot of the bed."

NINETY-EIGHT

"I'll call San Gabriel," said Tino, "you call Jessica and the boys?"

"Jessica and the boys are just one call," said Kendra.

"So is San Gabriel," said Tino. "Mom will call everyone else."

"I'll call Carmen," Kendra said. "She and Isabel together can alert the rest of the siblings."

That it was twenty to four in the morning was entirely irrelevant. Tino and Kendra both knew that the entire family had to be notified immediately. Kendra was quietly satisfied to have this responsibility, just at the moment. The huge fact, the immense reality – David lying lifeless in the hospital bed – was more than she could absorb right now. She could report this fact to the family. She could not take it in herself, let alone deal with it.

"You know," Tino said, "we really don't need to wake Solange. She had a long day."

"Oh I think we'd better," said Kendra. "Especially given that the whole family will be here in an hour. I've gotta call Matt, too. He would not like being left out --"

She stopped and looked at Tino, who had suddenly clapped his hand to his mouth, choking back a sob. The effort failed.

Kendra drew him close. He wept quietly in her embrace. She thought once again of the little boy in trouble with his father, of the high school sophomore taking pictures at the opening of the

341

Century City restaurant, of the sad seventeen year old, talking with her over the sushi about his parents' separation, of the college freshman who longed to be alone with her. She felt Tino in her arms. He was a man now, thirty-two. But he wept for his beloved uncle like a little boy.

"Maybe you should call Maribel," Kendra said, after a moment, as Tino's sobs subsided.

Tino shook his head, recovering himself. "No, no, too early."

"My guess is she'll respond the way Matt will – some friends really are family, you know." She smiled at him. "Especially when they hope to become family."

Tino shrugged, wiping his eyes. "Speaking of friends," he said. "How did Linda know?"

NINETY-NINE

Linda drove her cream-colored Camargue in a state of deliberate, even artificial calm. The surface streets between Bel Air and Brentwood were quiet and still, lined by darkened showcase homes and sleeping gardens. She needed to concentrate on the road, she had to pay attention to what she was seeing.

But she could not let go of what she had seen. David. At the foot of the bed. "David!" she'd cried. He'd smiled. And then he was gone.

Only an instant. Over almost before she knew it had happened. But it had happened. She had not just seen him. She had felt him. Felt his friendship. Felt his love. It was so real she had been about to ask how he got there. And then he was gone. And it only now occurred to her that it was not the David of yesterday afternoon, David in the sickbed in the office, David who had only fourteen hours ago told her that he had seen Damien. It was not David the wasted-away victim of cancer who had visited her but David as he had been fifteen years before, strong and vital and handsome. And yet at the same time it was David as he had never been, David as she had never seen him. Radiant with joy, serene in a light that was a mystery in itself, for the bedroom was dark. The light was something David had brought with him. Or maybe it was the light that had brought David with it. She did not know and in any event, it did not matter. What mattered was that at the moment of his death David had come to her.

She drove on through the dark, quiet streets, concentrating on the road, trying deliberately not to be carried away by the images within which nonetheless spilled forth: images of her parents and

343

siblings at Christmas when she was a little girl, her father's smile the day she made cheerleader sophomore year, her first college lover, her first job as a loan officer at a bank on Michigan Avenue, the splash and sparkle of the downtown fountains that sunny September day that she met Sam. She was twenty-three and in love.

It all came cascading back, her life in serial images and with all the emotions, all the circumstances, all the people who'd played a role in all those moments. Their wedding day at St. Thomas Episcopal since Sam had not annulled his first marriage; could not marry her in the Catholic Church. Gianna, Sam's mother, silver-haired and in spangled peacock blue, assuring her that Maureen, Sam's ex-, and the kids would eventually accept her. How she'd dreamt that day of the life that lay ahead with Sam; a child, she thought, a child soon to complete their happiness. She and Sam had discussed the vasectomy, she understood that it was reversible, she asked him only for one child, secretly wishing for, hoping for, secretly planning for two. The subsequent reality, Sam's equivocation, his allegedly conflicting reports from the MDs; her sad and gradual accommodation to the facts: had he lied to her about the vasectomy or about being open to children with her? The years stretched on and her hope faded, her dream of her own family was not so much dashed as gradually released, gradually lived beyond, left behind.

She hardened herself in response, after all, what else was there to do? Fall apart? Throw pots and pans, scream? Divorce him? By the time the thought of divorce began seriously to occur to her she was thirty, and living in southern California, Hollywood was her new life and she liked it, she liked her new friends, screenwriters, actors and directors, brilliant people, fascinating people, people who amused her. Besides, Sam was solid, stable, a sure thing: she was going to throw him over? For what? Another leap in the dark, for what else was marriage, after all? How would the next guy let her down? How would he support her? For she liked comfort, she had grown accustomed to it already in Chicago, and then, she was thirty, thirty one, one strike against her for Los Angeles was full of bright-eyed, talented and scheming twenty-three olds; if she were also a divorcee, two strikes. She thought of leaving, but calculated her relative advantages and risks.

She stayed with Sam. But she made him pay. She stuck it to him and how. He paid in jewels, he paid in designer gowns, he paid in furs (PETA had no influence with her fashion choices), he paid in luxury cars and the boat, in weekends at La Costa and winter stays in Palm Desert, he paid with first-class all the way whether for a week in Chicago or for a month in Paris, Aix and Nice. He paid. She saw to that. If her life were not to be filled with the love of a child, she would fill it with everything Sam's money could buy. Sam had plenty of money, and she had plenty of things. Bored with it after a few years, she looked for something to learn, something to do, something to take her mind off the emptiness, to distract her from the lasting disappointment at the heart of her life. She got her license and went to work in real estate. Emptiness was replaced with busy-ness; she was good, she rose quickly, she began to make her own money and in substantial commissions. She liked it. She liked the work itself, the houses and the gardens and their potential to be more than they were, given the right buyers. She liked the esteem of her peers and the fact that she was considered a professional by professional friends such as Kendra and Matt. She liked the fact that her afternoons were no longer silent and sad.

Why then the urge, almost overwhelming and moment-to-moment as she drove the dark streets, Bel Air to Brentwood, to break down and weep? Whence this surge of feeling, from her deepest self, to simply sob out loud, let the grief and anger and heartbreak come flooding irresistibly forth?

It was the light. The light which had surrounded David, more than surrounded him, which had held him and shone through him. It was the light, Linda knew, that had lit her up within, shown her her life in a flash, and released the feelings, set free the torrent she had

345

held back, she now realized, for more than twenty years. Was she sad? Was she angry? Did she hurt? Yes, yes and yes. The light showed her all that.

It showed her some other things, too. It showed her Maureen and the children; Sam's embittered first wife. She had not returned Maureen's hostility, but she had held it against her, unforgiving, for twenty-seven years. Well, after all, could she not spare some understanding for Maureen, for the children, in the break-up of their family? Linda had had nothing to do with that, it was over when she met Sam, but could she spare no empathy for a middle-aged woman with three teen-aged children whose husband one day comes in from the office and tells her he wants a divorce? Could she find no generosity in her heart for shocked and abandoned Maureen? For the children who suffered the emotional earthquake of that contentious divorce? No, they were not kind to her. They were still suffering, that's why. Their wounds, after all these years, were still unhealed. Was that a reason to secretly despise them? Should it not have been rather a reason to double-up on kindness, on gentleness, on understanding? They were still hurting a quarter of a century after the fact. She might have been an agent of grace and healing in their lives; they would not have made it easy for her, all the same she might have tried. She had not tried. Not at all. Could she spare them no mercy in her judgments? Could she not find room in her heart, to forgive and forebear?

There was more, in the light. There was much more. There was the whole reaction to Sam's deception, if indeed, deception it had been. Things. She had deliberately set about to fill up the emptiness with things. Honestly, some of the things she had bought over the years she didn't even particularly like; she just liked the fact that she could buy them. Their house in Bel Air was a collector's dream, for before she had taken refuge in real estate, she had spent a lot of her time decorating the house. She looked now at six-figure expenditures for pieces of furniture – furniture! – and she stood appalled, condemned in her own self-judgment. "It's an investment," of course, was always how the dealers justified it. Well, she supposed that such extravagances had to be justified one way or another, if they were to be lived with.

There was Sam himself. She had made him pay. And he had paid. Paid not just because he could afford to do so but also because he could not afford not to do so. For he was very much in love with her. She had never doubted that, and he gave her evidence of it day-in and day-out. The years went on and his devotion strengthened and deepened, rather than waned; Linda was inclined to think that his steadfastness was partly fueled by the deep guilt he carried in having misled her about children. She saw Sam's love, she gently but firmly ruled him through it. Yes, there was Sam himself. She had never really forgiven him.

The light showed her deep truths from dark places long left undisturbed, but tonight, in the aftermath of what she had seen, what she had felt, David, alive, strong, radiant, tonight as those deep truths from dark places came inexorably forward, she was loathe to send them back. She wanted them exposed, exposed to the light, shot through with the light, and not so much the truths themselves, but her response to them transformed in the light, transformed by the light. And that longing, that desire for transformation, she realized, is what made her want to weep. Oh!, to be able to take back the hurts she'd inflicted on anyone, the neglect, the judgment, the condescension. To be able to soothe and comfort another human heart, rather than dismiss and bruise it.

Somehow, the light, David's gift to her, his last gift to her, seemed to promise this.

She had reached Brentwood some minutes before. She was now turning onto Kendra's street. She guided the quiet car past the familiar houses and gardens, and pulled in at Kendra's, hearing the gravel beneath the tires. She looked up toward the house, dark but for a couple of dimly lit windows downstairs. The light through those windows was coming from the back of the house, from the sickroom, no doubt.

She parked the Camargue and sat staring at the house for a moment. She took a deep breath, opened the door and stepped out onto the gravel. The gravel; for the safety of the children. So that they would not play in this driveway. David and the children. Kendra and the children. How well they had done by the children, both of them.

She buckled against the door. She was ready to sob, sob for David, sob for Kendra, sob for the children, and she was ready to sob for herself and Sam, for what they had not done together, for the children who had never come, for the punitive extravagances and deliberate excesses, the futile attempt to get past that empty place, that sad and silent place, that place where no child had ever played.

"Pull yourself together," she snapped inwardly, stopping the first tear before it fell. "This won't do. This is no time for you to fall apart. You need to be strong for Kendra."

Kendra! Kendra her friend, Kendra her sister, for by God if there were one thing she knew how to do, if there were one thing she had gotten right in life, it was how to be a good friend. She loved Kendra and Kendra loved her.

And she did sob now, thinking of Kendra. She braced herself against the car, a hand covering her face. She wept, the tears copious and flowing. Her body trembled with the force of her grief. Yet she wept silently, as if afraid of waking neighbors an acre away.

She recovered herself after a moment, reaching a tissue from her purse and drying her eyes. She looked up and saw the stars despite the urban haze and for the first time in her life she was consciously aware of a depth, a space, if you will, beyond the depths of space.

The universe itself was held in that greater depth, in that space beyond space. It was a sudden and clear understanding, though she would have been hard-pressed to articulate it. Space-time itself held within that deeper realm, that limitless realm, eternity.

There, she thought. That place beyond the stars. That is where the light has come from. That is where David has gone.

So then, really, was it all true, after all? That light, the light in which David had stood, that light which had shown her her deepest self, was it from eternity? Her whole life shown to her in an instant, all times and places suddenly present, alive in that light, an eternal moment here in time. God, no longer an intellectual proposition about which one could speculate, but living – and loving – light? Could it be that there really was an all-good, all-knowing, all-powerful and above all, all-loving Intelligence, speaking to us from beyond the quasars?

Get a grip, girlfriend. Thank God, if there were one, for her rational mind. Get a grip. An overworked imagination, a sense of imminent and irretrievable loss, the loss of a lifelong friend, and after all, hadn't Isabel also seen Damien a few days after the funeral? What did Jessica say this afternoon, at the pool? The brain produces the image – but…no.

No. She knew what she saw at the foot of the bed. She knew who she saw. She knew what she felt when she saw him. And she knew that David was standing there at the foot of her bed in Bel Air at the very moment of his death here in Brentwood. Find your rationalizing way around that. The instant of his death. How could she have known? How could her brain have 'produced' the image at the precise instant of his death? Explain that, girlfriend, she said to herself.

She realized that she couldn't. And what's more, she realized as well that it didn't matter. It didn't matter at all that she could not

349

explain it. Physicists can explain the birth of the universe from a singularity but they can't explain the singularity. How was there ever anything other than nothing to begin with? Who knows, who cares? She didn't need to get this figured out tonight. So there is a deep mystery at the heart of life itself? Why shouldn't there be? She had not created herself; why should she think she would be capable of explaining it all away rationally? To Hell with her rational mind.

Well, no, not quite that. She didn't want to go off the deep end here. She didn't want to end up doing circle dances in the redwoods under a full moon. No, not entirely to Hell with her capacity for rational thought. She needed it. She was grateful for it. But it could only serve her greater understanding so far. Where it left off, well, she supposed something like faith would have to take over.

She looked again at the stars. She was suffused once again with peace, the peace that had radiated toward her, flowed through her the moment she saw David. She was loved – she was loved! In all that she had done, in all that she had not done, she was loved. It mattered only that she let this peace, this serenity, this light from beyond the stars embrace and enfold her. She leaned back against the car resting in that peace. She might have rested a minute. She might have rested an hour.

A sound from the street, a quiet engine, headlights turning into the drive. Linda looked toward the street, squinting in the brightness, trying to identify the car. Suddenly conscious of herself again, she straightened up, pushed her hair back, reached for a tissue from her purse and dabbed her eyes with it. A slate blue BMW. Matt. Thank God, Matt! He pulled alongside her, gave her a wave, then pulled ahead and parked. He got out of the car.

"Linda," he said.

She started across the gravel toward him.

"You are one beautifully ravaged picture of grief," he said, taking her in his arms.

"I'm a mess," Linda said.

Tears streaked Matt's face. "God, I hate this," he said.

"I know, baby," Linda replied, and wiped his tears with her hand. "I know. But you know what? 'This' is more than we know."

Matt looked at her. A small, wondering smile came over his face.

"Girlfriend's had an epiphany," Linda said.

"Really?"

Linda patted his arm. "We'll talk," she promised. "Meanwhile, Kendra needs her best friends."

Matt offered Linda his arm. She took it. They started across the gravel toward the darkened house.

Jessica and the boys arrived a few minutes after Linda and Matt. Solange opened the door to them.

"Daddy was smiling," Solange said, leading them down the hall to the sickroom. "He opened his eyes and looked at Kendra, and he smiled. Then he closed his eyes."

Matt and Linda were in the room with Kendra and Tino. Everyone got up as Jessica and the others entered. Jessica crossed through the room like a guided missile, going down on her knees at her father's bedside, taking his hand in hers and beginning quietly to sob. Justin followed her, placing a hand on her shoulder. Jeffrey went to Kendra, and threw his arms around her.

"Mom!" he said, and hugged her close.

Brett and Monique stood behind Jeffrey and as Jeffrey too crossed to the bed, each in their turn embraced Kendra. Kendra felt tears welling up but they did not fall. Brett crossed to the bed, but Monique stayed with her mother-in-law, an arm around Kendra's shoulder.

"We will be here for you, Mom," Monique assured Kendra. "We will be in Los Angeles. We will come out frequently. But you should also come to us. Come to Atlanta and stay with us, come to New Orleans and see my side of the family. They love you, you know."

The tears clouded Kendra's eyes so that the room before her blurred. She had found, in Monique, the love of a daughter that she had forfeited in Jessica.

As if reading her mind, Monique said quietly to Kendra, "We were talking, Justin and I, on the way over, just now. He said, 'We would be orphans now, except for Kendra.'"

Kendra blinked the tears back and managed a smile, it was a grateful smile and it was for Monique.

Jessica let go of her father's hand. She wiped her eyes and stood up. She turned and looked at Kendra.

Kendra's heart hurt, but she could not respond to it. She did not know how. She had been off-track with her step-daughter for the last dozen years.

Jessica crossed toward Kendra. Kendra wanted to cross to her and embrace her but resisted, placing a higher value on her step-daughter's sentiments than on her own.

Jessica reached Kendra and looked into her eyes. "Kendra," she said.

Kendra heard and felt the beating of her heart. Her lips trembled at the sight of Jessica's anguish.

"Kendra," Jessica said. "Thank you for loving Dad. Thank you for loving him. Thank you for loving us. Oh God, Kendra!" she suddenly cried, and her voice gave way, and tears rolled down her cheeks. "Where would be, if not for you? Thank you for loving all of us! Where would we be, if not for you?"

And, astonishing Kendra, Jessica fell into her arms, sobbing.

"Jessica!" Kendra said, and held her close. "Jessica, Jessica, Jessica." She could say no more. For the floodgates at last were open. Hugging Jessica tight, Kendra wept.

Brett looked to Monique, who was silently crying, still at Kendra's side. And suddenly, tears streaked Brett's face as well. Justin and Jeffrey, at the bed, turned and looked at their sister and Kendra, hugging each other so tight, so close, sobbing together. They looked at each other, a little astonished. They crossed silently to Kendra and Jessica and stood with them. Monique held out her hand for Brett, forming a protective family circle.

Linda with one glance and raised eyebrows, indicated the door, and she, Tino, Matt and Solange quietly left the room.

"Where would we be, if not for you?" Jessica asked Kendra, hugging her.

It was not a question Kendra could have answered, but in fact, had Kendra not been there, had Kendra decided, on discovering David's affair with Chrysta, to leave, an alternative family history would have developed.

David would have died ten years earlier, at fifty-five, not sixty-five, in the crash of a small plane in Colorado, flying home from the Sundance Festival. Kendra's leaving had rocked his world, the divorce had left him broken and embittered. He dealt with the teen-aged rebellions of Jessica and Justin alone, and not well, for much of what his children themselves were dealing with was Kendra's abandonment of them. David threw himself into his work for consolation, and he found a new lover, a blonde starlet the kids despised. It was the screening of one of her films that had brought David to Sundance, but they argued there, and she flew home on a commercial flight the same day David died in the crash.

The loss of Kendra was devastating to the children, the cause of many problems in their teen years. With the death of their father while all three were still teens, Jessica, Justin and Jeffrey found themselves orphaned in a world that seemed to offer only insecurity and heartbreak.

Jessica looked for solace in men, but her neediness and her demands drove one lover after another from her life. She twice became pregnant and was twice abandoned by the men involved, resulting in two abortions and an even deeper sense of helplessness and near-despair. In fact, she would pull herself out, she would reach deep within herself and find the strength to change her entire approach to living her life; she would graduate from college and get to law school and she would now, at twenty-eight, be a successful, if scarred and hurting, law student, still looking however, for the love and security which had eluded her it seemed, all her life.

Justin's teen-aged flirtation with drugs and alcohol spiraled out of control following the death of his father. No amount of family intervention could reverse the trend and only when he woke up one morning in the Los Angeles County Jail would he begin to take his problem seriously. Justin, too, would straighten out eventually, and now, at twenty-seven, he would be finishing his college degree and applying to law school, his dreams running a parallel to Jessica's. He would never have met Monique.

It would be Jeffrey, however, who would suffer the most, following the divorce. Kendra had been his rock, the only mother he had ever known, Lana having died when he was only two. He would never recover emotionally from the shock of Kendra's leaving, and with the death of his father, Jeffrey's very character would be adversely affected. Once easy and calm and secure in his relations with others, Jeffrey would henceforth be needy, easily disappointed, frequently suspicious and finally, withdrawn. Falling in with some of Justin's crowd in his mid-teens, Jeffrey would develop a dependence on drugs and alcohol, and spend several stints in rehab. His young life would be brought to a point of tragic no-return with a felony drunk driving causing serious injury charge. Out on bail and seeking the comfort of his old friends and habits, seeking as well escape from the black hole which his life had become, he would die, at twenty-three, as his mother had so many years before, alone in a hotel suite from an accidental drug overdose.

Jeffrey's death would leave a scar on Kendra's heart that she would take to her grave.

Nor was it only David and the children who would be so negatively affected by Kendra's decision to leave. Without Kendra there to help David process his anxieties, Damien and David would square off over the latter's questions about the financing of Jean Marc's market and bakery, on Melrose. The family would divide down the middle, Ramon and Raquel with Damien, Carmen and Tino with David, Ana and Isabel caught in-between and attempting unsuccessfully to negotiate a family peace. At the time of the plane crash, David and Damien would remain unreconciled. Damien would ache over this fact the rest of his life, but the plane crash had a second cause of sorrow for him.

Tino, bereft of the firm but gentle influence of his aunt, would have drifted gradually into David's orbit, alienated from his father. Tino would have agreed to appear in a film, after all, the same film David's blonde lover was starring in, and which was screened that winter at Sundance. Tino boarded the small plane with his uncle, for the flight back to Los Angeles.

He was the wreck's only survivor. His back broken, and with a number of other injuries, Tino would be months in the hospital and rehab, gradually regaining his strength and mobility. Anguished at the death of his uncle, scarred by the warring within the family, and limping the rest of his life from his injuries in the wreck, Tino would nonetheless eventually meet Maribel; he would reconcile with Damien and take over the management of both restaurants, working hard to bring the family back together in the wake of the shock of David's death.

Such would have been the history of the family, had Kendra decided to leave. Such would have been the answer to Jessica's question, "Where would we be, without you?"

This alternative family history never came to be, of course, because one sunny spring Friday over lunch Kendra talked with Linda about her options. She saw that the possibility of her leaving shocked Linda. And in Linda's surprise, Kendra had her answer. She and the children ordered both pizza and Chinese that evening, and watched THE KARATE KID. And Kendra stayed.

ONE HUNDRED-TWO

It was almost half an hour before Kendra and the children emerged from the sick room. Carmen, Ana and their husbands, driven over in the pre-dawn hours by Rico, had arrived. On being told that Kendra and the kids were having a private moment in the sick room, they immediately set to work on breakfast preparation, breaking eggs into bowls, laying out bacon, cutting fruit and cheese, slicing bread, mixing the ingredients for pancakes and French toast. Solange had put coffee on as soon as she came downstairs, and had a second pot brewing as Kendra came into the big kitchen, so strangely lit, busy and alive, given that it was just past five in the morning.

Linda and Matt were talking quietly over coffee at a table near the windows. Tino and Rico were slicing vegetables for omelettes. A tall, slender girl, her dark hair up in a bun, was working alongside the nephews: Maribel. She was rolling refried beans into tortillas for the breakfast burritos. Kendra stood at the entrance to the kitchen for a moment, just looking at her family. Jessica and the others flowed into the kitchen, and hugs were exchanged all around.

"May we go in?" Maribel asked Kendra.

"Come," said Solange, and Maribel, the sisters and their husbands followed down the hall to the sick room.

Rico stayed with Tino and the vegetables. "You don't want to go in?" Tino asked.

Rico shook his head. "I want to remember Uncle David as he was," he said.

Hearing this, Kendra crossed directly to her nephew. Rico turned to her with tears in his eyes. They embraced, a long and strong hug.

"The mortuary's been called, baby, Camden and Shire," said Linda, looking across the kitchen to Kendra, who remained in Rico's arms. "They did such a beautiful job with Gianna's services, you remember," she added, speaking of her mother-in-law. "I talked to Paul myself; he called me on his cell when he heard it was David. I asked him to give us two hours. Gives everyone time to get here."

"And I left a message with Nick," said Matt. "He'll handle the press release."

"Thank you," said Kendra and in her gratitude went virtually limp in Rico's arms. Then, "This looks like quite a feast," Kendra said, of all the preparations.

"Everyone is coming," said Rico, gently rocking Kendra and himself.

And as he spoke the doorbell chimed. Kendra crossed through the rooms to the foyer. It was unlit and she noticed in the darkness that dawn was breaking beyond the windows. She opened the door to Isabel, Ramon and Sandra. As they stepped in, another car pulled into the drive.

Isabel and Kendra hugged.

"Three more cars behind us," said Isabel. "We caravanned over. Anyone who can get here this morning will be here."

Kendra directed the newcomers to the sick room. "Breakfast in a bit," she promised.

She waited at the door as the second car came to stop, as the doors opened. Raquel and Juan; Javier and Angelo. Kendra crossed the verandah toward them. They saw her and waved. She crossed her arms against the cool dawn breeze, for she was still only in her robe. The garden was beginning to show its colors in the pale light. Among the trees, birds were singing. The gravel crunched under the footsteps of the new arrivals. Kendra crossed down the steps to greet them.